He took her face in his hands and brought it closer to his own. The moment his mouth covered hers, his hands slipped beneath her cloak so he could hold her pressed tightly against him.

He kissed her deeply, showing her with his tongue what he would like to do to her with another part of his body. He felt the heat in her burst into flame, and he remembered how she was always like dry kindling, ready to catch fire whenever he touched her. With a groan, he pushed her back against the embrasure and dropped his hands to cup her buttocks and lift her against him.

He did not kiss to seduce. He was far beyond that now.

Mastery was what he was after, and he meant to show her that she belonged to him. He wanted to delve into the very soul of her, to place his mark there, branding her for life, and ruining her for all time for the touch of any other.

He felt her hands slide beneath his doublet, and he could not help the response that made him press himself hard against her. He wanted her to the point of insanity. The thought of making love to her again drove him past all caution. He wanted her enough to take her here, on the battlements, in the middle of the falling snow.

His hand slipped hungrily downward until he could touch her and feel her pressing against his palm. He tugged her skirts upward until he found her leg and then followed it, going higher still, until he found the damp lace he searched for, and knew so well.

Also by ELAINE COFFMAN

LET ME BE YOUR HERO
THE ITALIAN
THE FIFTH DAUGHTER
THE BRIDE OF BLACK DOUGLAS

Watch for the next book by ELAINE COFFMAN

BY FIRE AND BY SWORD

Available April 2006

ELAINE
COFFMAN
THE
HIGHLANDER

MIRA®

ISBN 0-7783-2391-9

THE HIGHLANDER

www.MIRABooks.com

Printed in U.S.A.

THE HIGHLANDER

One

Trust not the horse, O Trojans. Be it what
it may,
I fear the Grecians even when they offer
gifts.

—Virgil (70-19 B.C.), Roman poet.
Laocoön, from *Aeneid,* Book 2

Grampian Highlands, northwestern coast of Scotland, autumn 1740

She was not utterly naked. But she was damnably close.

He did not know why he chose to ride along the narrow strip of beach that day, for he usually took the winding track that curled through the rugged granite peaks nearby. Perhaps it was the working of divine providence that sent him cantering over the sand, then caused his horse to rear suddenly and turn sharply away.

Otherwise, he might have ridden right over the woman lying there.

Who was she? he wondered. Some mythological figure escaped from a Renaissance painting—one of the three Horae, perhaps? Clad only in a thin, wet shift, she lay in a cradle of rocks and sand, imbued with melancholic beauty, her body provoking, and yet chastely invisible. Still and pale, she reminded him of an ancient statue—for her beauty could have inspired some venerable sculptor to immortalize her in marble.

Tavish Graham dismounted and walked toward her, puzzled by this mysterious woman. How did she get here?

She had no name and nothing to identify her, nor was there any clue as to where she had come from—nothing, save the shift she wore and the pure lambent reality of cold, naked flesh. Incredibly young, and fair of face, she was slender as a reed, with a body to arouse envy in the female heart, and lust in her counterpart.

She did not move, even when he dropped down on his knees beside her. He put his head to her chest and listened, for he hoped to hear the beating assurance of a heart that said she lived.

He heard nothing.

He dusted the sand away and was about to listen again, when the exquisiteness of her face distracted him. She had a pureness of beauty quite unlike anyone he had seen. It brought to mind the dim, smoky light of taverns, where nudes reclined on canvas, and licentious thoughts were given free rein—to look, to touch, to make advances, or simply to toss the woman over the shoulder and carry her away.

She was far too lovely to die, he thought, as he lifted a bit of seaweed clinging to her pale lips. He inhaled sharply when he saw she was staring at him, as if just awakening from a deep sleep.

Her skin was like ice when he laid a palm along her cheek. "Who are you?" he asked. It was as if she came vividly to life before his eyes, and with elegant hands and masses of chestnut hair she modestly tried to cover her nakedness.

"Have no fear, lass. Ye are safe. I have come to help ye."

He saw a tear roll from her eye. She whispered something inaudible and closed her eyes.

She was not dead, thanks be to God, but she would be soon if he did not get her dry and warm.

He looked around him, but saw no signs of anyone having been here, nor did he see any bits of wreckage that could have come from the ship that went aground the night before.

He knew not where she came from, this nameless beauty shrouded in mystery. He only knew she had not been in the water long, or she would be dead.

Which she would be soon enough, if he did not get her warm.

He was puffing vigorously by the time he wrapped her in his plaid and carried her to his horse and placed her in the saddle. He mounted behind her and pulled her close against him, so the heat from his own body could offset the icy chill in hers.

He turned his horse, ready to continue on his way, when a moment of indecision furrowed his brow.

Where should he take her?

He feared it was too far to take her to his home at Monleigh Castle. With her so wet and cold, he doubted she would make it that far. His only hope was to make it to Danegæld Lodge. His brother Jamie had gone there two days ago to have peace and quiet.

Tavish did not stop to think how Jamie would

react to having a half-drowned lass interrupt his quiet retreat, or left in his care. But then, Tavish rarely thought of such things for he was the youngest brother, and the one to use his charm to manipulate others—the one who saw his way as the right way.

Tavish turned his horse toward Danegæld and rode at a gallop, for he knew that soon the cold, dampening fog from the North Sea would begin to creep inland, and it would carry with it a cold chill.

As he rode, he thought about the woman in his arms, and the inexplicable aura that surrounded her. That he did not know her captivated him. He had been away at the university in Edinburgh for most of the past three years, so it was possible a lass or two could have escaped his attention—even one as bonnie as she.

Night descended upon them and the weather turned colder. Tavish pulled the plaid more tightly around her, until only her face and a few wet curls were visible.

"Clk...clk..." He urged his horse forward and kept up a steady pace, riding toward the dark edging of trees in the distance where a stingy moon hid behind the clouds, throwing everything below into deep shadow.

Soon, they began to climb the flanks of the mountains that rose like a buttress against the powerful North Sea, as if commanding the churning waters to come no farther.

The woman stirred and moaned something inaudible. He knew her position was not a comfortable one, but Tavish did not let a thing like pity slow him down. She needed a warm place more than she needed comfort.

Still, the knowledge that she might need soothing did not prevent him from offering a few sparse words of comfort in that awkwardly tender way men sometimes have—gentle words, gruffly spoken. "You are safe now, lass."

Her cold hand fell limply against his and he slowed long enough to tuck it beneath the plaid. Overhead, the moon outran the clouds to illuminate her blue lips, and fell with lifeless color upon a face as pale as ashes.

He could feel the cold numbness of her body reaching out to him through the plaid, and could only hope that some of his own body's warmth would pass into hers, before they both froze. He urged his horse into a faster pace.

The trail was uneven and rough, strewn with large boulders, some so close together there was barely enough room for a horse to pass through.

It slowed their progress, and his horse pricked his ears forward and stepped gingerly over the rocks, made slippery by a heavy mist that descended upon them.

Ahead of them, Tavish saw where the trail took a sharp turn and dropped steeply toward the river. Once they were around that, it would curve away and upward and they would begin to climb again.

"Hold on, lass. 'Tis no' so far now."

A soft mist began to scatter droplets about, and he cursed his luck. She was wet enough. Saints above, the last thing she needed was more water.

The track dipped into a narrow ravine, and they rode along the river until they came to a shallow ford. He slowed his horse to cross with the hope no water would splash upon her, adding to her discomfort.

He paused a moment on the other side, hearing only the sound of the harsh breathing of his horse as he watched the steam rising from his wet hide. Tavish felt almost apologetic when he resumed his pace and urged his horse into a gallop along the narrow trail. He was thankful the lass in front of him slept on, for he knew if awake she would be complaining mightily.

Gradually he could feel the warmth beginning to gather between them, and he felt relieved that at least the part where their bodies touched was losing its chill. He tried to shift his position, but the lass was all dead weight.

"Och, yer a hard one to budge," he said, not really realizing he had spoken aloud until he heard her reply.

"Where are you taking me?"

Her voice was soft, and her accent went straight to his groin. Seductive as hell, it was. He glanced down at her, almost too astonished to answer. "What difference does it make? You should be glad to go anywhere, as long as it is dry."

"I want to know where you are taking me."

She might be half dead, but she was persistent. "I am taking you to my grandfather's house, Danegæld Lodge."

"Why?"

"'Tis where my brother is, and I canna think of naught else to do wi' ye."

"You could put me down."

"Nay, lass, I couldna do that. Yer sure to freeze in this night air, not to mention that ye have little on, save yer hide, which is little protection against any dragoons or Black Watch that might be about."

"You speak English, but your accent is peculiar."

"Peculiar? Ach, I suppose 'tis."

She said nothing more after that, and he thought she was asleep until some time later when she asked, "Are you a Scot?"

"Aye," he said, feeling the word rise up proudly inside him. "That I am, and if you dinna mind my saying so, you've got a verra peculiar accent of yer own."

She did not respond to that but simply asked, "Where are we?"

"On the road to Danegæld."

"I mean where...what country?"

"You mean ye dinna know where ye were afore I found ye?"

"No."

"How can that be? How can you no' remember where you were going?"

He was thinking she was not going to answer him, but after a little time passed, she said, "I don't seem to be able to remember much of anything."

"Well, don't fret about it now, lass. Yer in Scotland, and that should give you a great deal of comfort," he said, feeling somewhat befuddled over this conversation that raised a lot of questions and provided precious few answers. God's knees—it was a conversation that seemed to be going nowhere. Like talking to himself, it was.

"Do you have no memory, lass? Do you have no recollection of how ye came to be in the water wearing scarcely more than yer goose bumps?"

"Non, monsieur."

Now, that was decidedly French, he thought. "Yer a French lassie. Am I right?"

"Perhaps…I cannot seem to remember very much."

"Och, 'tis like talking to a vapor. The question lingers then disappears without an answer," he said, having decided he liked her better unconscious. "Dinna fret, lass. Yer memory is probably frozen like the rest of ye. Why dinna ye try to sleep for a while? It will make the trip seem shorter."

"Why are you taking me to your brother?"

"Because my brother is the chief…"

"Of what?" she interrupted.

"He is Chief of the Clan Graham, ye ken?"

"Why can't you help me?"

"I'm on my way back to the university in Edinburgh. Besides, I only rescue lasses. I dinna solve their problems."

"I don't have a problem."

"If ye dinna ken who ye are, and ye dinna ken where ye come from, and ye dinna ken where ye were going, then ye have a problem. Besides, a lass what looks as good as ye is bound to cause problems afore long, even if she has none at the moment."

"What will your brother do with me?"

"Chain you in the dungeon and ravish you periodically for as long as you please him," he said, hearing her gasp. "Now, be quiet, for yer blethering is distracting."

He smiled in spite of himself and hoped that frightened her sufficiently to keep her quiet, at least for a while.

It did…for a time, but before too long, she asked, "Can we not stop for a little rest? I am growing numb all over. It's so cold."

He could hear her teeth chattering. "Aye, I ken ye are cold, lass, and so am I. I would stop if I thought it was safe to do so. You would be colder if we stopped, for there is no place of shelter in these parts. We need to keep moving."

She turned, pushing against him as she shifted her position.

Och! He wished she had stayed where she was, for now her hipbone was pressing against a place that made him very mindful that he had a near naked woman in his arms.

He was certain she could feel him rising hard against her in response. He nuzzled her ear. "Keep wiggling like that and I may ravish you before my brother has the chance."

"Go ahead," she said, sounding so grumpy, he chuckled. "I'm so cold I wouldn't feel a thing."

"Och, 'tis just as well. We've no time for ravishing right now, but if you can wait until I'm home next, I will gladly oblige you," he said.

"When will that be?"

"Not until midsummer, so ye have a while to anticipate it."

The track began to climb upward steadily. "Danegæld Lodge is just ahead, at the top of the mountain."

Her teeth were chattering loudly now, but she still managed to say, "I th-thought we were g-g-going to your grandfather's."

"Aye, it was my grandfather's home afore his death, and quite a magnificent place it is, too. My mother was the daughter of the Duke of Lochaber. He was one of the wealthiest men in the Highlands. After he died, Jamie made some changes to it so we could use it for a hunting lodge, but you will still see the gilded garnish of its magnificence."

He caught the way she looked down forlornly at the sodden scrap of wool he had wrapped around her, and how she tugged at it where her pale, bare legs gleamed in the moonlight.

He wanted to tell her that if she stopped wiggling about, the plaid would stay tucked around her, but he decided not to mention anything that would sound like a reprimand. "Dinna worry about the way ye look, lass. There is no one there but Jamie and the staff."

As they climbed higher the trees began to disappear, and they followed the trail along a steep ridge of solid rock, strewn with large boulders that probably had fallen from the higher ridges above. She wished the moon would go behind the clouds again, for she could see the terrain that lay before them was as bleak and cheerless as her future, and she imagined herself riding back into time, into the past of this barbaric country, where there resided only strangers, with odd ways and peculiar speech.

She ached in every muscle—at least those that were not so paralyzed with cold that she could still feel. She no longer had any sensation in her fingers and her body began to shiver uncontrollably. She began to despair that they would ever reach the place where they were going. She felt as if she had been cursed and turned into an icy block of stone—her punishment for rebellion.

Every extremity was heavy and leaden, and her

mental alertness began to suffer greatly, to the point she wondered if she were slipping into a stupor. She did not feel so cold now. It felt like her body was warming. She was deliriously sleepy.

Her head nodded a time or two, before it dropped to rest upon her chest.

Tavish must have sensed what was happening, for he shook her roughly. "Och now, we'll have none of that, lass. Ye canna sleep just yet."

"I can't help it. I'm so slee…py." Her last word dwindled away to nothing.

"Aye, 'tis the cold making you sleepy, but you dinna want to give in to it. Sleep now, lass, and ye will never wake up."

"Mumph…" She was too drowsy to speak legibly.

"Ach, so that's the way it is? Well, I dinna mind telling ye that is what I like—a lass that is all warm and willing to please. 'Tis a bonnie good way to warm ye, I ken."

She felt a hand brush over her breast. "Why dinna ye tell me ye were so willing earlier?" he said, nibbling at her ear. "I ken we can find a verra good way to make us both warm."

Her head snapped up. She slapped his hand away. "You take liberties you have no right to take."

"That's a good lass," he said, and then he laughed and spurred his horse.

She had to grab the pommel to keep from losing her balance. She had a strong suspicion he had infuriated her on purpose: the sleepiness had passed, and with it the feeling of warmth.

Now she was trembling from the cold again, and wide awake, feeling miserable and capable of crying with very little urging. And still her teeth chattered.

"It's been a long, hard ride and I apologize for putting you through it, but if it makes you feel better, you've come through it as well as any man and, most important, yer still alive, so count your blessings, lass, and take heart. We have arrived at our destination at last."

It was bad enough that this man had seen a great deal more of her than any man had, but the thought that she was about to undergo the same ordeal again made her uneasy. "I am shamed for my appearance. What will your brother think when he sees me?"

"He will think I've brought home a half-naked, frozen lass taken in a raid."

"Hmm, a raid…you still do that sort of thing?"

"Aye, 'tis still done, though not by me personally, ye ken."

She turned her face against his chest seeking his warmth, for her face felt as though it might crack. Her voice was muffled as she said, "That's the first good news I've heard since I met you."

"Och, lass, I dinna remember meeting you at all, for I don't even know yer name."

A moment later, he dismounted and held his hands up to lift her from the saddle. When her feet touched the ground, she found she did not have the strength to stand.

Her knees buckled and she dropped, as if the world had disappeared beneath her feet.

He barely caught her before she hit the ground. "I pegged ye for a troublesome lass," he said, "so I am no' surprised I will have to carry ye." He chuckled. "Although I canna say I am disappointed." He swept her into his arms and carried her up the steps. "Light as goose down ye are."

He called out his brother's name when he reached the top step. "Jamie! Open the door. I've got a lass half frozen to death."

While he waited for the door to open, he said, "Allow me to correct my bad manners. I am Tavish Graham. Tell me your name, lass."

She had her face tucked into the cove of his

neck and shoulder, seeking warmth. "I must have a name, but I cannot remember it."

"Dinna ye worry about that, lass. I ken my brother can frighten it out of you afore long."

Two

A liar should have a good memory.
—Quintilian (c.35-c.100), Roman rhetorician, *De Institutione Oratoria* (c.90)

If there was anything Jamie Graham detested more than being roused from sleep, it was being greeted with a surprise.

To have both happen in one night did little to sweeten his mood.

When he heard Tavish call out that he had a half-frozen lass in tow, Jamie knew his carefree brother had become enamored with some tavern doxy and was smitten enough to drag her here with him, when he should be on his way back to Edinburgh.

He grumbled as he climbed out of bed, wrapped his plaid around himself and went below stairs. "Must I be at everyone's beck and call…day and night?"

He jerked the door open.

"It comes with the title, Yer Earlship," Tavish said, and grinned up at his brother.

"Hang the title from the nearest gibbet." Jamie paused when he saw the girl in his brother's arms. "You better have a good explanation for this, or by the cross of St. Andrew…"

He paused midsentence, for whatever he expected, it was not the sight of the half-naked, shivering woman that greeted him. He looked from the girl to Tavish and asked, "What is this?"

Tavish glanced down at the girl lying silent and still in his arms and grinned up at his brother. "I believe they are called lasses."

"Is that all they have managed to teach you in Edinburgh? To be impudent when sincerity is called for?"

"I am being sincere. This lass *sincerely* needs help. Now, are ye going to keep me standing out here all night in this freezing drizzle, or can I come inside?"

Jamie opened the door wider. "Then by all means help her."

Tavish stepped into the room. "I think you are more equipped to handle this than I am. You're the chief."

Jamie barely took notice of the ragamuffin is his brother's arms. "Don't try to foist your obligations off on me. Our tastes were always different."

"I didn't bring her here for me."

"Well, I hope you didn't bring her for me. I came here to get away from one woman. I dinna need to replace her with another one."

"She won't be any trouble. She needs help. You willna believe where I found her."

"She's a woman. She will be trouble. And I dinna care where ye found her. Take her back."

"That might be harder than it sounds." Tavish lowered her to a chair in front of the fireplace.

Jamie observed her critically. She appeared to be naked under the plaid that was wrapped haphazardly around her. His gaze followed the curve of her thigh, down her bare legs to the shoeless feet.

He was about to inquire about the lack of clothes and shoes when Tavish said, "We need to get a fire going. It is as cold as the North Sea in here. Where are Angus and Mary?"

"I dismissed the staff."

"Why?"

"You are all questions tonight. Do you remember my telling you I was coming here for a few days to be alone?"

Tavish rubbed the woman's hands briskly, trying to warm them. "Aye, you did, but I didn't know you meant to turn yerself into a cloistered monk."

Jamie's gaze was still lingering on her long, bare legs. Just how high did they go? "*Hermit* would be a better choice of word, since there are some of the more carnal things in life I don't intend to give up."

Tavish gave him a teasing grin. "Och! I ken ye will talk differently after ye wed and have a wife to box yer ears when yer eyes start to roam."

"Only until I have an heir."

Tavish turned his attention back to the girl and tucked the plaid around her.

"I had no idea you were so motherly," Jamie said, his tone heavily laced with mockery.

"Make light of it if you like, but I will not be a party to it. Can ye no' see that she is chilled to the bone? Would you rather that I had left her, to freeze to death?"

Jamie narrowed his eyes, suspicion playing with his thoughts. "By God, you haven't married the doxy, have you?"

Jamie heard the lass gasp a split second before Tavish leaped to her defense. "It is not what you think. She isn't some tavern wench I picked up."

Jamie took the poker and began to stir the dying coals in the fire. He placed a few sticks of kindling over them and watched them burst into flame. He shook his head trying to clear away the last residue of sleep. "So tell me, brother, where *did* you find her?"

"Weel, half of her was in the North Sea. The other half was lying on the beach. I would have ridden right over her, if my horse hadn't shied away at the last minute."

His brother's words pricked his interest. He saw the wet hair, the bits of seaweed still clinging to it. "You pulled her from the sea, you say?"

"Aye. I thought she was dead at first, and when I realized she was still alive, I knew I had to get her to a warm place with all due haste. I thought at first to take her to Monleigh Castle, but then I began to fear she would never survive a journey of that length."

"Where exactly on the coast did you find her?"

"Near Ravenscroft."

Jamie's eyes glazed with thought. A frown appeared between his brows. He walked over to stand before the girl. "What were you doing in Ravenscroft, or better yet, in the water?"

"I do not recall, *monsieur.*"

"Where do you live?"

"I have no memory, *monsieur.*" She continued on in French, but speaking too low for Jamie to catch much of what she said.

He rubbed the sleep from his eyes and gave his head a shake. "Could you speak English? I fear I am not up to unraveling the mystery of who you are and why you are here in a language other than my mother tongue—at least not this late at night, and me with a damnable headache."

"If you don't like having a headache, then why do you drink?"

"Who said I drank?"

"I am not a child, *monsieur.*"

Jamie purposefully allowed his gaze to roam leisurely over her, so he could watch her response. "Ye dinna have to convince me of that," he said. He was thinking she had lovely eyes, as light and blue as the waters that lapped gently at the shores of the Greek islands.

No, he thought. She definitely is not a child.

Tavish was scratching his head as he studied her thoughtfully. "We dinna have much to go on, do we? That is aside from the fact that she is a female and in need of our help. Do you think she is French?"

"Just because she speaks French does not mean she is French." Jamie thought about that for a moment. She had exquisitely fine-boned features, and if he were judging by looks alone, she very well could be French. He had studied in France and Italy for several years before his father's death. Based on his knowledge of the French language and his familiarity with native speech patterns, there was little doubt in his mind that the language was her mother tongue. Although she did speak English well, it was strongly accented with French.

Damnably seductive it was, too.

Those captivating, siren's eyes of hers made it difficult to keep his mind focused on what he was about. "Since French is obviously her mother tongue, it would seem highly probable that she is French."

Tavish grinned widely and slapped his leg. "I knew it! So, at least until we decide differently, we will say she is French. What happens next?"

Jamie turned back to the girl. "What is your name?"

Her lips were trembling, but she answered him clearly. "I do not remember."

Tavish was right. She looked frozen to the core of her. He had never seen lips so blue, but he had to know something about her. It would not do to welcome a spy in their midst. "All right, then how about your last name? Do you remember that?" When she did not answer, Jamie raised his voice. "Your last name! What is it?"

"I..." She stopped suddenly and looked down at her hands, which were clasped together in her lap.

"Go on. Your last name...what is your last name?"

"I...I do not know." Her voice was soft and lilting.

"You were about to tell me a last name a moment ago, then stopped. What made you change your mind?"

"I did not change my mind. Sophie is all the name I recall."

"Sophie. It isn't much, but at least it is a start," Tavish said.

"Something isn't right about all of this." Jamie glanced at Tavish. "A moment ago she said she did not remember her first name. Now she does."

She knew he was waiting for her to explain, but she said nothing. The one called Tavish seemed kind and jovial, but his brother was hard and suspicious. She did not want to stay with him, for she feared what he might do if she did not give him the answers he sought.

Jamie turned back to her and spoke slowly. “I will give you one more opportunity to answer. Tell me now or, by God, I will toss your shivering carcass outside and leave you there.” He saw the way she was twisting her hands, the fear in her eyes. He was not swayed. She could wring her hands until doomsday, but he would have the truth out of her or else. “I will warn you, mistress, I am not easily duped by a woman’s beguiling ways. Answer me,” he demanded.

“I did not tell you because I did not recall it at the time.”

“So, you miraculously remembered it when I asked for your last name?”

She nodded.

Jamie turned to Tavish. “She lies.”

“I think you have frightened her,” Tavish said. “You can tell she’s scared. Look at her. See how she trembles, white as a sheet. I worked hard to make her relax, and now you have terrified her. She is near to fainting with fear.”

Jamie did not bother to look. “Do not fall into that trap. She strokes you with her words and beguiles you with her alluring ways, but I warn you now, a false face hides what a false heart knows.”

“I am no’ so captivated that I cannot see the

truth," Tavish said. "She has been through much. Grant her leave, Jamie. Is there no kindness in your heart for someone less fortunate than you? Och! I have never seen ye so hardhearted."

"Stop your caterwauling. I am not going to serve her for breakfast. All I want is the truth."

"Aye, and where were we? Sophie…her name is Sophie. She is French. We have that much. It is a beginning." Tavish gave her a smile.

"Aye, and it is not much to go on," Jamie said, not bothering to hide the skepticism he felt. "The name, by the way, is of Greek origin. It means wise, sensible or discerning, which she does not appear to live up to."

"She has no' been here an hour," Tavish said. "Give her time. Sophie could be a French name, too, don't you think?"

"Aye, it is a common girl's name for both the Dutch and French." He turned back to her. "You don't remember anything save your name, prior to my brother finding you?"

"*Non, monsieur,* I regret to say that I do not. *Je suis désolé.*"

Je suis désolé… He did not think she was sorry about anything, but he had to confess her words curled seductively around him. Even in her state she was a charmer, and it did not hurt that she had a husky voice that made her accented English quite arousing.

Still, something was not right. Jamie was uneasy about her sudden appearance from the sea, when any mortal would have died from the cold. He was not one to ignore his misgivings.

He spoke to Tavish. "We have no idea how she came to be in the water. It does sound a bit preposterous, does it not? A woman who looks like this doesn't randomly fall out of the sky and land at one's feet now, does she?"

"Not unless you are verra lucky," Tavish said as he gave Sophie an encouraging look. "I guess you didna hear about the shipwreck. A ship—the *Aegir*—ran aground late last night, on the rocks below Monleigh Castle. Some of our men were out there until morning, pulling bodies and belongings from the sea. There were no survivors."

"I doubt she was on that ship because you said you found her near Ravenscroft. That is at least ten miles south of Monleigh. She couldn't have survived the extreme cold temperature of the water long enough to reach Ravenscroft alive."

"The ship was bound for Norway," Tavish went on, as if not listening to what Jamie said. "Perhaps she managed to crawl onto a piece of driftwood or perhaps a boat, and floated farther down the coastline with the current."

Jamie shrugged. "Anything is possible, but the only survivor? It sounds too incredible to be true."

"I thought the same at first, but what other explanation could there be? She isna a silkie."

Jamie spoke to the girl again. "Have you no memory of being aboard a ship?"

"*Non,* I remember nothing."

"You better be telling the truth." Jamie spoke the words sharply and grasped her beneath the chin, in order to lift her face to his. She could be lying. She could be a spy. She could be many things—but most of all, she was someone they could not trust.

He studied her eyes, as if searching for the accuracy of her words. "Gloriously deceitful and a virgin renowned forever," he said, recalling the words of Horace.

"What are you thinking?" Tavish asked.

"Have you considered the fact that she could be a spy?"

"A French spy?"

Jamie nodded. "Or English. It is not unheard of, you know. There have been numerous French spies captured while looking for support for the Jacobite cause, and the English have had their spies everywhere, looking for them."

Jamie waited to see how she was taking all of this, but all he saw was the exhaustion, and the drain on her body the extreme temperatures had taken upon her. "Enough discussion for now. We can find out where she is from, and why she is here, at a later time."

"Aye," Tavish said, "she needs to rest. We canna leave her sitting here, shivering and half naked."

Jamie turned and jerked another plaid from a nearby hook. "Remove that wet plaid," he said to Tavish.

"*Non.* I am not dressed, *monsieur.*"

"I can see that, but getting you dry is more important than modesty at this point." He unwrapped his brother's plaid from her and was glad to hear that Tavish's gasp masked his own.

"*Mon dieu!*" she exclaimed, and tried to grab the plaid to cover herself, but Jamie held it away and out of her reach.

She looked at him beseechingly, distress plain on her face, and his only thought was that she was exquisitely beautiful, with a body a man would gladly go to war for. "Well, judging from her reaction, we have learned another thing. She isna a whore."

He caught her chin and held her immobile. "'Was this the face that launch'd a thousand ships, and burnt the topless towers of Ilium? Sweet Helen, make me immortal with a kiss.' "

"Now you *have* frightened the wits out of her," Tavish said. "She is on the verge of tears. Are ye daft, brother?"

Aye, he was seriously beginning to doubt his own sanity, for now he not only had a half-drowned lass to reckon with, but the lust thundering through his veins, as well. All in all this was fast proving to be a trying night.

Yet, he could not ignore her rare beauty—looking up at him with a misty-eyed radiance, virtue simply oozed from her. She might be the object of any man's desire, but something about her screamed innocence, and a long-buried tenderness flared briefly within him. He regretted the aching need within that tempted him, when he should remain perfectly neutral. With a sort of self-inflicted irritation, he quickly covered her, but not before he had a fleeting glimpse of generous, rose-tipped breasts, a nipped-in waist and the flare of feminine hips...and the corresponding rise of his own erection.

With a muffled oath he turned to pick up another log and tossed it on the flames, more because he needed a distraction than from any real need to build up the blazing fire. He did not miss the way she jumped when the vivid show of sparks exploded with loud popping sounds.

"Why are ye so nervous, lass? Are you hiding something?"

"I am not nervous. I am tired. I am cold. I am hungry. I am tired of answering questions. And I grow quite weary of bandying words about with you."

Ever on the defensive, Tavish sprang to her defense once more. "Dinna be so hard on her, Jamie. Can ye no' imagine what she has endured? She hardly looks like a criminal, or someone you should harbor grave doubts about."

"I am too much the skeptic to overlook the possibility of anything. It is my job to be suspicious."

"Aye," Tavish said, "and burned by false fire, mayhap?"

"I take full responsibility for my actions," Jamie replied. "And it might behoove you to remember that I am trying to cope with the paradox of being a loyal Scot, the chief of the clan, the laird of the castle, a man and a brother, while trying to cope with a deeply felt moral obligation toward this lass I find myself responsible for."

"You may be responsible, but you could also be wrong. She could be telling the truth, you know."

"Aye, then perhaps I should be more like you, irresponsible and always right."

Tavish was grinning now. "Aye, ye should, brother. And a wonderful feeling 'tis, ye ken, to always be right."

Sophie sat silently, her attention focused on the two men wrapped in yards of fabric, with legs exposed. A sight such as this—a man's bare legs—was something new to her. They did not dress like the men in France, nor did they resemble the men there in other ways, for they were both more rugged, such that it made her conscious that they were men, and she was a woman, and she needed to cover herself.

There was a sort of physical rawness about them that seemed to permeate everything—an awareness she was never far removed from.

Her attention kept going back to the one called Jamie. With his tanned face, the stubborn chin and high cheekbones, he could have been a gypsy. His hair was long and as black as the night that surrounded them. But it was the smoky-green eyes that captured hers and held her transfixed. They were not the eyes of a gypsy, but the devouring eyes of a man who left no doubt that he was accustomed to being in charge.

She would have to admit that he was devilishly handsome, with classical features and an arrogant nose, which seemed perfectly suited to a man filled with overbearing pride. If she had met him at another time—if the circumstances were different—he would still be full of overbearing pride, she thought.

It was at this point that she realized their gazes had locked, and the way he watched her made her wonder if he was privy to her thoughts, for he almost growled his next words.

"If you are trying to size me up, I can tell you now my heart is as hard as Grampian stone, and if it's my soul you are trying to delve into, it is too dark to see anything...black to the core, it is. That said, I would warn you that you have one last chance to tell me the truth, and if you still persist in not knowing anything, you better pray to whatever god you claim that I never find out differently."

"What is that supposed to mean?" Tavish asked.

"I believe in giving fair warning."

"You obviously believe in playing the bully," she said, and slipped lower into the chair.

"Careful," Jamie said, "you could still find yourself tossed out on your delicate...ear."

Tavish laughed and said, "Don't let him frighten you, lass. He's as harmless as a kitten."

When she did not answer, they both looked and saw she was asleep.

"Get her undressed and into something warm—one of Arabella's gowns, perhaps. Then put her to bed," Jamie said.

Tavish looked aghast. "Me? I brought her here to you. You are the clan chief and the laird of Monleigh Castle. She is your charge now. You undress her."

"I'm about to be betrothed, if you remember."

"I did not ask ye to make love to her, just to take care of her until she's better. Look at it as an act of charity."

"When did you become so shy? It's not as if you didn't spend half your time in Edinburgh undressing lasses."

"At least the lasses there are awake. Undressing an unconscious woman doesna seem right now, does it?"

"You wouldn't really be undressing her, since she's practically naked anyway."

Tavish shrugged. "Then you undress her."

"Has she had anything to eat?"

"Not since I found her," Tavish replied. "We didna stop. I was afraid she would freeze to death on me, so I rode straight through."

"There is some soup left from dinner. It should still be warm. Give her a bowl."

Tavish shook his head. "I dinna have time. I

need to leave my horse and take one of yours, and then I must be off to Edinburgh. I need to make up for some of the time I lost."

"Your horse is lame?"

"No, just worn down keeping up such a pace, with double the load."

Jamie nodded. "Take one of my horses then, but not Corrie."

"That devil-eyed brute? I would walk first," Tavish said, and turned to Sophie. He placed a hand upon her shoulder as gently as he could, but the moment he touched her she jerked in response and her eyes flew open.

She had that dazed expression as if she did not know where she was.

"I apologize for waking you," he said, "but I must be on my way back to Edinburgh. My brother is the Earl of Monleigh and an honorable man, so you have no worry from that quarter. You will be safe here with him until you are able to travel, then he will take you to Monleigh Castle. Have no fear. He seems fierce, but his heart is good. You will be safe, and well cared for under his supervision. Dinna worry about that."

Tavish slapped his brother on the back. "I will see you at Christmas, then."

"Aye, and bring my horse back when ye come."

Tavish laughed. "If I don't lose him gambling," he said, and slammed the door behind him before Jamie could say anything more.

Three

How, like a moth, the simple maid
Still plays about the flame!
—John Gay (1685-1732), English poet and playwright. *The Beggar's Opera* (1728)

With Tavish and his light touch of humor gone, the room soon fell into silence. A tense quiet hung uncomfortably, wafting over her. She felt skittish as a newborn colt trying to stand on wobbly legs. She knew he was watching each breath she took, waiting as a spider waits for some insect to land in its web, so it can kill with the kiss of silken thread.

She could feel her body stiffen with expectancy. This man unnerved her. There was something about the almost melancholy expression on his proud face that touched her, for it was a look that hinted at deep sorrows nobly endured, and she wondered if his destiny was a tragic one, or if she was a part of it.

On edge, she sank deeper into the chair, fighting the uneasiness she felt at being alone with him. He was nothing like the fops she knew at court, and he was nothing like his carefree brother. When he entered the room, one was instantly aware of his physical presence. He aroused feelings she did not understand. She could almost imagine his face close to hers, then closer still, until his warm lips were covering hers. Her body trembled and she wanted him to lie beside her, to give her his warmth.

She blinked her eyes and welcomed the return to reality. This was not the dreamy infatuation of a convent-reared girl. The circumstances were far different, just as the two of them were more than simply a man and a woman.

They were two people who could not trust each other. He had his suspicions that she was lying, that she was not what she appeared to be.

And he was right.

But, she also had her suspicions about him, as well. She did not know if he was someone she could trust—in spite of what his brother said—and consequently they were caught in a stalemate, each determined in his own way to prove the other false.

The truth was, she was frightened of him. Even the tone of his voice alarmed her. There was nothing kind or gentle about him. She was in a strange country, fearful for her life, with no clothes, no money, and she feared what could happen to her if he found out who she was. Under any other circumstances, it would have been the perfect time to cry, but tears would not soften him, and she would not give him the satisfaction of knowing he terrified her that much. It was best to appear confident and unafraid.

She could see the fire was fully blazing now, but she was unable to tell if it did anything to alleviate her cold, numb state. Yet she welcomed the fire as a diversion, which kept her mind off the fact that she was in this strange place with this strange Scot, completely alone, and completely at his mercy—which she had already decided was something he did not have.

His brother said he was an honorable man, an earl, and someone she could trust. Another glance at the long-shanked body that looked as rock hard as his face, and she wondered about that last statement.

He did not look very trustworthy to her.

And it surely looked to her as if he was staring straight at her breasts. Embarrassment rose quickly, and she pulled the plaid higher. He was such a beautiful man—wholly masculine—but beautiful nonetheless. It was a pity he did not have the manners or the disposition to match it.

She wished Tavish had been the one to stay with her. She liked his jovial manner much better. This man was his brother's opposite, for there was nothing about him that was not dark, hard, and as coldly tempered as the swords hanging on the wall.

At last, unable to stand it any longer, she broke the silence. "I can tell by your expression that you are not happy about my being here."

"Aye, I did not come up here to play the nurse. I've more important things to do with my time."

"I never asked to be brought here, you know. If you are going to be angry, be angry with your brother. He should have left me where he found me."

"If he had, you would be dead by now."

"I don't see that my present circumstances are any better. I am cold. My skin is shriveled from so much water. I have been jostled all over creation on the back of a horse, riding in the freezing rain, only to arrive here to be greeted by an ogre. You never asked if I was tired or wanted to retire. I have not been given anything to eat or drink. I have been accused of lying, and having a poor memory, of being a spy. I have been undressed, threatened, ogled and insulted. Compared to all of this, being dead does not seem so bad."

"You would be wise to hold your tongue."

"And you would be wise to learn how to treat a lady," she said, afraid she had angered him now.

Jamie grunted his opinion of her declaration, then said, "I will get you some soup."

"Merci," she said, trying her best to emulate his irritated tone, and at the same time, immensely thankful that he did not strike her or toss her out into the cold.

If she had not been so exhausted and numb she would have tried to leave, but she was not so foolish as to believe she would make it ten paces before collapsing. Besides, she had just come in out of the cold and rain. She had no desire to turn around and face the elements again.

And where would she go?

While he was gone Sophie remained still, staring into the fire in a daze, looking but not really seeing, while exhaustion played with her mind. Barely conscious of the noise he made banging about in the kitchen, she was almost to the point of using up the entire stock of her mental and physical resources. She felt groggy. Her thinking was becoming muddled, and the thought of death, which had been with her throughout her ordeal, stayed with her, to imbibe her with a kind of drowsy cheer.

Would it be warm and peaceful to be dead?

She was in the twilight of evening, where everything is faint and diffuse, her mind somewhere between wakefulness and sleep, when he brought the soup and put it on a small table that he placed before her.

She opened her eyes and inhaled the fragrant warmth, then realized she was ravenously hungry. Perhaps that is a good sign, she thought, although of what, she had no idea.

Jamie grabbed the spoon and thrust it into her hands. "You can stare at it of course, but it will do you more good if you eat it. You do know how to use a spoon, don't you?"

Without giving him a reply, she picked up the spoon and began to eat.

"I will get a bed ready for you," he said, and grumbling, he left her in the room alone.

Later, when he returned, she was fast asleep with her head resting on her arm. The spoon was still in her hand, but the bowl was empty.

"Och, ye are a wee thing," he said, looking at her. A moment later, he scooped her into his arms, lifting her so easily that she might have been a sack of down.

Sophie stirred in his arms and said with a long, stretching yawn, "I can w…alk."

"You can't even talk. Go back to sleep."

Her head flopped against his shoulder in spite of her determination to stay stiff, with her head erect. She felt as if her bones had grown as soft as her brain. It was simply too much effort to even think.

He slid his hand down, over her derriere. "I think you are getting colder if that is possible," he said in a husky, desire-laced voice that was both teasing and confident.

As a way to get her attention, it was effective. Unbelievable, she thought. Is he trying to shock me? Or is this his way of thawing me out—with heat-impassioned words?

Held securely in his arms, she felt as though she was floating up the stairs. Once they reached the top and turned down the corridor she was dimly aware of the thud of his steps on the wooden floors, as well as the erratic thumping of her heart.

Sophie's volatile emotions were running away with her. A man had never taken her in his arms and carried her like this before, and she found it altogether a pleasant experience. There was so much strength in this man, and in the feelings he evoked within her. She seemed at war with herself. He was overwhelming, and she could not deny his looming presence in her mind, any more than she could ignore his presence, or her preoccupation with it.

It left her both attracted and frightened.

He pushed the door to the bedchamber open with his foot.

Sophie opened her eyes to mere slits, just enough to see a candle burning on a table next to a very high bed, turned back, with clean white sheets that looked better than anything she could ever remember seeing.

He dropped her on the bed and she rolled over and burrowed into the sheets. She gasped, for they might look inviting, but they were icy cold. Her skimpy clothing was still clammy and damp beneath the plaid, and she could not control the spasm of shivering that overcame her quite suddenly.

"You are cold to the bone. It will take a lot of heat to warm you."

She hoped he was not going to offer his own body for warmth, for she was so cold, she would have found it more than difficult to turn him down.

She burrowed deeper and reached for the covers.

He grabbed her hand. "Not so fast. You canna sleep in damp clothes." He picked up a nightgown from the end of the bed. "This belongs to my sister. It should fit you."

"Your sister is here?"

"No. I came alone this time." He grabbed the end of the fabric, and for the second time that night unrolled her from a plaid.

Beneath his gaze, her body felt like it was melting from the inside out.

"Is that shift all you have to wear?" he asked.

Shivering violently now, she grabbed at the sheet and tried to cover herself.

He cut her off, and removed what was left of her shift with one yank.

Any other time, Sophie would have fought him to the death, but she was weak as a moonbeam, and her teeth were chattering so loud she feared they might crack. She knew any resistance would be pathetic at best, and could only serve to prolong the period she lay naked and exposed to his eyes.

Her second choice was to snap her eyes shut, for she could not bear to see his face during the most humiliating experience of her life. Please, God, she thought, let this be over as soon as possible, and let him not remember a thing about it on the morrow.

When her humiliation was over and he had the gown pulled over her head and her body covered, she heard his chuckle as he said, "You can open your eyes, lass."

He was buttoning the gown with total indifference, but when he reached her throat, he paused to lift the small gold medallion that hung on a delicate gold chain around her neck.

His expression changed immediately to a hard grimace. "Where did you get this?" he asked, his words clipped and cold.

"I...I don't know for certain, but I think it was given to me," she said, her teeth still chattering.

"By whom?"

"I seem to have the feeling I was a lady's maid, and that perhaps she gave it to me."

"You seem to have a very odd way of remembering things and having an explanation handy when it is necessary."

"I have heard it said that the mind works in strange ways," she said in her defense.

"Aye, and it was beyond strange how your mind conveniently conjured up a memory of being a lady's maid when you had no recollection of it earlier."

She was afraid to look him in the eye, but after a few seconds of silence, she could not resist. When she saw the cynical look of detachment, she shivered. "Of course, that is only a guess, a feeling," she said.

"Of course," he said, and dropped the medallion where it rested on her gown, and it seemed to burn into her flesh on contact.

She pushed it back beneath the buttons and out of sight.

He picked up a decanter of wine resting on the bedside table. He poured a glass and handed it to her. "Drink this. It will warm you."

"I'm not thirsty."

"I didna ask if ye were thirsty, lass. Now, drink it," he said, "or I'll pour it down your throat. You are too pale. It will warm you and put some color on your cheeks."

Her hand came up to touch her face. "I can't even feel my cheeks, so why should I care if they have any color or not?"

"Drink it. It will warm you."

She did not take the glass. "If stripping me naked won't put color to my cheeks, I don't know what will. Do you think I was on that ship? The one that wrecked?"

"Aye, and washed ashore like so much wreckage. It is the only explanation, so it must be the one we accept for now." He thrust the glass of wine toward her again. "Drink it," he said. "I won't tell you again."

She had a vision of him pouring it down her throat as the French do when force-feeding geese to enlarge their livers to make *foie gras.* There was little doubt in her mind that he would not hesitate to do as he threatened.

She scooted back to rest against the headboard and accepted the proffered glass of wine. He pulled the covers over her and tucked them in before he took a seat in the chair beside the bed.

"It really isn't proper for you to be in my bedchamber, even in Scotland."

"Hang propriety. This is an unusual circumstance. I want to make certain you drink the wine...all of it. Besides, if you are a lady's maid like you claim, there isn't anything to worry about, is there? In fact, I could ravish you right here and now, and nothing would come of it. It's the privilege of rank...the same as it is in France, but of course you don't remember anything about that, do you?"

Sophie gasped, took a hurried sip and choked. When she finished coughing she took another sip, and another, until she finished it.

He took the glass from her and placed it on the table. "You don't drink wine like it's medicine. I would think a citizen of France would know that."

"Perhaps I don't care for wine." She stretched and slipped her feet into the depths of the enormous feather mattress and gave a gasp of shock. "Brrrrr. I do not think the wine is warming me at all. It's still very cold."

Jamie mumbled something about being a maid and strode to the fireplace, only to return a moment later with a warming pan. "Move your feet," he said, and after he thrust the pan beneath the covers, he began to move it around slowly.

After a short while, he carried the long-handled pan back to stand it against the hearth.

"Mmm," Sophie said as she pushed her feet down into the warm sheets of fine Holland linen. Before she realized what she was about, she said, "All I need now is a nice hot bath."

"I stop at warming pans," he said and then, as if he had realized the harshness of his tone, his voice softened somewhat. "Perhaps you can have a bath tomorrow, if you are feeling better."

"Oh, yes, a bath! The thought of it makes me feel better already."

"It's a good thing you had the wine. Your cheeks are getting some color."

She hated to tell him it wasn't the wine at all that brought the flush of color to her face, but for some reason she could not seem to find her voice. It only made things worse feeling the burn of his green gaze, hot upon her skin.

He picked up the glass and stood. "I will bid you good night, lass. We are an honorable clan. Ye have nothing to fear from us."

"Unless I am not telling you the truth."

His eyes searched hers. "Aye, unless you are not telling us the truth. Sleep as long as you like on the morrow. I will rise early to hunt."

"Thank you, for your help, and your kindness."

He started to blow out the candle.

"Leave it, please," she said, "until you have quit the room, and then I will douse it."

"Don't forget and fall asleep first."

"I won't."

She watched his long-limbed body as he left the room, and continued to stare at the door, long after he had closed it, until the sound of his retreating footfalls faded away completely.

She lay there, staring up at the ceiling, until the fire in the hearth was dying and the sheets were growing cold again. Her hand clutched the golden medallion, and she rubbed her thumb over the raised image of a *fleur-de-lis*.

Was he familiar with the icon? she wondered.

She prayed Jamie Graham had no knowledge of the heraldic symbol, with its three tapering petals tied by a surrounding band, long used by the kings of France.

A sigh escaped her lips. If he only knew…

Visions came to her… Of a ship foundering in the storm and breaking up against the jutting rocks, the icy cold of the water as she was thrown into it, and the heavy burden of her clothes, like leaden weights pulling her down… down…down…

And then she could see her father's face before her, calling out to her, much as he had done when Sophie had fallen out of a boat when she was a small child, and her father watched helplessly from the shore.

"Take off your dress, Sophie. You cannot swim because of the weight. Remove it! Quickly, child."

Sophie had obeyed her father's command and swum to shore and into his loving arms.

She did not want to think about her father or the shipwreck. She closed her eyes and wished for sleep, but all she saw were the dark, icy waters of the North Sea closing over her head, and the way she struggled to remove her clothes, so terrified that she would drown before she could do so. By that time, she was already so very cold that she had difficulty with the buttons, but she finally managed somehow to rip the dress from her body and kick off her shoes.

When she surfaced at last, she no longer heard the screams of the other passengers. All she could hear was the pounding roar of the sea thrashing, and dashing itself against the rocks. She wondered if she could make it to shore when she was struck by the bow of a small boat, and felt someone grab her and pull her aboard.

She vaguely remembered hearing a male voice and that he wrapped her in a dry blanket. She huddled in the bow of the boat, water streaming from her nose and mouth, while the wind and the sea seemed determined to drive them straight to the bottom.

She must have dozed off at some point, for she the next thing she remembered was being hurled forward as the boat struck something, and the sound of splintering wood echoed with a deafening roar through her ears.

The boat bounced and then crashed back into the rocks, and Sophie was thrown into the sea once again. She struggled to keep her head above water and called for help, but she never saw the man or the boat again.

The current was strong and at first she tried to fight it, but then it occurred to her that the boat had struck a rock, so that must mean the current had carried the boat toward the shore. She began to drift with the current, until the numbness began to slow her. She had only a vague recollection of her feet scraping against rocks, her body being washed ashore, and then the feeling that she was going to die, surrounded by nothing but bitter cold and a driving wind.

Her hand came up to the medallion once again. She rubbed her hand over the *fleur-de-lis,* as she had a habit of doing since her father had given it to her.

"It belonged to your grandfather, Sophie," he said.

It wasn't until Sophie was older that she realized the importance of her grandfather, and what it meant to be the granddaughter of Louis XIV, the King of France, and that he had worn this very medallion before giving it to her father. As a child, she was told how very fortunate she was to be the granddaughter of the Sun King.

Having a beautiful face and being the granddaughter of the King of France carried a double curse, Sophie learned later, when she became the pawn of kings.

Enough, she told herself. That part of your life is over now. No one will ever know of your royal blood, if you do not tell them.

She doused the candle and slipped farther down into the bed, wondering how much warmer she would have been if Jamie Graham were lying here beside her.

Her thoughts were foolish, she knew, yet she could not help wishing for human contact, and even his presence—warm, strong and protective. At least she would not be alone if he were here.

Her heart cracked at the thought, for it was true. She was completely alone, in a strange land, and her heart felt as abandoned, lonely and as bleak as the windswept crags of the cold mountains that surrounded this place.

She knew she should harbor no illusions about Jamie Graham. He would have no use for her when he learned the truth; when he discovered she was the granddaughter of the Sun King.

That thought carried its own warning, and she reminded herself that her life may be in more danger here with him than it would be with the English, or the French.

She had to congratulate herself, for she always managed to get herself in a silver-lined dilemma. And what was she doing romanticizing about a grim Scot, when she should be concerned for her life?

Because there was no help for it; she simply could not stop thinking about him, even to the point of infatuation, for she had to admit he was quite probably the most impossible, terrifying, deliciously beautiful man she had ever seen.

Why was he not the man the King of France chose for her to marry instead of that unspeakable villain, the Duke of Rockingham?

She could not forget the smooth, sensual lips, the proud nose with the aristocratic slant, the hair as black as the devil's own heart, and those eyes that missed nothing. And when he walked from her bedside to the door, she could almost hear music playing, for he moved with such a graceful, sensual ease that it made her want to call him back.

But she could not call him back, for it would do no good. He was an honorable man, a leader who would never trust her, because he did not believe her lies. She wished that she could take back everything she had said and start over. Would that she could simply tell him the truth—but she knew she could not. No, not yet, for she had no way of knowing where his loyalties lay.

If he were loyal to the crown he would turn her over to the English in a heartbeat. If he was a Jacobite, and a follower of the man they called Bonnie Prince Charlie, he would turn her over to the French. Either way, she would lose, for either of these choices would soon land her in the Duke of Rockingham's bed. She shuddered at the thought of being the wife of such a horrid excuse for a man.

The only way she could get any sleep was to resolve this issue once and for all, so she told herself that once she learned of Jamie Graham's leanings, and had the inward assurance that he would not hand her over to either king, she would tell him the truth. She hoped when that happened, it would not be too late. If she waited too long and he found out the truth for himself, he would turn his back on her, and she would never, ever stand a chance to gain his help, or win his heart.

A man like Jamie Graham would love and love deeply, but even that would not be enough to hold his heart if the woman he loved ever betrayed him.

If only it were possible. If only he was a man like those of the legends of yore, a man who would defy heaven or hell to love and protect her, and keep her forever by his side.

She drifted off to sleep, feeling acutely the loss of love, before ever having experienced it.

Four

Not all that tempts your wand'ring eyes
And heedless hearts, is lawful prize;
Nor all that glisters, gold.
—Thomas Gray (1716-1771), English poet.
"On a Favourite Cat, Drowned in a Tub of Gold Fishes" (1748). *The Poems of Thomas Gray: William Collins: Oliver Goldsmith*

Jamie went below stairs and poured a glass of wine, then slumped into an empty chair—the same chair Sophie had sat in earlier.

His mind quickly went over the assorted array of thoughts vying for attention, the primary one being his suspicions about the sudden appearance of a certain French lass in his life and how she managed, in a short while, to complicate everything.

He knew so little about her, which naturally fueled his suspicions. And there was the fact of her lack of memory, and the vagueness of some of her answers. Yet his doubts isolated him, for there was no lonelier feeling than to distrust someone you desperately wanted to trust and believe in.

He had a responsibility to his country, his clan, his family, and even to the lass now in his care, and that made him wonder how much more complicated things could become.

The situation in Scotland was tenuous, and likely to get worse, for Bonnie Prince Charlie was stirring things up with his claim to the British crown. Because he had many followers in the Highlands, the British were worried. If Charlie were to win enough French support, he could attempt to gain the crown.

In the British mind, preventing a war was much easier than winning one, so they attempted to trample all Stuart support into the ground, before it became a greater threat.

Jamie knew they would not stop until they reached their ultimate goal—the complete annihilation of the Highlanders. The names of acquaintances arrested as Jacobites was growing, and he rarely picked up the newspaper without seeing the name of a friend who had been imprisoned.

Spies were everywhere. He would not put it past the English to send a beautiful temptress to ferret information, under the pretext of being a shipwrecked lass, for they had been guilty of much worse in the past.

Whenever he looked at Sophie's angelic face, he wanted to trust her, wanted to believe everything she said. He could not allow his desire—to help her or to bed her—to rule his head, and neither could he allow his heart to acquit her because he found her desirable.

And therein lay the crux.

How could he accuse her unjustly, and call her a spy, without proof?

He had practically betrothed himself, only two weeks ago, to a woman he did not love, and then the ideal mistress floats out of the North Sea and into his life. She was the kind of woman a man wanted to keep all to himself, and the thought of making love to her nightly held an inordinate amount of appeal.

He could not erase the memory of her sweet body and innocent face, the full lips made for kissing, and the long legs that would fit so perfectly around a man's torso. She was as rare as virgin's milk.

He shifted his position, feeling uncomfortably hard. Thoughts of her had a way of doing that to him. Desire for her was like a snake that coiled around him, sinuous and subtle, charming him and catching him unawares, until the fatal bite.

How could he ever be satisfied with Gillian, the woman he thought to make his wife? Gillian, who managed to arouse nothing in him, save his temper...

As always, his thoughts could never reside with Gillian for long, and now thoughts of Sophie were beginning to supersede them. He thought about the way Sophie said *Oh, yes,* and how her sultry voice aroused him instantly, and stirred impassioned thoughts as he wondered what it would be like to copulate with her and have her whisper *Oh, yes,* in exactly that way the moment he came inside her.

The idea of making love to her was elbowing its way to the forefront of his mind, for all thoughts seemed to eventually wind up there. Naturally, that made him consider the probability of it happening. She thought she was a lady's maid, and, if so, he could have her at will, but there was something about her that made him suspect she might be more than a lowly maid.

She seemed too refined, too genteel.

Oh, he wanted her to be a lady's maid, and wished for it to be true, for then he could go ahead with his plans for marriage to Gillian, and when his obligation there was done, and an heir was born, he could seek his pleasure elsewhere, and he knew without a doubt that when it came to Sophie, she would be all pleasure.

It occurred to him also that if she was not a lady's maid, and if she was of a higher position or, God forbid, a member of the peerage, then having her here alone with him had already compromised them both.

Well, it was a little too late to think about that now. The oarless boat was adrift in the water, and could not be called back. If Tavish had taken her to Monleigh Castle instead, things would be different. But he had not, and now she was here.

There was a reason this lass came into his life, at this particular moment, and whether it was to turn his world upside down or to fit smoothly in his plans to keep her beside him for as long as it pleased him, he had no idea. He could only wait and see which one it would be.

He hardly slept that night, for it was difficult to sleep when he knew Sophie was lying in another bed alone, and not very far away. All he had to do was go to her. Somehow, he knew—call it instinct—that she would not turn him away.

By the time morning came, he was tied in enough knots that he decided a cold swim would shock some much-needed sense back into him and cool the raging lust that roared for attention, for it would not serve the Earl of Monleigh well to go about as besotted as a schoolboy, with the front of his kilt raised up, especially when he was only two weeks into the idea of marriage to someone else.

Gillian came briefly into his mind but could not linger, so overpowered she was by the lustful image of a French lass.

Sophie… Ah, Sophie. The superlatives came easy when thinking of her. A natural beauty, she could have descended from Aphrodite herself, for she possessed all the qualities of beauty, being both pleasing to look at and desirable to touch. A beautiful woman was something to be enjoyed and he intended to do just that. A few simple thoughts of her aroused a wild sort of heat within him that he felt with sharp intensity.

The sun had not been up long when he slipped away and made his way down to the narrow shallows of the river. He stepped into the icy water, submerged himself and walked back to shore, droplets of water sluicing down his naked body.

By the time he picked up his plaid and began wrapping himself in yards and yards of fabric, the rivulets of water had pooled into a single channel that ran, straight as a pine, between the muscles of his chest and abdomen.

He followed the line of water until it disappeared and saw that the cold swim had not had the desired effect. He was still hard. He tried not to think about the best way to rectify that. Slinging the water from his hair, he took long strides back to the lodge.

He was surprised to find her sitting in the chair by the fire when he walked into the kitchen.

"What are you doing up, lass? I have no' yet had time to build up the fire. Right now, it is putting out a sorry amount of heat."

"I have been here only a few minutes, and I do find the kitchen to be much warmer than my room."

"Aye, 'tis the warmest room in the house. With the staff is away, I dinna bother to light fires in the other rooms."

He stirred the coals and added some kindling, which ignited immediately. He continued to poke at the fire for a while and then, with a satisfied grunt, he stacked three logs over the flames. "It should start getting warmer soon. Are ye hungry?"

"Yes, but what I would really like is a bath. I still have all this salt water in my hair, and bits of debris and sand, too. When I awoke, I found a piece of seaweed stuck to my cheek."

He wanted to tell her it would take more than seaweed to mar her beauteous face, but he decided against it, knowing it would only make her uncomfortable. Instead, he simply watched as she tried to smooth her curly, matted hair back from her face.

When she saw he was watching, she said, "I fear I am a frightful sight, rather haggard-looking, I know."

"Och, lass, it would take more than a wee bit o' seaweed or tangled hair to mar beauty such as yours," he said, having decided it was a statement that needed saying.

She dipped her head and he marked her shy, realizing she had not been able to completely ignore his comment.

"This is one time I am thankful there is not a looking glass about," she said.

He did not want to tell her that his opinion was better than any reflection in a looking glass. He wondered at her reaction if he were to tell her she looked good enough that he could easily throw her over his shoulder and carry her up to his bed without hesitation. Or that he would pause only long enough to warm her up, so she wanted him as much as he wanted her, and that she would be crying out for him when he took her.

"If it's a bath ye want, lass, then a bath ye shall have. I will heat some water for you."

She glanced down at the gown she was wearing, and he did not miss that she had wrapped his plaid around most of it. "I was wondering if your sister might have something here that I could borrow to wear."

"While you are bathing, I will go above stairs to see what I can find."

"It will be heavenly to have a real dress to wear—and a clean one. It is not easy to keep everything covered with a bolt of cloth. *Mon dieu*, I don't know how you do it."

"It bothers you more than it does me. As far as my taste is concerned, I would find it far more pleasing to the eye to have you going about in nothing at all. I find myself hoping that might happen."

"I fear I shall dash all your expectations then, for that is highly unlikely."

"I will remind you of that one day, lass. Have no doubt about that."

It was obvious she made a great effort to ignore both him and his comment, and he was unable to read what she was thinking in the smooth contours of her lovely face.

He said nothing more as he filled the large kettle with water and pushed the hook so the pot was centered over the hottest part of the flames. While the water heated, he set about making a simple breakfast of ham and oatmeal.

The food was ready before the water was hot enough, so he placed a bowl of oatmeal on the table, with a side dish of ham next to it. He made her a cup of tea. "Do you take honey in your tea?"

"Yes…*merci,* but I truly would like to bathe before I eat."

"You should eat first so you don't lose what little strength you have when you step into that warm water."

He offered her his hand and helped her to her feet. He led her to the table, for it was obvious she was still a bit light-headed, and he wondered at the wisdom of letting her in a tub of warm water, but he doubted he would have much luck with talking her out of it.

Once she was seated, he took the seat opposite her and ate his oatmeal. After a few minutes, he sat back to observe her while he drank his tea. She was a dainty eater, and well mannered. She knew the proper way to use a utensil, and he noticed how she never put her elbows on the table. If she was a maid, he decided it had to be in the service of a woman with a title—someone with breeding and a thorough knowledge of social graces.

"How is your memory this morning?" he asked.

"My m-memory?"

He did not miss the shocked, uncomfortable expression that moved rapidly across her lovely features, to be replaced by one of outward calm when she caught the meaning of his question. "Oh, you mean my *lack* of memory?"

"Your inability to recall past experiences would be one way of putting it. The Greeks have a word, *amnestia,* which means forgetfulness."

"Which comes from *amnestos,* which means not remembered."

"Interesting that you can recall that," he said. "You are in possession of an unusually good knowledge of languages for a maid, wouldn't you say?"

"Perhaps, but who knows? I might have been a lady's companion, or a governess. I really do not have a firm recollection of that part of my life. As I told you, it is only a feeling I have that I was in some type of service to a lady...one of high regard, I think."

A sardonic smile came and went quickly, and he doubted she had even noticed, but she surprised him.

"The name for your smile, *monsieur,* has come via my own language—the French word *sardonique,* which ironically comes from the Greek word *sardanios,* which means…"

"Scornful, which originally meant Sardinian."

"Ah, yes, like the Sardinian plant, which if eaten makes terrible contortions on the face. Is that what you had for breakfast, milord?"

She had a fine mind, and he enjoyed playing these word games with her. She was his equal in that. He wondered in what other areas she would be a good match for him. "I would cast my lot with governess," he said. "'Tis more than obvious that you are no common maid."

"My oatmeal grows cold," she said, and began to eat.

He cleared away his dishes and dipped a finger into the kettle to check the temperature. He yanked it back quickly. "Your water is hot. While you finish eating, I will fill the tub."

He knew he made an inordinate amount of noise, banging the large copper tub about, but this was not the sort of thing the Earl of Monleigh usually did. However, by the time she finished eating he had the tub filled, with a drying cloth and a slice of soap sitting nearby. "Need you any help?" he asked, almost leering at her and feeling his teasing her like this was becoming a regular habit and something, he had to admit, he rather enjoyed.

Something akin to amusement danced in her eyes. "Thank you, no. I have been bathing myself for some time."

"Perhaps I should wait here, to make certain you haven't fainted once you are in the water."

"There is one way to find out, isn't there?" And with that, she stood and went to the tub, and dropped the plaid before she stepped in.

"You aren't going to remove your sleeping gown?"

"I will once you have left the room. It needs washing, anyway."

All Jamie could think about was her sitting in that bathtub a few minutes from now, bare and beautiful, with her soft skin shimmering with all the richness of the finest pearls. He called to memory the image of her the night before, when she lay completely nude in her bed, eyes closed, while he pulled his sister's gown over her head and buttoned it.

That had taken a mountain of will, for it had not been easy to resist the temptation to put his mouth over her breast and to try his own method of warming her.

"I will leave you and go in search of something suitable for you to wear," he said at last.

He did not have to turn back to look at her to know she was watching him. He could feel it. He smiled. He was never one to disappoint a hopeful lass, so he gave her something to look at when he let his plaid slip as he went around the door.

Five

When Love's delirium haunts the glowing
mind,
Limping Decorum lingers far behind.

—Lord Byron (1788-1824),
English poet. *Answer to Some Elegant Verses Sent by a Friend*

She might be a maiden and untouched by human hands, but one would have to be a blithering idiot not to know that she had just been given a good look at the Earl of Monleigh's well-muscled buttocks, and just a glimpse, mind you, of that part of his anatomy that lay on the opposite side.

That in itself was shocking enough (although she would never admit that she enjoyed it immensely), but the worst part of it was, she knew he had done it on purpose, just to shock her and see her reaction.

Shocked she was, but she would not give him the satisfaction of letting him know she had even noticed.

Truthfully, she was wishing by this point in time that he had walked a little slower. After all, if he was going to give her a look at his privates, why not give her a good look?

She knew he was doing his best to seduce her, by giving her a glimpse of what exactly he had to offer. Dangling his wares before her as he had, she was reminded of the fisherman who baited his hook to catch the big fish.

Only she was not biting.

By the time he returned with a dress slung over his shoulder, a slow-spreading smile on his sensual lips, Sophie was out of the tub and wrapped in his plaid. She was leaning toward the fire, fluffing her hair to dry it. He crossed the room and placed the dress, undergarments and a pair of slippers on a chair, before he thrust a comb in front of her face. Then he said, "I thought you might need this."

"A comb! *Oh! Merci...merci beaucoup.* I was finding it quite impossible to get the tangles out with my fingers."

He took her hand and pulled her to her feet. Without releasing her, he sat down in the chair and pulled her into his lap. Before she had a chance to squeal her dissatisfaction with the arrangement, he began to comb her hair.

"Just to conserve your strength," he said.

Sophie could only manage a muffled "Hmm..." as she closed her eyes and let herself be completely seduced by the warmth of the fire, the nearness of him, and the luxury of having a man who looked as good, and smelled as fine, as he did, comb her hair.

She had no idea how long his hand had been there when she opened her eyes and realized his hand was cupping her breast. Her heart began to hammer so furiously she thought for a moment it had sprouted wings and would fly right out of her chest. Her first thought was she had fallen too quickly into a comfortable place with him, and now he had closed the gate and locked it, trapping her inside.

She turned her head to tell him in so many words to remove his hand from her breast, but when she whipped her head around, her lips collided with his. The next thing she knew his hot tongue was inside her mouth, and he was kissing her as if a ban on kissing was going into effect tomorrow.

There was no knowledge of the exact moment he slipped the plaid from her shoulders, only the memory of a cool draft upon her skin, and the feel of his arms lifting her and carrying her down with him, to lie on the hearth rug before the fire.

How he managed to unwrap miles of plaid so deftly, she would never know. He had to be part sorcerer—a descendant of one of those mystical beings that roamed the moors centuries ago, casting spells hither and yon, bewitching the unsuspecting.

He dug his fingers into her hair, telling her how beautiful she was and how much he had wanted to do this since the moment he first saw her, half-naked and in his brother's arms.

All of a sudden, none of it seemed to matter to her.

She did not care that his hand was on her breast, or that his tongue was in her mouth, or that he had peeled away the layers of his plaid until she lay completely bare before him, warmed only by the heat from the fire, and the heat that was even more intense that came from Jamie himself.

He had the hands of a magician, for he knew just where to touch her and how to make her want him with a deep yearning—with a fierceness she had never known before.

From somewhere deep within her she felt the first stirrings of a sweeping response for which she was totally unprepared—a naked awareness of intimacy that called to her like beckoning fingers, urging her to follow his lead. She was slowly being consumed by a lazy awakening of desire that urged her to turn her back on caution and go with him, only to have him leave her trembling at the entrance to a new world of yearning and delight that yawned wickedly before her.

Her only fear was that it would completely engulf her and leave her bound as tightly as a slave to him.

Out of the impassioned blur, his face began to take form above her, like a vision, and she remembered her days in the convent when she was taught the devil could take many forms.

Oh, my, was that she who was making that whimpering sound?

She decided it must have been, for he stroked the sensitive lobe of her ear with his teeth and whispered, "Don't be afraid. I would never hurt you, lass. Never."

Her first impulse was to fling her arms and legs to the four winds and let him have his way with her, but her uncertainty about exactly what all *his way* involved, she allowed her more chaste thoughts to overrule her melting-hot impulses.

He kissed her deeply, and caressed her until she was close to tossing her chaste thoughts out the nearest window.

What was that digging into her hipbone?

When sudden understanding came to her, she wondered why women used the word *prick* as a term of endearment, for she could find nothing endearing about the knowledge of just what part of him was rudely pressed against her hip.

His tone was comforting, his hands gentle, his words soothing, and soon she forgot about the discomfort to her hip, or rather she found that some things can walk a fine line between pain and pleasure, for now the knowledge she had previously shunned was giving her a feeling of power, and it washed over her warmly. She learned, too, that there is no aphrodisiac like power.

Oh, he knew what he was about, and although she knew he was beginning to draw her under his powerful control with the innocent reassurance of his kiss and the gentle stroke of his hands, she was powerless to stop him, because deep, deep down she wanted this, and had wanted it almost from the first.

She was as ripe as a fig ready for the plucking, and she knew it the moment his hands touched her.

Faintly aware of the sound of rain tapping at the

window, she responded passionately when his mouth came hungering, but this time he did not kiss her with the same intensely hot kiss as before, but a kiss that merely brushed her lips lightly, teasing and drawing her out to make her yearn for it, driving her to seek the heat, the searing heat that he had branded her with earlier.

She moaned her disenchantment and pulled his face down to hers, until their lips were touching.

This time, it was he who groaned, and the feeling of having this power over him returned, and with it the deep craving for more. As if sensing her frustration, he brought his fingers to her lips and with subdued pressure parted them, before replacing his fingers with his mouth, and reducing her to a molten lump of yearning.

She never knew there was more to kissing than simply bringing two sets of lips together. His kisses were plundering, consuming, and evoked all kinds of responses from her she never knew herself capable of making.

Oh, please, she thought. That cannot be me moaning again.

Why would anyone whimper when they kissed? And why did it make one's heart beat faster? Or their lips feel all swollen and hot? She remembered the women at court and the countless affairs that went on all around her. She called to mind the men who made it their profession to seduce women. And lastly, she recalled the way they would leave soon after the conquest, to seduce someone else.

"Please..." she whispered. "Oh, please stop."

Her words seemed to drive him onward with renewed vigor, and she was already dizzy from the rush of the last onslaught. She could feel the smooth hardness of his muscles beneath her hands, as his own hands slipped lingering over her torso and down the flat surface of her stomach. She could feel his prick hard against her hip again, and gasped when his hand slipped lower to the vee between her legs—although she had to admit that it fit so perfectly there—she wondered if it had been created for that specific purpose.

His hand began to emulate perfectly the thrust and rhythm of his tongue, and her body seemed to take over and do her thinking for her, which was all right, since she was completely incapable of thinking of anything at the moment save all the delicious things he was doing to her and the way her body seemed to blossom under the touch of his hand.

A booming clap of thunder saved her virginity.

At least that is what she thought later, for there

was little doubt in her mind that if it had not ripped across the sky at that particular moment to rattle the panes of glass at the windows, she would have ended up flat on her back, legs spread wide, with Jamie Graham teaching her everything he knew about lovemaking, which would probably take eons.

Dizzy from the sudden jerk back to reality, she pulled back from him and brought her hands to her temples. She had come dangerously close to being completely absorbed by him, and on the verge of losing her common sense along with her virginity.

Did she not have enough troubles without giving in to more?

She had lost her country, her home and her family. A day ago she had almost died. She was living a lie and pretending to be something and someone she was not. Her very life was at stake, and what was she doing? Becoming awestruck and completely captivated by a man she had known only a few hours.

All she had was her virginity, and she had almost begged him to take that.

Kissing was one thing, becoming a *courtisane* was something else entirely. She would have to be very, very careful around him from now on.

She made the mistake of taking no more than a quick peek at him and saw those green eyes of his missed nothing, for he seemed to look into her very soul, probing for answers to questions only he knew. She did not understand why she kept having the same feeling around him that she had when she was being sucked under the waters of the North Sea, afraid she was drowning and incapable of saving herself.

"It's raining," she said, needing some diversion and time to regroup. She desperately needed to recover and plan her defenses for the onslaught of his next attack—which was surely to come.

"Aye, lass, I ken it is raining," he said, the drone of his Scots burr coming like a purr from deep in his throat. "You will become accustomed to it in time."

"It rains a great deal, does it not?"

"Only twice a year—October to May, and June to September."

She laughed, thankful for the gift of humor that was suddenly bestowed upon her. "Well, at least it is easy to predict the weather then."

"Aye, if ye can see the Grampians it is going to rain. If ye canna see the Grampians 'tis already raining."

She stared at him, wide-eyed, and completely captivated by his chiseled features. All this and humor, too, she thought.

He kept her under his scrutiny for a moment or two, then kissed her lightly on the nose before he stood and pulled her up with him.

"You should get dressed. I need to see to the horses and bring in more wood."

She pulled the plaid around her and gathered up his sister's clothes that he had brought down for her.

It felt strange to think about wearing another woman's undergarments as well as her clothes, but Sophie was thankful that Jamie's sister was about her size, and that her taste in clothing was very similar to hers. Considering the fact they were of very different nationalities, she found that one little tidbit made her feel optimistic. Perhaps they might have a few other things in common, as well.

As she made her way trudgingly up the stairs and down the hallway to her room, she could not help wondering about this strange, enigmatic Scot. Who was Jamie Graham really? One moment she felt as if she had known him forever and that she could practically see straight into his heart, only to find the next moment he had become a complete stranger—cold, aloof and distant.

Once in her room, she saw he had built up the fire and the room was much warmer than when she had left it earlier. The fire was warm and tranquilizing, and the bed so inviting she could not resist. She decided to lie down only for little a while, not to sleep, mind you, but simply to rest her eyes.

The moment her head touched the pillow, she was overcome with drowsiness.

When she awoke, she knew she must have slept longer than she should have, for the sun had dropped lower in the sky, and the fire that had burned so brightly before was now nothing more than smoldering ashes.

Although still plagued with a feeling of fatigue, she did feel a bit better. As she donned her borrowed gown and dressed her hair, she wondered how long she would continue to be exhausted of both strength and energy. She knew it was vanity on her part to long for a looking glass so she might see how the dress of gold brocade looked on her. And for a moment her weariness was forgotten.

Feeling like a woman for the first time since her ordeal, she went below stairs. Jamie was not in the kitchen, so she wandered about, looking in several of the rooms. Sophie ended up taking a rather lengthy tour of the beautiful rooms that made up the first floor of Danegæld Hall, although she still did not find Jamie.

It was only when she returned to the kitchen that she found him standing in front of the window with his back to her.

She glanced at the table and saw two places set. A pot bubbled merrily over the fire. The kitchen was warm, she was clean and wearing a dress. She inhaled the delicious fragrance of food, unable to believe she was feeling famished again.

She would have felt the promise in the moment, but when she looked back at the black silhouette of him against the pale gray of the sky outside, he appeared touchingly solitary to her, and something about it reached out to her.

As if drawn to him by some unknown force, she crossed the room quietly, her slippers making no sound, and came within mere inches of his back.

She lifted her hand to touch him but stopped short of doing so. She had no idea why she'd come so brazenly to where he stood, or what she expected to happen now that she had been so bold. It was as if something or someone had taken control and was guiding her steps, and she was powerless to do anything but obey.

What was the commanding influence that gave him authority over her and seemingly negated her own will?

* * *

He did not hear her enter, but he sensed her presence.

Still, he did not turn toward her, for he preferred to wait and see what she would do. He had been thinking about her during her absence, and went so far as to go to her room to see about her when she did not return after so long a time.

When he'd opened her door, he saw immediately that she was sleeping, and upon closer inspection, he saw the dark circles beneath her eyes, the fatigue that went to her very center. Her ordeal had weakened her, and it would take some time for her to fully recover the loss of so much of her vitality. He thought of how close she had come to dying, and was thankful Tavish had found her when he did.

He wanted her. It was obvious to him the moment he returned below stairs, for the rooms seemed suddenly empty and cold without her. He did not understand it, for he could never remember being so preoccupied with a woman before.

He regretted he had allowed his desire for her to build into a driving need to copulate, just as he was sorry that it pushed him to the point of almost seducing her—when she was still weak of body, and inexperienced when it came to lovemaking. A woman like her deserved more, and yet, around her he was a predatory animal.

It was all pure lusting instinct and the need to possess. Yet, he knew once would never be enough, for she was the kind of woman a man kept beside him.

In the back of his mind, he kept asking himself if he frightened her. It had all happened so fast that he did not have time to consider anything except making love to her. It had taken a bolt of thunder to bring them both to their senses, although he considered all the blame to be his.

Still standing behind him, Sophie lifted her hand to test the texture of his hair that was tied back with a leather thong.

He turned suddenly, and tried to understand what was happening here. This strength of feeling, this compelling desire, the tender emotion was both alien and strong, and it lodged like the sharpest lance in his heart.

She was wearing Arabella's dress, but his sister had never looked so good in it, for the deep gold color was not as becoming to her coloring. But on Sophie, it only served to draw out the golden tones of her skin and the warm brown tones of her chestnut hair. The light from the fire illu-

minated her with a pearly glow, and he found h
so lovely he ached to take her in his arms.

The moment he turned, she dropped her hand and stood quietly before him. She seemed uncertain, and thoughtfully quiet, and he found this unsettling, for it was he who was so uncertain. "Ye fear me."

She did not answer him at first, and he was about to turn back to the window when she said, "I do not fear you, but who I am—what I become when I am with you."

"You are still the same person, in my presence or away from it. You have not changed. Only your circumstances have."

"No, you are wrong. I have changed a great deal, and there is no going back."

"What do you mean, 'changed'? How so?"

"I know things. I feel them. There is now awareness where there was nothing before."

"What kind of things?"

"Knowledge…the forbidden fruit. It is as if I have been locked out of my own world. I no longer know myself or my capabilities."

"Ahh, you feel…"

"Immoral."

He frowned. *Immoral?* That was not the word he was thinking of. "You aren't immoral, you are only awakening to your own wants and desires that have been dormant since you were born. Clear your mind of any prudish thoughts. There is a first time for all of us."

That brought a smile to her shapely, made-for-kissing lips. "Somehow I cannot believe there was ever a first time for you. I think you are superhuman, a being beyond ordinary understanding. I do not think you were ever an apprentice. You are like Athena, who leaped forth from the brain of Zeus, mature and wearing full amour. Oh, I do not know what I am saying. I rattle on like a babbling drunk. I keep having the compunction to speak, even when I have nothing to say. Perhaps I swallowed too much seawater. I hear it does strange things to the mind."

He took her in his arms and pulled her close. "Is that better?"

"No, it is worse. My heart is beating so fast, and I feel I must speak faster to match pace."

He pulled back enough to see her face and saw immediately the inner chaos, the conflict of emotions that fought for control. He felt an odd sort of curiosity to keep her with him long enough to see which one would emerge the victor. Would it be the pride of overcoming tears of humiliation, or the final succumbing to the power of breathless desire?

"Your sister's dress fits me perfectly," she said,

looking down to smooth the fabric that did not need smoothing, not that it mattered, for he knew she was only mentally groping for something else to say.

"Aye, lass, I am not a man to miss such as that."

He knew his inquisitive visual caress sent a responsive wave of pleasure rippling across her. He was glad it unnerved her. He wanted her senses acutely tuned to him. He wondered if she, like him, relived the moments when the two of them lay on the floor in front of the fire, and if the recalling of it swirled around her like an opium cloud, desensitizing her and making everything else in the world seem oddly distant.

He was so wrapped up in the nearness of her and his own desire, that he did not at first notice the fine beads of perspiration that suddenly appeared on her face, or the absence of color there.

He was about to ask how she was feeling when she gave him an empty look and said very softly, "I don't think I feel very well."

And she fainted dead away.

Six

I shall not say why and how I became, at the
age of fifteen,
the mistress of the Earl of Craven.
—Harriette Wilson (1786-1846),
British writer and courtesan. Opening of
book. *Memoirs of Harriette Wilson* (1825)

He caught her before she hit the floor.

He gathered her close and carried her up the winding staircase, castigating himself as he went. He should have noticed the change in her before she collapsed. He could have given her a chair, or a glass of wine, but he was too preoccupied with his own thoughts.

He carried her into her room and placed her

gently on the bed. He stood over her, watching her beautiful breasts rise and fall with each breath, and was about to splash a little water on her face when she stirred and said, "*Non... non...non... Je ne veux pas me marier.*"

I do not want to marry? Was she betrothed? And if so, to whom?

He dipped a cloth in water and bathed her face and, as he did, he wondered what demons tortured her, or if she would recall what she said when she awoke.

She looked so small and terribly young lying in repose, and he felt a strong sense of protectiveness toward her.

He should take her to Monleigh Castle.

He knew that, but he could not bring himself to do it. He wanted to keep her here with him, to have her all to himself, if only for a little while. It was simply that he wanted to be alone with her, for as long as he dared to think he could get away with it. Opportunities for a man of his class to be alone with a woman were practically nonexistent and, when he returned to Monleigh with her, there would be few opportunities to be with her alone there, in the midst of all the family members and clansmen crowded about.

It was at this point that he found he was glad

for her fainting spell, for it sanctioned his decision to keep her here a few more days.

He studied her delicate features, the flawless skin and the perfectly shaped features that lodged so symmetrically on her oval face. She had unbelievably long lashes, and he wished they would flutter and her eyes would open.

He placed his hand on her forehead to be certain she had no fever, and the moment his fingertips brushed her skin, she mumbled something and opened her eyes.

She blinked a few times, and he imagined she had opened them into a hazy fog of blurred images. She blinked again and looked around, as if trying to decide where she was.

"I don't remember coming up here."

"You didn't. You fainted and I carried you up here."

She looked quickly down and he knew she was checking to see if her clothing had been rearranged.

He smiled, unable to hide his amusement. "I never take advantage of an unconscious woman."

"And I never faint."

"Is that something else you remember, or is it another one of your intuitive feelings?"

"I have no idea. I only know I am not some

fainéant aristocrat with nothing more to do than go around fainting all the time."

"So, you are an aristocrat?" he asked.

Panic gripped her. *Stupide!* she thought. You let your guard down. Do not allow yourself to become too comfortable with him. You must remember what you are about. One small error in judgment could land you in Rockingham's bed. With an inaudible gulp, she composed herself. "It was a figure of speech, not an indication of my status, nor evidence that my memory has returned."

"Smooth recovery, flawless presentation. No tripping over the tongue for you, is there?"

She made a move to get up.

"Not so fast." He placed a restraining hand upon her shoulder. "You aren't as strong as you think. Stay here awhile and rest."

"I'm not tired."

"You may not be tired, but your body has suffered a terrible ordeal. It will take some time to restore your strength and endurance to the level it was before you almost froze to death."

"I know I am a terrible burden and a responsibility thrust upon you that you did not want. Caring for me is keeping you from the things you came here to do. Perhaps you should take me to the nearest village. I am—"

"Enough of that. We will go when and where I say, and whenever I feel you are a bothersome burden, I will tell you. Make no mention of it again."

Looking at him thoughtfully, she said, "I suppose you think I am being very rude and unappreciative, but I am not trying to be. It is simply that... Oh, I don't know what I'm trying to say," she choked out.

She should have been more appreciative of the smile that formed across his lips. It was not his customary smile, for it did not carry the hint of mockery. Instead, it was what she would call a knowing smile, as if he not only sensed her uneasiness at being on the bed with him so near, but also understood the cause of it.

"You are nervous about being here alone with me."

It was a statement he was making, not a question he was asking, yet she felt compelled to answer it. "Yes. It would be very unwise for me to stay here any longer."

"Probably."

"If anyone should learn of this, it would be very damaging for both of us, I would imagine."

"Aye, what you say is true. But tell me, lass, why are you nervous about being here with me?"

"You are a man. I have no way of knowing your intentions."

"No, I suppose you don't."

"You could, this very moment, be planning any number of things."

"Such as?"

"You could send me on my way."

"I would never even think about it."

"You might turn me over to the English."

"Something that I would never consider."

"You could even be planning to seduce me."

"Now, that has crossed my mind," he said.

"Thank you for adding to my discomfort."

"You prefer dishonesty? If I said I was not interested in taking you to bed, would you believe me?"

"Until you gave me a reason not to."

"You should not be so trusting."

"And I am sorry you have forgotten how to trust. If I had to choose one over the other, I would always choose to trust."

"Then you would be a fool."

"Perhaps, but I cannot help feeling it is worse to distrust than to be deceived."

"And comparing lies to the truth? Have you any inclinations on that subject?"

"I think it is my turn to ask a question. You said

you were recently betrothed. Won't she be worried when you do not return?"

"Not particularly."

"It must be a strange betrothal."

"It is not an official betrothal, but more of an understanding of long duration. It is the title that Gillian is after. Unfortunately, I come with it."

"Then why did you ask her to marry you?"

"Did I say I had asked her?"

"I do not understand."

"It's a long story."

She shrugged. "I've plenty of time. I'm not going anywhere."

"You are a persistent wench."

She smiled. "Drops of water will wear away a stone."

His expression turned intent and unreadable, and she heard him say her name softly, as a child would do when trying out a new word. Her smile vanished and a tight constriction gripped her throat. Her senses flooded with a sort of conscious perception.

She was aware of the play of light coming through the window to slide along the dark strands of his hair, aware of the incredibly long lashes, thick and black around the moss-green eyes.

And his lips…oh, his fine lips, smooth, firm, and far too close to hers.

Those fine lips brushed against hers, softly—once, twice, three times, moving slowly, lingeringly, with tender intent. Blinding, dizzying seconds ticked by, and still he teased her with his kisses, making her wonder what he would do next, or where he would touch her and for how long. She tried to hold on to herself, to get a firm grip on her sanity, but he seemed equally intent upon drawing everything away, save for the blinding need to kiss him back.

He lifted his head and she felt the sharp stab of loss as his lips left hers. Her heart began to ease its frantic beating, her blood began to cool, and she wondered why her brain was so slow to chastise her once again—always succumbing as easily as a *courtisane* to him.

"Y-you were going to tell me a long story about you and Gillian," she said, praying he did not look at her as if she were an idiot, and chastise her for being such a scared simpleton.

A favorable answer to her prayer was immediate, for he gave her a lopsided grin that so captured her heart that she would swear to her great-grandchildren fifty years hence that it was the instant she knew she had fallen in love with him.

"For a long time now, Gillian has been what you would call a friend of the family. Her family's estate borders Monleigh. My siblings and I played with her when we were children. Our parents would often say that Gillian would probably end up marrying one of the Graham boys, and Gillian would always say she would marry James, because he was going to be the earl. Everyone would laugh, for it was humorous to hear a girl of ten say such, but there came a time when her determination to be my countess ceased to entertain me."

"If that is true, why would you entertain the idea of marriage to her?"

"If I had my way, I would never marry, but it is my responsibility to produce an heir or two, and Gillian was willing...and convenient."

"And she does not mind that you are marrying her for her reproductive capabilities?"

"It is the way of things, is it not? A man offers his title, his wealth and his protection in exchange for the heirs a woman will give him. It is a business arrangement, nothing more. She gets what she wants, and so do I."

"It seems awfully cold to me."

"It is cold, but much simpler than marrying for love and knowing that at some point, one of you will suffer."

"It doesn't have to be that way."

"Let me tell you something. Marriage is like a

new pair of shoes. They may look good to the average passerby, but they rub blisters and they always pinch somewhere."

"I do not know where your hostility toward marriage came from, but I pity you for having it."

"Don't," he said, "for I have a very valid reason."

She turned her face to the wall. "I think I will rest now."

She heard the sound of his steps as he walked to the door, but instead of opening it he paused, then turned and walked back to her bedside.

She gasped when she felt the bed sag. Dear God, she thought, he hadn't sat down on her bed with her in it, had he? Perhaps he'd only propped his feet on the bed. She turned her head and saw him lying next to her.

"You take liberties you have no right to take."

"It's worth it, whatever the risk," he said, placing his hands on each side of her head and leaning over her.

"What do you think you are doing?"

"I'm looking at your lovely face."

She snorted her disbelief and almost laughed. "Flattery is an overused tool to seduce a woman."

"Perhaps you are right. The straightforward approach is always best. I want to kiss you until you beg me for what we both want." He leaned forward and she knew he was going to kiss her, but he stopped mere inches away. Sophie could not move even if she wanted to, for everything within her seemed to fold in on top of her.

It occurred to her that this was the situation every girl in the convent dreamed about, and prayed would one day happen.

Would she be a fool to end it now?

She felt no shame in staring directly into eyes as green as the grass at Versailles. And she thought it utterly sinful for a man to have such eyelashes—when most women would die for half of what he had.

His mouth was so close to hers, all she had to do was pucker and they would smack together. She could feel the warm sweep of his breath dancing over her cheek. She wanted him to kiss her, wanted to feel the hard press of his chest against hers. She wanted him so much that merely thinking about it made her lips burn for his kiss and her breasts harden, while farther down, everything seemed to melt.

She sighed with relief when he claimed her mouth, and she dug her fingers into his hair and pulled him closer and kissed him back with all the passion and feeling she possessed.

His hands were beneath her now, holding her firmly against him as he stroked and caressed her until she could feel his arousal was as great as hers, and the proof of it pressed hard and hot against her.

She wanted to mate with him, and his body's reaction told her he wanted to make love to her. She arched against him, feeling a sense of frustration. She wanted…she wanted…

Only he knew what it was that she wanted. Only he knew how to ease the pain of desiring someone to the point of desperation. She tried to hide her discomfort, but it was obvious she was too unsophisticated when it came to lovemaking, or concealing anything from him.

As if reading her thoughts, his hands began to caress her with a slow, escalating tempo, dropping lower with each rotating move. Warm, firm hands cupped her buttocks and lifted her upward and inward until their bodies were aligned perfectly. Through layers of dress and bedding she could feel him, harder now than before.

The pressure of his kiss increased, and all her defenses melted at the onslaught. Where did he learn to do all the things he did with his hands and his lips? She felt like a rag doll without the stuffing. Her body was limp now, and she relaxed beneath him.

He seemed more intensely aware of her now, in the physical sense at least, and his reaction to her sent secretive little cries pulsing from her throat. Bathed in a sense of warmth and faint excitement, she felt a deep, throbbing sensation of desire begin to swell and expand, until she felt the slow, steady build of inexplicable pressure.

For a brief moment she had an inkling that Jamie knew exactly what was happening to her and knew, as well, what to do to stop this maddening spiral of acute desire that seized her.

Never had she known a man could be so gifted with the touch of his hands. The indolent movement of his palm traced heated circles against her sensitive skin. Their bodies might not be joined, but she knew that somehow they had reached a point of fervent mating of mind and passion.

He wanted it.

And she wanted him to take it.

It was somewhere between the mating of mind and passion that a cooling draft of air washed over her and she realized he had smoothly exposed one breast. Now she was torn between showing him her horror at what he had done, and praying he would go on and make it a matched pair.

He took the decision away from her when he caught both of her hands in his and drew them over her head, holding them captive, while he lowered his head to slowly cover her breast with his mouth.

And then, as quickly as he had made the move he pulled back, as if something had cautioned him against going any farther. She was about to ask him what had happened when he said, "Get some rest, lass. I will be below stairs if you have need of me."

She was too stunned to speak and could only watch, openmouthed, as he quit the room.

She pounded the bed in frustration. *"I will be below stairs if you have need of me."*

Did he not he understand she had need of him now?

Seven

Licence my roving hands, and let them go,
Before, behind, between, above, below...

—John Donne (1572-1631), English metaphysical poet and divine. *Elegies*. "To His Mistress Going to Bed" (1633)

Jamie wondered if Sophie had any inkling as to the battle that was going on inside him. Was she even the least bit cognizant of the fact that she had managed to take complete command of his thoughts in an unbelievably short period of time?

If anyone had ever suggested him capable of such, he would have labeled them daft. Him, the Earl of Monleigh, a man who heretofore took pride in the fact that he was always in control.

And look at him now....

Obsessed, he was, with a water sprite from France, who had no belongings, no past and no memory—or so she claimed.

There was still something not right about all of this. It was too easy, and she was too permissive.

Women were either easy or impossible.

The easy ones were harlots or mistresses, and the impossible ones were not. Yet, he would swear she was a woman of fine breeding and a maiden.

Damn him for a fool, but he had not been able to decide on precisely which she was. The maiden bit was easy to prove, of course, but the other? One minute he believed her, and the next he was convinced she was lying in order to conceal the truth.

Question was, which was the truth, and what exactly was she hiding?

The most likely answer was simply that she was a spy. That would explain her opening to him like a flower in warm water, for what better way to gain privy to a man's thoughts than by warming his bed?

If that were true, the setup was brilliant, for who would suspect a shipwrecked French lass who was a maiden of being a spy for the English?

He wanted to believe her, and probably would have if it were not for her story about being a lady's maid. Nothing about her validated this claim. Her soft hands were not the hands of a servant. Her language was too refined. She was too educated and well mannered to be as she claimed, and yet, he was reluctant to condemn her on the sole basis of his own convictions.

He tried to believe she was a governess.

What he needed was proof.

Further complicating things was the fact that it was becoming increasingly difficult for him to remain detached. He desired her, wanted her in his bed, and that added another dimension. So far, he had been the honorable man, at least in part. He had not given in to temptation completely.

But that did not mean he did not harbor desires and secret thoughts, or that he would be able to withstand indefinitely the power of attraction.

For the past two hours, he concentrated on doing his best to drink enough to forget the temptress in the bed above stairs.

It did not help.

Over and over, he tried to lay everything out in his mind, but always the same problematic set of circumstances emerged. And being a man, he tried to organize his life much in the same way he bred his cattle.

It was like trying to add two and two, and then

being angry when it came out to be four, simply because he wanted it to add up to five.

As it always happened, his thoughts soon wound their way back to Sophie, and the tempting serpent of desire began to coil itself around him until he could think of little else, save her. He was drawn to her, yea, captivated by her, but he could not let desire rule his head. He could not toy with the idea of marrying an unknown waif, no matter how beautiful she was, or how much he desired her.

Gillian was the sensible choice. Sophie was pure fantasy, something to be indulged but never taken seriously. She was a commoner, and without title, and therefore not the perfect wife for an earl.

But, she would be the perfect mistress.

He must stick to his original plan to marry for the sake of his title, and never allow his feelings, or his desire for Sophie to stand in the way. He would marry Gillian and give her the title she wanted. Once she was his countess and had given him heirs, she would not care if he had a dozen mistresses. He did not feel bad in the least about such a cold, calculating reason to marry, for Gillian's reasons were just as cold and calculating as his. She wanted all the things his title and wealth would give her. Once she had that, she would ignore any indiscretions on his part. No, there was no love between them, just as there would be no guilt felt by either of them. It was an arrangement, nothing more.

It all seemed so simple. All he had to do was convince Sophie.

A vision of her came into his mind and he went along with it to see where it would lead him. Imagination is a strange thing and, before long, he saw himself going up the stairs and down the hallway to the room where she was sleeping.

Without waking her, he began to unlace the golden dress of Arabella's that she wore, and then he slipped it down over her shoulders until the soft mounds of her breasts were completely exposed and she was, as he wanted her to be, bared to the waist.

Her skin was soft and warm, the velvety drag of his tongue over her breasts brought the desired reaction, and he felt them harden to tight crowns. He groaned with a drugged feeling, heavy and filled with desire.

He pushed the dress down farther, past the smooth planes of her flat stomach over the juncture of her thighs and down the firm legs that parted slightly when he stroked them with his palms. Taking his fingers and placing them on each side of her, he parted her gently until she was open to him completely. He covered her with his mouth, finding the point of her desire and touching it until she moaned in her sleep and spread her legs wider, allowing him to thrust into her deeply.

He replaced his tongue with his fingers, found the barrier of her virginity, and felt a surge of pride that he was at the portal of her awareness, where no man had ever been.

After some time, he withdrew his hands and kissed her again, touching her until she began to writhe beneath him as he found the rhythm and she began to move with it, faster and faster, until she began to convulse and cry out, her body jerking with spasm after spasm that washed over her.

He released himself from his pants, covered her with his body, and began to stroke himself against her until she was writhing beneath him again, continuing until he was dangerously close to losing control completely, then at the critical moment, he pulled back and spilled himself in the soft cove of her belly.

Knowing she was aroused and wanting him, he lowered his hand and touched her, until she opened her legs wide, enabling him to stroke her until she was unbelievably ready. Still, he did not stop, but kept stroking her until she began to pant and press against him, thrusting her hips wildly until she went over the edge, shattered and crying out his name.

He lost count of how many times he brought her to this point, for his mind was saturated with the knowledge that he was right.

She would make the perfect mistress.

There was a sort of truce between them for the next two days, while Jamie made a valiant effort to busy himself with hunting and a few meetings with the clansmen who cared for the grounds.

Sophie spent her days reading and resting as she began to regain her strength and to feel like her normal self.

On the third day, Jamie returned from his morning hunt with two fat rabbits, which he cleaned and dressed down at the river. One he placed on the spit over the fire. The other he cut up and cooked in the kettle with a few vegetables.

The delicious smell permeated the kitchen and drifted up the stairs.

A short time later, Sophie entered the room.

"You are looking better, lass. I think you are on the mend. Did ye sleep well?"

She felt a warm flush rise upward and hoped the

telltale stain of red did not color her cheeks. She knew he had no way of knowing how much she thought of what happened between them, or how the erotic memory of it occupied her thoughts. She had never had such wanton thoughts before, and could only speculate as to why she would have such thoughts—with vivid details of him making love to her—after it had already happened.

He was watching her with an odd expression that made her wonder if he could have some inkling as to what she was thinking. He had not mentioned their amorous encounter, and the tension of it began to wear on her. Why was he avoiding her?

"I'm sorry," she said. "Did you say something?"

"Aye, I asked if you slept well."

"Yes, I suppose I did, for I do not remember waking even once. I think the rest has been good for me, for I feel better today, and stronger. However, I do not think I will ever feel completely warm again. I didn't realize it could be so cold here in the autumn."

"Aye, it can be quite cold in the Highlands," he said.

She had taken a seat near the fire, not far from where he stood. She was holding her hands out, seeking warmth, when she heard dogs barking outside.

She saw him turn quickly to glance through the window, and then he turned back to her with a smile. "They have treed the barn cat," he said.

"Are they your dogs? I have not seen them in the house."

He must have seen the look of fright in her eyes, for he gathered her into his arms and sat down to cradle her against him. He held her easily, as if it was something he did daily. "Aye, they live here, although they think they belong to Angus, the gamekeeper, for he is the one who cares for them. They are not really pets, for they were bred to alert us to any unfamiliar types who might be about. I think the last time they came inside was when my sister, Arabella, was fourteen."

She worked her face into the cove of his shoulder and her mouth close enough to his ear to whisper, "Are you sure it was only the barn cat they found?" she asked.

"Aye."

"How do you know it was not a person, or a wild animal?" she asked. "Have you ever caught someone prowling?"

"Aye, there have been occasional raids or cattle thieves."

"You don't think they could be out there now, do you?"

"Nay, lass, I saw Tam barking at the cat. Besides, Tam's bark would have been different had it been intruders."

"Do you suffer that sort of visitor often?"

"Often enough. Mostly it is the MacBeans, or the Crowders, but it could be any number of Highland clans. These are hard times, and the clans are always warring with one another and stealing cattle, as if we dinna have enough trouble with dragoons patrolling the area."

"Life here faces too many unknown perils. How can you bear it?"

"You have to learn who you can trust, and who is on your side. Even then, it is not unheard of for a man to be betrayed by his best friends. There are many spies about and many ways of hearing."

She shifted her position. "I know I ask too many questions."

"Not too many, although you do ask your share."

She shifted her weight as she tried to get a more comfortable position.

"You would do us both a service if you didna wiggle so much, considering the place where ye are sitting. It makes it damnably hard to keep my mind on consoling ye."

"I know I must be heavy."

"Nay, lass, 'tis not that you are heavy, for in truth you dinna weigh more than a bag of turnips. It has more to do with that part of me that ye are sitting on. Has a mind of its own sometimes, and when in the close proximity of such a fetching derriere… Do ye understand now?"

Everything between her ears turned scarlet, but she did manage a nod and a weak "Yes."

She was about to ask him how he fared on his morning hunt, when his body tensed, as if listening.

Sophie listened as well, and was aware that it had grown very quiet outside. Her mouth felt dry, and the sound of her heartbeat hammered in her ears.

His hand whipped out suddenly and clamped over her mouth, and when she turned startled eyes upon him, he motioned for her to be quiet.

He removed his hand.

She remained as still as a chimney, and strained her ears to listen. In the distance, she heard the sound of hooves, coming closer.

Jamie eased out of the chair and went to the peg near the door, where he had left his sword.

With a sense of dread she watched, dry mouthed, as he buckled the sword around his waist.

The hoof beats grew louder now, and then as if passing by, they began to fade.

He turned back to her. "If you are feeling up to it, you can fill a couple of bowls with rabbit while I go outside to have a look around."

She nodded, her heart not really dedicated to the prospect of serving rabbit, when her first inclination had been to run above stairs to find a good place to hide like one.

After he had gone, she decided she did not want him to think she was a coward, so she found two bowls and an equal number of spoons. She filled each bowl with the thick, savory broth and vegetables, mixed with ample chunks of rabbit. It was similar to what they called a bouillabaisse in France, although she had no idea what the Scots called it.

She placed the bowls on the table and sat down to wait, and grew increasingly nervous with each moment that passed. She wondered what she would do if something happened to him, and realized how important he was to her survival. What would I do? she wondered.

The thought of being here without him made her realize he was all that stood between her and the English.

She wished she knew more about life here in

Scotland, and what the ordeals and harms were that these hearty Scots faced each day. In France, she had heard a few vague stories about Scots, especially those in the Highlands, and how they were only one step removed from barbarians, but that really gave her no idea what trials and perils Jamie was likely to face.

Occasionally, a story would reach France about the hatred most Highlanders had for the English, and the atrocities the English committed against them. There were other stories, too, of how the Scottish nobles usually sided with the English, even to the point of betraying their own countrymen.

She wondered if perhaps this was why the French were generally sympathetic toward the Scots. Strange though it was, it did seem that it was human nature to sympathize with those battered down by misfortune and cruelty more than when they were triumphant.

While she waited for Jamie, Sophie went back to drumming her fingers on the table and busied herself with looking around the kitchen.

It was a comfortable room, and not too large like some castle kitchens she had seen. It also had two nice windows, which castles also lacked. Two long tables were pushed against one wall, and one larger table with a top of smoothly polished stone stood in the center of the room.

Near the fireplace, the bowls of rabbit sat on a smaller table, surrounded by eight chairs. Two dark chairs, ornately carved, were placed side by side opposite the table, separated by the hearth rug.

She could see why Jamie liked to spend time at Danegæld. All the rooms of the lodge were cozy and of a good size, and comfortably furnished in a manner that was luxurious and lavish but not overdone.

She heard him approach and stomp his feet before he opened the door. A few flurries of snow blew in, and the sudden gust of air caused the flames in the fireplace to burn more brightly, fanned by the sudden updraft.

"You should have eaten," he said, when he saw the bowls and Sophie waiting for him.

"I thought about it, but I dislike eating alone."

"Aye, to pass the meal in the company of friends is always preferred."

"I was worried. You were gone a long time."

"It was not as long as it seemed. Time always seems to pass slower for the one who is left behind."

"Did you see anyone?"

"Aye, there was a platoon of English dragoons

on the trail less than a mile from here. 'Twas the rattle and clink of their equipment that set the dogs to barking." He spoke each word carefully, all the while keeping his gaze focused upon her to judge her reaction to the news.

Her response was more explosive than he anticipated, for her head jerked up quickly, and when she brought her hand up to her chest, she managed to hit the spoon. It did a somersault when it flipped out of the bowl, and sent a shower of rabbit bits and vegetables across the room.

By the time the spoon hit the floor with a hollow clang, the anxious look was gone, and she was having a devil of a time suppressing a laugh, for a carrot disc rested rather precariously upon his shoulder.

Apparently, the lofty earl did not share her amusement. "I did not know you were so terrified of the English. Why is that?"

She shrugged. "I have no idea why, only that I am." She barely paid any attention to what she said, for the carrot was a distraction.

"Do you find something amusing?"

"Yes. You have a carrot on your shoulder."

In a tavern a few miles away, Major Jack Winter of His Majesty's 7th Dragoons was drinking a pint of ale with two fellow officers.

Lieutenant Peter Hastings held the attention of his two compatriots. "I say it is impossible that she could have survived when everyone else on board perished. Why must we continue to look for her?"

Captain Geoffrey Wright had an answer ready. "Because they want us to keep looking until we find her or until her body washes ashore."

"We don't know for certain she was even on that ship," Lieutenant Hastings said.

"It seems we do have confirmation of that now," Major Winter said. "It seems her cousin has admitted that she accompanied Mademoiselle d'Alembert on board, and that she left shortly before it sailed."

"Perhaps she changed her mind after her cousin's departure, and left the ship. It could have happened that way," Hastings observed.

Major Winter nodded. "It's possible, but one would think she would have been seen leaving the ship."

Wright glanced at the major. "In the meantime, we must continue to look for her."

Major Winter nodded. "Until I receive orders telling us otherwise."

Hastings put down his pint. "How large an area must we patrol?"

"We must thoroughly search a radius of twenty

miles," the major said, "but regiments across Scotland are on the alert, as well as our spies."

Wright whistled. "Someone must want the chit badly."

"Oh, they do," the major said, while tapping his fingers on the table. "They most certainly do."

"But why are we looking for her?" Hastings asked. "We aren't in the habit of helping the French. Who is it that is so interested in locating her?"

"The Duke of Rockingham," the major said, and then he laughed at the expressions on the faces of the other two.

"I almost feel sorry for her," Captain Wright said, shaking his head.

"Perhaps I would as well, save for the fact that she is French, and since I have nothing but animosity for them, I say she deserves whatever she gets, and that includes the likes of Rockingham," Hastings added. "But what I don't understand is, why is Rockingham so interested in her?"

"He's had his spies hunting down the Jacobites in France for years," the major said. "It seems on one trip to France, he saw her and was completely captivated. She is reported to be a great beauty."

"Not bad," Hastings said. "A beautiful face and the granddaughter of Louis XIV." He paused as if considering something, then asked, "You don't mean Rockingham had thoughts of marrying her himself?"

The major nodded. "Oh, yes, and not just thoughts. He was cunning enough to offer his assistance to the French crown, and the result was his betrothal. It was my understanding she was to be sent to England to marry the duke. Of course, at the time all of this transpired, Rockingham was in good standing with her cousin, Louis XV. Now I hear the Louie does not think as highly of Rockingham as he once did."

"Wait a minute," Wright said. "Something isn't right here. You said her cousin accompanied her aboard, then left the ship before it sailed. Why was she sent unaccompanied to England on a ship bound for Norway?"

"The French had nothing to do with that," the major said. "It seems the mademoiselle had plans for her life that did not include marriage to the Duke of Rockingham. She took matters into her own hands and planned her escape to Norway before her cousin could order her to England. The ship she boarded was never scheduled to sail to England."

Hastings nodded with sudden understanding. "And now no one knows where she is...*if* she is still alive, that is."

"Exactly," the major said, and raised his tankard.

The three men laughed and gave a toast to have the good fortune to locate the wench, or her body, soon.

Eight

The Devil, having nothing else to do,
Went off to tempt My Lady Poltagrue.
My Lady, tempted by a private whim,
To his extreme annoyance, tempted him.

—Hilaire Belloc (1870-1953), French-born British writer. *Sonnets and Verse.* "On Lady Poltagrue, A Public Peril" (1923). *Complete Verse* (1991)

Sophie had been at Danegæld a week, when she sat dejectedly on her bed. She was beginning to feel like a prisoner. She had not been outside since Tavish had brought her here.

Jamie had knocked on her door earlier to inform her he was going fishing, before he gave her the same instructions he gave her each morning when he departed. "I will be back before the noon meal, lass. Stay inside and do not open the door to anyone."

She was feeling much better, which was probably why she was beginning to feel bored to her toes. Not particularly inspired to do much of anything, she decided to go down to the library to find a book to read and perhaps, if she was very fortunate, she might find one in her native tongue.

It was the first time she had really taken in the fine architecture of the magnificent lodge, and the lavishly decorated interior, resplendent with scalloped walls done in the ornate rococo style, ball finials and ornate urns.

From the window in the Banquet Hall, she could see part of the formal gardens of the park—what they called a *par terre* in France, as well as a courtyard.

Everywhere there were themes of hunting, feasting and the seasons displayed in profusion, yet they did not detract from the portrayals of Roman gods, Bacchus and Diana in the ceiling panels of the Banquet Hall.

Later, as she did a bit of snooping, she discovered that these were the same themes carried out in Jamie's own apartments.

By the time he returned, she had taken a thorough tour of the house and was walking in the *par terre* when he rode up on a gray stallion.

Her heart still beat with excitement at the sight of him. Would she always feel this way around him? She reminded herself that it really did not matter, for she would not be around him much longer. Soon, she would have to leave.

If the English were not yet looking for her, she knew they soon would be. In the meantime, she would have to consider her next move, and where she could go where no one would find her.

He had been her constant companion these past few days, and she realized now how much she had grown accustomed to being with him and, when he was gone even for a short while, how much she missed his powerful presence.

She was comfortable with him, and his absence in her life would leave a gaping hole she feared no one would ever be able to fill.

She brought her hand up to shield her eyes from the sun as she watched him ride toward her—a sight she would never tire of seeing.

Today, he had his hair tied back with the leather thong, and the wind had loosened a few strands giving him a look of raw masculinity. She noticed he wore his sword and that his pistols were in the saddlebow, and she wondered if he had taken these things fishing. Or, had he gone to the great house and found her missing, and brought them along to search for her?

The corners of her mouth lifted into a smile, which soon faded when she saw he did not smile back, but regarded her impassively. He pulled the horse to a stop beside her, folded his arms over the pommel and leaned toward her. "I thought I told you to stay inside, lass."

"You did, but…"

He threw his leg over the saddle and was off his horse in an instant. He grabbed her by both arms, and gave her a good shake.

"When I give a command I expect it to be obeyed."

"Obeyed?" she repeated, totally shocked at his choice of words. "I did not realize you were the emperor."

"I am king of this lodge, and king of Monleigh Castle, and chief of the Graham clan, and anything I say in regard to any of those is to be obeyed."

"I am not one of your possessions."

"If I remember right, you don't know what or *who* you are. I do not expect you to understand everything I say to you, nor will I tolerate you questioning the decisions I make. Your role is to be submissive, nothing more. My word is law. Our clan has lived by that code for centuries. There is no other way. You will do well to remember that."

"I am not a member of your clan," she said, thinking this was not going at all the way she had hoped.

"As long as you are in my care, you are part of my household."

"Then it must be time for me to leave. I am feeling better. It is time I took care of myself."

"You will go when I give you leave to go, and not before."

"You can't hold me here against my will. I may not know who I am, but that does not make me a prisoner."

"Oh, but you are. You are my prisoner, and I will keep you here for your own good and personal safety until we unravel this mystery of who you are, where you have come from and how to contact your family. Now, stop being sullen. I am being more than fair by giving you this warning. Had you been a member of the clan, you would have been beaten."

She sucked in a breath. "You will never lay a hand on me."

"Disobey me again and you will see the way of it, lass."

"I suppose it is my fault for not realizing that the only way you can hold a woman is by keeping her against her will." She jerked her arms free and was about to turn around with as much drama as she could muster, and leave him talking to himself.

She never made it that far, for he grabbed her by the arms and prevented her from taking even one small step. He watched her through narrowed eyes for a moment, as if disbelieving what he heard her say.

She was aware that she truly was his prisoner, in every sense of the word, for he had all the advantages, and she had none, save the pitiful fact that she was a woman—something she thought he would honor, only when it suited him.

"One other thing," he began. "When I want to keep a lass, I don't have to make her my prisoner. Warming my bed is much more binding than leaving a lass locked in her room, yearning for the unattainable."

Yearning for the... She had never been humiliated like this, and she toyed with the idea of slapping him, and would have, but she was not too certain that he would not slap her back so, instead of that, she said, "You are vile."

"Nay, lass, not vile...truthful."

She opened her mouth and then closed it, having decided it was in her best interest not to anger him further. It was much more effective, in her estimation, to remain sullen and quiet.

"You must realize you are no longer in France, and that in Scotland things are done differently. When I tell you something, I expect it to be obeyed. You might not like it, and you might not understand it, but you will do as I say. If you start to second-guess me, or go against my directives, it could be the death of either or both of us. This isna France, and we are no' in possession of so civilized a form of government. You are a lassie with a free spirit, and I admire that in ye, I truly do, but there are situations where a man must be in control, and that means ye will have to do as I say, like it or no'."

"All right," she said, obviously angry. "I'm sorry I came outside to get some fresh air…for the *first* time since I came here."

"That is what I mean. You say one thing and believe another. What I am telling you is you must believe what I say, and trust in it with all your heart, no matter if you want to or not. It is your obedience I want, lass, not your apology. You will not set foot outside Danegæld until you prove your willingness to carry out what I demand or order, without question. For your sake, I hope this doesna happen again, for if it does, I will punish you. Have no doubt about that."

She was thinking about kicking him in the shin when he said, "Now, come here and I will give you a hand up and you can ride the rest of the way back wi' me."

"I prefer to walk...if I may have your royal permission."

"When ye find yer mark and stand on it, ye are a hard lass to move. Stick like a burr, you do."

She pointed her uplifted nose toward Danegæld and began to walk.

He did not go after her, as she hoped, and that infuriated her even more.

By the time she reached the graveled drive that led to the lodge, the sun was almost gone and it had begun to snow, and enormous, fat flakes fell slowly around her.

She pulled the sides of her borrowed cape closer together, thankful for the fur lining.

From the corner of her eye, she saw Jamie ride toward the stables, but she did not turn to look at him, preferring to walk on with the snow melting on her face. She found herself wishing she would freeze, just to get her point across, but soon realized there would be precious little feeling of victory if she were a dead woman encased in a sarcophagus of ice.

Personally, she hoped he would sink up to his eyeballs in one of his soggy peat bogs. To think she had actually considered telling him the truth about her past and the reason she left France.

Ha!

As if he would be capable of understanding anything except brute force. She smacked herself on the forehead. How could she be so stupid? How could she think him capable of either compassion or understanding? Sometimes she felt as if she were depriving some village of their idiot—she could be so *stupide*...

He would not understand if she spoke of her own loneliness, or the death of her beloved father, any more than he would care to hear how her mother married again, and to a man who tried to use Sophie to gain favor with the king. What would he care that Rockingham gave the king lavish gifts and large amounts of gold, and how it made her feel to know she had been sold into the slavery of marriage to a man the age of her father, a man she despised?

No, she would not tell him of her lonely life growing up with only one brother who was considerably older than she, and the years spent in the convent where she prayed that one day she would find her own hero.

She knew he could not understand how she dreamed that he would be a man with long black hair and a strong profile inherited from his Viking ancestors; a man who would love and protect her, and keep her always by his side, because he saw her not as a chattel, but as his equal.

She felt the warm trail of tears that mingled with the cold, melted snow on her face. There was so much love inside her that she wanted to give to the man of her dreams, only now she understood that she had been wrong to think that man would be Jamie.

She came upon a fountain and stopped to look at the ice crystals that formed around the edges. Out of the corner of her eye, she saw Jamie come out of the stables and walk toward her.

She did not want him to see her like this.

She wiped her eyes with the back of her sleeve, and cursed the Bourbon blood that ran in her veins, as well as the burden of unhappiness it carried with it.

Feeling the need to destroy something besides her hopes, she tore at the buttons at her throat and searched for the gold medallion around her neck. When her hand closed around it, she gave the fragile chain a hard yank and hurled it into the fountain, as if that one act could change who she was, and what she was running from.

She gathered up her skirts and ran the rest of the way back to the lodge, not stopping when she reached the staircase, but continuing up as fast as her legs would carry her.

Once she was back in her room, she stood with her back to the door, her eyes closed, gasping for breath.

As he walked toward the fountain, Jamie watched her run the entire distance to the lodge, having decided to let her go. He could not allow her disobedience, and knew she had to sort through all of this by herself.

She would not welcome his intervention now. She was too angry at him, and her feelings were too raw.

No, he would not chase her.

Not this time.

That did not mean he did not want to go after her. He wanted her too much, and he thought of little else than making love to her. No matter what he did, he could never erase the memory of her slender nakedness, the yielding alabaster of her breast, the little panting cries that came from deep in her throat.

She was an enigma, a distraction, a mystery, a headache, and as stubborn a lass as he had ever encountered.

And she sure as hell was not a lady's maid.

She could have been a courtesan, save for the fact that he knew somehow that she was untouched.

She ought to be married…

But not to him.

She would probably be a good wife…

To someone else.

He should let her go…

But not just yet.

Desire for her pierced him like an arrow, and the shaft had driven deep into his heart. Her image was always before him, shining and bright as a candle in the dark, until the looming shadow of distrust doused it.

He could not love a woman he did not believe.

Restlessness seized him. He shoved his hands deep into his pockets. He laid his head back and inhaled deeply, needing the return of orderly control. He felt out of balance. He would probably stay that way until he knew what she was hiding. He wanted to help her, but she had to trust him enough to let him into her life.

He could not correct the wrongs if he did not know what they were.

Never in his life could he remember being in a situation like this, where he had no answers, or worse, did not even know what the questions were.

He would have continued ambling along, lost in his own musings, if he had not noticed something shining from the bottom of the fountain.

When he fished it out, he saw the *fleur-de-lis* on the chain. He knew it had to be the same one Sophie wore around her neck. His first thought was it might have slipped off her neck due to a broken clasp, but when he saw it was broken in the middle of the chain, he knew it must have come off by force.

But how?

And why?

He could think of no apparent reason for her to rip her necklace from her own neck and toss it into the fountain. Yet, there was no one else here who could have done it.

He dropped it into his pocket, curious as to why she had thrown it in the fountain instead of taking it with her, for he was certain it had to hold some special memory for her, otherwise she would not wear it.

Damn puzzling, infuriating woman that she was.

Nine

Quarrels would not last so long if the fault were on only one side.

—François de La Rochefoucauld (1613-1680), French writer. *Reflections, or Sentences and Moral Maxims* (1665)

Sophie locked the door and then, for good measure, she kicked it.

He was the most infuriating man she ever had the displeasure of meeting. She hoped she never saw him again, and to prove her point, she pushed the trunk away from the foot of the bed and shoved it against the door.

"There," she said as she dusted her hands, and wished that she could dismiss him just as easily.

Her heart was pounding, both from exertion and from anger. Still in her cloak, she began to pace the floor, cursing him in French and calling him every vile name she could muster.

When that did little to ease her passionate fury, she threw back the doors that led to the balcony and stepped outside.

The wind was rising and began tearing at her cloak, blowing it back over her shoulders. She placed her hands on the balustrade and turned her face into the wind to feel the sting of snow, wanting the physical pain to match that which she carried inside, not knowing it was her own tears, and not the snow, that turned her face wet.

She brought her hand up to her hair and felt its stiffness, and wondered what it would be like to lie down and slowly freeze to death. She had been told that it was a painless death—you simply went to sleep and never woke up.

Of course, she had had a good inkling of what it was like the day Tavish found her and brought her here. One had to endure a lot of aching cold and shivering before reaching the point of falling asleep, and that was enough to send that thought on its way.

Sacre bleu! She had never felt so desolate.

She could not return to France for her cousin,

King Louis, would say she had insulted his honor, and he would immediately send her to England and Rockingham. She could not remain here, for the English would surely find her before long.

Yet, where could she go?

She had lost everything…her clothes, her money, her past, her future…everything, when the ship broke up on the rocks. Today she had learned the English were patrolling the roads, and she was not so naive as to think they were not looking for her.

She had committed a grievous affront in the eyes of two countries. They would not let her get away with it. They would want her brought to task, and they would find her.

It was only a matter of time.

Lost in her own grief, she did not hear him approach, and had no inkling he had even come into the room until she felt a warm presence against her back, and knew instinctively that it was Jamie.

"How did you get in here?"

"I have a key to the door. As for the trunk, it is easily pushed aside."

He put out his hands to grip her shoulders and, turning her, pulled her against him. He caught her chin beneath his forefinger and turned her face up to his. When he kissed her, his hands went under her cloak and a shower of snow swirled around them as he held her against him, tightly, as if he feared he would lose her if he let go.

If kisses were books, this one was an epic, for it was long, educational, adventuresome and impressive, and she was a heroine of sorts for surviving its onslaught.

His lips touched the hollow of her throat.

She swallowed and swayed against him, unprepared for the sudden surge of feeling that washed over her at the feel of his tongue touching hers, probing, encouraging, tempting…

She understood now what he meant when he said "Warming my bed is much more binding than leaving a lass locked in her room, yearning for the unattainable."

Her hands dug into his arms as the world seemed to fall from under her feet. A warm, liquid heat pulsed through her body, humming like the husky tones of a violoncello. Her flesh burned beneath the touch of his hand, and she found herself wanting to get even closer to him, needing the comfort and the protective hardness of him.

She was vaguely aware of the sound of the wind hissing through the doors as he closed them, leading her into her chamber.

"Sophie…why were you standing out there?

You are soaking wet, at least in the places that are not frozen stiff. What are you trying to do? Kill yourself?"

He removed her cloak and dusted the snow from her head. He left her for a moment, only to return with a length of cloth. Neither of them spoke as he gave his attention to drying her hair.

After a while he made a satisfied sound, apparently pleased with the results. He then wrapped it around her head, turban style, before he began to briskly rub her hands to warm them.

She was barely aware when he stopped rubbing and began kissing the tips of her cold fingers, one by one, and her thoughts began to pull away from him and back to another time.

"I remember someone…my grandmother, I think. She used to do that."

"What? Kiss your fingers?"

"Oui." She nodded and her head fell against his chest. He pulled her close and rubbed her back briefly before he picked her up and carried her to the chaise in front of the fire.

He stirred the embers and put on more logs, then drew the fur coverlet over her, lifting it long enough to join her and take her in his arms.

He kissed her cheek. "Tell me what bothers you, besides your anger at me."

She no longer felt angry and tried, without success, to find the words to put it all into perspective, but her thoughts seemed incapable of connecting with the words jumbled in her mind.

He kissed her lips softly. "Why canna ye trust me?"

Tears burned and blurred her vision. She wanted to tell him. She needed to tell him and feel the assurance that he would protect her. Yet, she could not tell him, although it grieved her. Her future, even her life, was at stake.

She could not be too careful.

She did not answer but asked him a question instead. "Are you going to make love to me?"

"Yes, but not right now." He had such a beautiful smile—one that drew attention to his perfect teeth, as a frame enhances a portrait.

She studied his eyes, fascinated with the mossy, yellow-green color. She wanted to speak, but the knot in her throat would not budge, and the breath lay trapped somewhere in her lungs.

She doubled her fists and pressed them hard against her stomach, and rolled toward him. She was tired: tired of running, tired of lying, tired of trying to fight archaic laws, tired of thinking she could outsmart the might of two powerful countries. She wished she was a child again, or that her father had not died, or that she had been born ugly, or at least the daughter of paupers.

She wished wishing would, just once, solve her problems.

She began to cry then, because it was too hard to talk, to think, or to give him any inkling of what she had been through, and what she feared might happen to her when they caught her.

Now everything was doubly complicated, and the frustration pounded like a hammer in her brain. She knew she was coming under this man's spell, as surely as she was falling in love with him. And that in itself, was another complication.

She tried to tell him she was sorry, that she was not normally a woman prone to lies, deception or tears, but the words tore at her throat and she felt as if she was bleeding inside.

Her eyes burned, and her nose, too. Her head ached, and her body was so cold she was numb. The only feeling she had at all was the raw burning at the place at her neck where she had ripped the chain away.

She swiped at her nose and began to shake her head. "This is all so pointless. I cannot stay here. This is not my home. I am a stranger, in a strange place, among strange people. Even the food is strange. I need to go…somewhere, and that is when the frustration sets in, because where do I go? Why don't I know where that place is?"

"Tell me. Tell me where you want to go and I will take you there. Tell me what you are afraid of, why you cannot remain here. With my last breath, I will protect you. Tell me and I will find a place for you. A place where you feel comfortable and safe. Do you want to go home… back to France?"

She shook her head. "No."

"What is happening to you?"

She started crying again. "I don't know. I don't know," she repeated, and buried her face in her hands.

"Cry then, for it cleanses a woman's heart in a way a man cannot understand."

That only made her cry harder.

How dare he understand women so well.

Yet he did understand, and he held her and let her cry, not asking any more questions, choosing instead to let her cry until there were no more tears to shed.

When she reached that point at last she felt better, but drained and achy all over. So here she sat, with her swollen eyes and her red nose.

Wouldn't it be wonderful, she thought, if she could wake up right now and discover this was only a nightmare?

When that feeling passed, she simply felt sleepy. "I must be getting warm," she said, "but I don't understand how that can be. No one is ever warm in Scotland." She yawned and nestled against him, and with her head on his shoulder, she slipped off to sleep.

There was no way of knowing how long she had slept, but she awakened as he was carrying her to her bed. She said nothing as he undressed her down to her undergarments, and pulled the blankets over her.

He sat down beside her and took her in his arms to cradle her against him.

"Are you going to make love to me?"

She felt his chuckle. "Yes, but not now. Go to sleep."

He stayed with her, not leaving her side even once, until she opened her eyes and scowled when she saw he was still sitting beside her.

"Are *you* still here?" she asked, sounding quite grumpy.

"Aye, I am still here. Are you still angry?"

"Of course. Nothing has changed that."

"I thought you were feeling better after your cry."

"I do feel better, but that does not mean I gave

up. I might be overcome—you are obviously bigger than me—but I will never yield," she said, lifting her nose defiantly.

He laughed. "We are not enemies engaged in a war, and I was not asking you to relinquish your life. Can we not call a truce?"

"You mean neither of us wins?" she asked.

"Or neither of us loses." He knew his smile made his eyes shine a little bit brighter, for he could not hide the pleasure he found in her—even when she was angry.

She could not know how she looked or how achingly beautiful she was with her lovely brown hair loosened in sleep, its long silky skeins wrapped around his arms and curling over her breasts.

One long curl had wrapped itself around her neck, and when he untangled it he saw the angry, red welt, raw and crusted with blood.

He ran his finger along the scratch and kissed it, but decided not to mention finding the necklace. He had not yet completely enticed her out of her grumpy mood, and he did not want to test how far he could go with her right now. The necklace could wait until another time.

He noticed she had narrowed her eyes with a suspicious look she was giving him.

"What? Have I done something?"

"I want to know what is it that you want."

His brows rose with surprise. "Do I want something? I do not remember saying I wanted anything. Why would you ask me that?"

"You are humoring me, and when someone humors a person it is because they want something."

"If I am being indulgent, it is only because I wish you to be happy."

"Why?"

"Because you are under my protection, and I am concerned for your welfare, and when you are happy the responsibility is much more pleasurable."

"You make it sound as though I am a great deal of trouble."

The smile that had been tugging at his lips broke forth with a chuckle. "Responsibility is not always a problem. Sometimes it can be pleasure."

When he lifted his hand to brush the back of his fingers lightly along the curve of her cheek, he saw the way the blueness of her eyes seemed to darken as she regarded him thoughtfully.

"Which one am I?" she asked.

He lifted one finger to trace down along a dark curl that lay like a question mark over her breast. He noticed the way she watched his hand as it toyed with the coiled lock of hair. "You are pure pleasure, Sophie. Always."

She was suddenly fascinated with her fingers and gave her nails a critical going-over. He took both of her hands in his, brought them to his lips and kissed each palm in turn. He kissed the soft, tender skin of each wrist and drew them up and around his neck.

This put his face close to hers. He saw her eyes widen. She had never appeared more innocent. "You are the most seductive woman, even when you are trying not to be."

His mouth came down on hers, his hands slipping around her and holding her close. The silken contact of her skin against his was overpowering. Even through their clothes, he could feel her shapely, feminine softness that mated so well with the hard musculature of his own body.

His hands moved in a gentle, questing odyssey over her, and followed each movement with a kiss.

"You are making it difficult for me to remember just why I was angry at you," she said.

"I know," he whispered, as his lips played with the sensitive skin around her ear. "If I said I apologize for anything I have said or done to hurt or offend you, would you forgive me?"

"I forgive you *this* time, but don't press your luck. *D'accord?*"

"Aye, I agree, you little witch."

She was watching him, with her soft lips half parted, and he knew the moment had come. He wanted his mouth against her, wanted the taste of her on his tongue, wanted her lips and her limbs open to him, of her own free will.

It had been a torturous two hours, holding her while she slept, the soft cushion of her breasts rubbing his arm with each breath like an invitation. Once, he had placed his hand over her breast and cupped it in his hand, content to simply keep it there because it was part of her.

It was a moment of pure truth, void of lust or desire.

Before long, the agony of her nearness became too much. He wanted her desperately. He wanted to turn her on her back and to lie on top of her, and press her mouth open with his, while his legs parted hers.

He knew now that he could never let her go. She belonged to him and with him. An eternity with her would never be enough.

How ironic he did not meet her until he fancied himself betrothed to someone else.

Ten

The best way to get the better of temptation is just to yield to it.

—Clementina Stirling Graham (1782-1877), Scottish writer. *Mystifications.* "Soirée at Mrs. Russel's" (1859)

Sophie knew he was going to make love to her. She knew she should stop him. She knew, too, that she would not.

Like him, she knew part of her motivation was pure lust, born of the strong physical desire to mate with him, without allowing all of the associated feelings of love or affection to guide her. She knew he wanted her, although she did not realize her yearning for him was heightened by his powerful attraction and sexual desire for her.

She never realized a man could be so sensual, and yet carnal minded, or that it would affect her so much emotionally. She only knew she felt herself wrapped in the magic glow of his desire.

It was a luxurious feeling, like soaking in a hot bath, or sleeping with the sun warm upon her face.

She wanted to mate with him, but she was not entirely certain it was purely her lustful desire for him that motivated her, for it had occurred to her that Jamie Graham might just prove to be her salvation and her protector...inadvertently, of course.

To make love with him carried the risk of becoming *enceinte,* but in her case that could be blessing, for it could deliver her from the jaws of a detestable arranged marriage, and a lifetime of marital slavery to a man she abhorred.

She dismissed the notion that she might be fortunate enough to have both Jamie—for it could happen that he would fall in love with her—and the end to her betrothal to that detestable worm, the Duke of Rockingham.

On the heels of that came the reminder of what her father once told her. "Blessings never come in pairs, Sophie, and misfortune never comes alone."

She knew better than to think of Jamie in terms

of her future. There was no future for them, just as there could be no feelings involved. He wanted her because he lusted after her. Therefore, she told herself, she wanted him because he was a necessary part of her plan for saving herself from the clutches of Rockingham.

They both had a need to fill, and it would be a clean mating, with no attachment, no feelings involved.

If Jamie were to get her with child, it was almost a dead certainty that the Duke of Rockingham would see to it that the betrothal was nullified immediately. No man as powerful as Rockingham would want the taint of a wife carrying another man's bastard—especially the bastard of a Scot.

Sophie was willing to withstand the shame, the humiliation, and even the turning away of her family and country, if it meant the wedding would not take place. She possessed a significant inheritance from both her mother and grandmother. She would be able to live alone quite comfortably for the rest of her life.

A piercing pain stabbed at her when she accepted the fact that to bear Jamie's child meant she would never marry. She hardened herself and pushed away the visions she had long carried in her mind: a loving and devoted husband, a long and lasting marriage and a house full of children.

A pang shot through her at the memory of moments with the father she adored—the busy duke who spent too many lamp-lit hours in the magnificent library at Châteaux Aquitaine. Few as those days had been, they were thick with memories.

One time in particular stood out in her mind, when she had left her bed and gone downstairs to see him. During their talk, he told her that there were times in life when people had to make decisions based upon the facts before them and not upon wants or desires.

"I say this, *mon trésor,* because I know you have a preponderance for pasting together what is true and what is false, and extracting what is plausible. No matter how much you may desire it, one cannot make a soufflé rise twice. Practicality, Sophie. Above all, one must always be practical. Do you understand what I am saying?"

"Yes, Papa. It is as Molière said, 'I live on good soup, not fine words.'"

Even now, she was warmed by the memory of the way her father threw back his leonine head and laughed heartily as he gathered her to him and gave her an adoring kiss.

Be practical, she reminded herself. She knew

Jamie was on the verge of marriage. Once their idyll here had ended, he would return to the arms of the woman he planned to marry, and she would be forgotten.

Yes, she would be practical. Above all, she would not allow herself to fall in love with him.

But surely it would not spoil things if she cared for him just a little, or if she desired him, for the door to passion had yawned wide open before her—too overpowering for her to close.

There was a part of her that was not born of lust or desire, but one inspired by the strong, and deep feelings she had for him. She had never been in love, and had no way of knowing if the things she felt were born of this deep abiding sentiment, or if it was simply the strong attachment and desire that might one day blossom into love.

The warmth of his breath washed over her, as if making room for the legions of goose bumps that followed when his lips began to make lazy patterns across her skin. Each sensation traveled farther and deeper than the previous one, and her breathing became more labored and shallow. She could see by the diffuse brightness in his eyes that he was reacting to her as much as she was to him, and the thought of it was as pleasing as it was powerful.

She closed her eyes, sensing the faint aroma of soap on his skin before she was gently encircled in warm, comforting arms. The heat emanating from his body relaxed her and she felt his gentle, caressing hands stroke her face and throat with inexhaustible patience, followed by a nuzzling kiss to the cheek.

That kiss, by virtue of its restrained gentleness, did what no amount of force could have persuaded her to do, and she lay unmoving, somewhere between the harsh and glaring lights of reality and the soft, muted colors of a dream.

"You know where this will lead?"

She knew what he was asking. How could she tell him that no matter how she might resist, there was never a time when she did not want him.

She gazed into eyes as dark as obsidian granite, almost liquid with desire, and said, "Show me."

"I want to make love to you, more each time I see you, but I want it only if you want me in return. I dinna want ye to look back on it and think it was against your will. I want you to know what is happening here. I want you to want me as much as I want you."

She studied the way candlelight tinted his dark hair with the sun's color and made his flesh gleam as if dusted with the finest gold. His hair carried the scent of pine and fresh air. His arms offered her comfort and protection, and she needed that so.

He held her close and her body pricked with awareness. Nothing seemed to exist beyond her need to have this time with him, to feel his body close to her, to know the touch of his hands upon her secret places.

She felt the change in his body, the tautness of skin and muscle born of hunger and desire.

"I need you," he whispered. "Now, Sophie. Now."

She quivered at the potency of his words of desire, whispered against her naked flesh, and realized he had removed the rest of her clothes, and she had helped him. Now she could feel the heat of his skin against hers, and knew he was as naked as she.

His warm tongue came calling and she melted against him and opened her mouth to his. She might have many nights such as this with him, or she might have only this one, so she decided she would hold nothing back.

She would have this one night to remember for the rest of her life…one night when she was young and impassioned, one night when she threw caution to the wind, one night when she let him take her to a mythical place where she would make love to a man she desired above all else.

It felt so perfect, so right. She had no shame of lying naked with him, or allowing him to do the things to her body that he was doing. She opened herself to him, softly whimpered, and clung to him because she knew it could not last.

"I could spend all night just kissing you… everywhere. I want to make love to you and cannot maintain my sanity if I do not. I have thought of little else since my brother carried you into my life. No matter how many times I take you, each time will be like the first."

He kissed her breasts, first one and then the other, and she felt the soft, breathing wetness that hardened them, and the muscles in her stomach grew taut in response.

"Your skin is like polished ivory, smooth, refined and cool against the fever I feel within."

He turned and shifted the angle of his body until he was lying full upon her and she knew the feel of the hard length of him, hot as a brand against her flesh. It felt so right to be with him like this, and yet, she fought against the temptation to boldly reach out and take him in her hand. Not because she was too shy to do so around him, but because she was a novice about such things and uncertainty manipulated her as if she were a marionette.

She did allow herself the liberty of letting her hands travel over the smooth musculature of his chest, where she could feel the power of tightly coiled muscles beneath the thin layer of skin.

He claimed her mouth with another kiss—this one longer and more intense—and she felt the rigid probe of him against her like a question.

"Yes," she whispered. "Please…yes."

He paused long enough to ask, "Are you sure, Sophie?"

She moved her legs farther apart and heard his responding groan.

There could have been no greater surprise in his estimation if she had pulled out a claymore and cleaved him in two. He knew this was new to her, and yet there was a wantonness about her that was arousing and it intensified his desire for her.

He could feel the soft pliancy of her breasts pressing against the bare flesh of his chest with each breath she took. His hands wandered at will over the gloriously undefiled beauty of her exquisite body, and the response from her—a soft rapture that washed over him because of the magnificent throb of her intense passion.

His mouth came to hers repeatedly before he dropped lower to kiss her breasts and take the hard points into his mouth. He wanted to touch her in all the places he knew would drive her wild, and at the same time he feared he was too raw with wanting her, too hungry for her, and needing her so much that he feared he could hurt her.

She was a strong wind that blew over the heated coals of his desire, and when her hand closed around him, he burst into flames.

Sophie…

He whispered her name as if it were a sonnet, then touched her as she had touched him, and her gasp was a mixture of pleasure and surprise that nearly sent him spiraling out of control.

"My lass," he said, and came into her, his hands gripping her bare bottom, holding her against him. He heard her moan and asked if he hurt her.

"Only when you stop to ask questions."

Flesh against flesh, warm, moist, fitting together in perfect union as if they had been missing, one from the other for all eternity, and now, after eons of searching, he had found that part of him that had been absent for so long.

He ground his hips against hers, and could hold back no longer. With a groan, he felt the surging release as his body tensed, and then enjoyed the luxury of moving slow, and relaxed inside her.

The sound of her passion went over him like a

whisper of silk and he thought there was nothing to match the joy of lying tangled in Sophie's fragrant hair.

They fell asleep for a time with that drowsy, sated feeling, and the joy that comes with lying together after passion is spent, and he thought this was the most perfect peace of all.

When he stirred and felt Sophie in his arms, he kissed her and nuzzled her neck as he scattered soft, breathy kisses where the delicate wisps of hair curled behind her ear.

Too strong…

His feeling for her was too strong, as if he had drunk a magic potion. Already he was hard again and yearning to take her once more.

Sophie must have known, for she turned toward him and whispered, "Make love to me again."

Later, when she lay nestled against him, her breathing even and steady, he held her close, afraid almost to let her go. Yet, in his moment of triumph, when he had accomplished what he wanted to do since the first, he could not put behind him the feeling that he had seduced an angel.

Would there be hell to pay?

Eleven

But I will wear my heart upon my sleeve
For daws to peck at: I am not what I am.
—William Shakespeare (1564-1616), English
poet and playwright. *Othello* (1602-1604),
Act 1, Scene 1

The Duke of Rockingham was in a fit of temper, and the sound of his angry tirade carried throughout the long, winding corridors of his castle in Yorkshire.

"I am sorry, Your Grace, but we have not been able to find any trace of her. We have spies and soldiers searching for her. Rewards have been offered, but there has been no response. We cannot find anything. There is absolutely no trace anywhere. Perhaps it would be best if you simply gave her up for dead."

Rockingham gripped the back of the ornately carved chair until his knuckles turned white. "Do not take it upon yourself to advise me, you vain, onion-eyed minnow. I alone will decide what would be best. I will not give her up for dead simply because *she is not dead,* do I make myself clear?"

"Perfectly clear, Your Grace."

"Her body was the only one that was not found," Rockingham said. "Do you not find that indicative of something?"

"It could have been borne out to sea with the current," Sir Giles Newland replied.

"You fool! It would be a bit ironic, wouldn't you say, that *hers* should be the only one not accounted for?"

Sir Giles started to speak, but the duke dismissed him with a wave of his hand. "It is time I changed my strategy, therefore I will have no further need of you. Tell my factor to pay you what you are owed, and then tell him I want to see him. Immediately."

Sir Giles bowed and backed toward the door. "As you wish, Your Grace."

Five minutes later, the duke was interrupted

when his factor, Jeremy Ashford, entered the room, bowing as he always did whenever he came into the duke's presence.

"You sent for me, Your Grace?"

Rockingham finished writing his signature to a bill of sale, and returned the pen to the inkstand. He sat back in the chair, made a tent of his fingers, and said calmly, "Yes, I did. I find I have need of a Scot."

"A Scot, Your Grace?"

"Yes, but not just any Scot. This one must be a Highlander."

"You want me to find a Scottish Highlander? Any Highlander?"

"Yes, any Highlander will do, only he must be a traitor."

Jeremy smiled, and then nodded. "Aah, a traitor, you say? Very well, I will see what I can do, Your Grace."

"And quickly, Jeremy. Time is of the essence, as they say."

"Very well, Your Grace. I shall do all I can to expedite matters."

The wind descended upon Danegæld with fierce determination, driving snow and piling it against the windows. Outside the windows were iced with frost, but inside, the massive fireplaces seemed to hold back the best Mother Nature had at her disposal.

Sophie stood at the window, watching for Jamie. He had gone to feed the horses, but it seemed to be taking longer than usual, and she wondered how long she should wait, before taking her cloak and going in search of him.

Her knowledge of this sort of thing was a collage of hearsay, vague book learning and what tidbits Jamie had provided her, for life here was so different from her life in France.

She did not see him come out of the storm, and did not hear him enter the house, until she heard the stomp of his boots on the stone floors. She tensed, waiting for the sound of his arrival.

Jamie dusted the snow off his plaid and came into the library to thaw his extremities before the fire.

When he saw her standing in front of the window, observing the inclement weather, he said, "This one is a true snowstorm. It could last for days." He rubbed his arms to get the blood flowing. "It is bitterly cold out there."

He went to where she stood, put his arms around her and drew her back against him. He scattered kisses over her neck. "I am as incapable of resisting you as I was the first time we made love. No, I think it is worse now. I think of little else."

He lifted her hair and kissed her neck again, beneath her ear, where he knew she was most sensitive. She moaned and rolled her head back to rest against his shoulder.

He unbuttoned a few of the top buttons on her dress and slipped his hand inside, where her full breasts lay warm and firm.

It was difficult to believe it had only been two weeks since their first lovemaking, and that the times he had warmed her bed since then were too numerous to count. "I could stay right here, holding ye thus for eternity."

She smiled. "Or until your feet begin to get cold."

"Are your feet cold, lass?"

"You still need to ask, when you know they have been cold since the day I came here? Sometimes I try to remember what it feels like to lie in the warm sun of summer, and to feel the kiss of the sun on my face. *Sacre bleu.* It is enough to have such bitterly cold weather, but why are we always denied the pleasure of seeing the sun? Is it always so dreary and so cold?"

"Aye, Scotland can be a dreary place, lass. The

stones hold moisture, and that is what causes the chilling dampness." He took her hand. "Come… stand in front of the fire, on the hearth rug. It is much warmer there."

She let him lead her to the great fireplace, and she held out her hands to warm them while she watched him remove his boots, and stand them before the fire to dry. The warmth from the fire began to dry his trews also, and soon they were giving off steam.

"When do you plan to return to Monleigh Castle?"

He was busy kissing her and did not answer right away. "Are ye anxious for us to go?"

"You know my anxiety, or lack of it, has nothing to do with it. You must return home sooner or later, or they will come in search of you."

"And you?"

"I must make my own way."

He pulled her closer. "Oh, I think not."

"I beg your pardon?"

"You cannot leave on your own. Where would you go? You have no idea who you are. You have no money. You are safe with me. Nay, you will not leave. When I return to Monleigh, you will go with me."

"Jamie, I do not think it would bode well for

you to return home with me in tow. It is bound to cause problems between you and Gillian, or have you forgotten all about her and your marriage?"

He turned her toward him. A dark scowl cut into his features as he gripped her securely by her upper arms. "I am the chief, the laird, and the law as it pertains to Monleigh and the Grahams. If I choose to bring you there to live, it is for no one to question. Not even you, lass."

"And Gillian? Is she not entitled to an explanation?"

"I answer to no one. Gillian knows this."

"And she accepts it?"

He made a scoffing sound. "Gillian wants to keep her talons hooked into the prey she has snared. She may not like your being there, but she knows there is naught she can do about it. Her ambitions do not run overly high. As long as she can become the Countess Graham, and mistress of Monleigh Castle, it is enough for her."

"There is a mean side to every patronizing disposition," she said, recalling the intrigue, the jealousy and the deceit she witnessed while attending court in France. She decided it must be that way the world over.

"Sophie, lass, all of this is no worry of yours. I have come up against worse and survived. It is nothing I want you to be concerned with, nor do I want to cause a frown between those beautiful blue eyes. Have no fear. I can protect you from the enemy, without or within my keep."

"I do not wish to reside in a place where I evoke hard feelings, and incite malevolence between members of your clan. I do not know how it would feel to know I had no friends, or to know everyone whispered behind my back. Malice can cut deep."

"Malice is a petty concern," he said.

"Yet it hath very long arms."

"What?"

"Nothing. It is something my father once said."

"Do you remember your father?"

A trap yawned at her feet. She had allowed herself to forget. "I remember things about him from time to time. Sometimes, I can even see his face, but I have no recollection of who he was, or his name."

"Was? He is dead, then?"

Her heart hammered. She could feel her palms growing clammy. "I have the feeling he is, but nothing more to go on, if that is what you mean."

She saw the hard-as-granite look in his eyes and knew the conversation was over, for it was apparent in the way he dismissed her.

She saw the muscle work in his jaw, only moments before he said coldly, "We will leave for Monleigh as soon as the storm lifts."

The fire sputtered with a flurry of snow that rode down the chimney on a downdraft. Overhead, the wind rattled the small windows that were set higher in the walls. It was as if the elements themselves were trying to warn her away.

Danger, they said. Danger lies ahead....

She knew she should not go to Monleigh with him. Everything within her being told her this. She would be publicly branded as his mistress the moment she crossed the threshold. There was bound to be strife.

Yet, how could she withstand him? Her only option was to leave, and what chance did she have in this strange land, fighting against the bitterness of the weather, the distrust of the Scots, or the English patrols looking for her?

Well, isn't that what you wanted, she asked herself, to bear his child and be branded a trollop? Remember, Sophie, and stay focused. The more maligned you become, the more your chances of being shunned by Rockingham will multiply.

She said nothing more, but simply watched him as he turned and left the room, the laughter gone from his eyes.

Sophie stood motionless after he left, not certain where she should go, or what she should do—not that there was an abundance of choices.

Her days were mostly filled with lovemaking and idleness, and when that did not consume the entire day, she filled in the empty places with playing the piano, and bouts of reading.

She clasped her hands together. Her fingers were cold as ice, and she realized she was not as good at all of this as she thought. Oh, it had sounded fine when she had laid it all out in her mind, but she was having difficulty with the reality of it.

She wished she could go after Jamie and then she would not feel so overwhelmed, but she knew he would not always be the pillar of strength in her life that she could lean on. At some point, she would have to go on alone, to straighten out her life and find her place in the world.

She must be careful now.

This was not the time to be filled with self-doubt, nor was it the time to allow fear to command her thoughts. She must be strong, for she was the one person who could mastermind her eventual undoing.

She wandered aimlessly around the room, picking up a figurine here, straightening a cushion there, until she realized she was unconsciously committing this place to memory. She understood the need to take in each dear feature she saw, for she knew this place would always be a treasure she carried close to her heart, just as she knew why.

She was young here; she had fallen in love here, and Danegæld is where she had learned what it meant to give herself completely, body and soul, to another. This house would forever be dear to her, and she took great care to study each beloved detail.

This house is where I became a woman, a hide-away where I gave and received to the fullest extent of passion, she thought. *This place is where we came together in the frenzied grip of burning obsession; the place where our hearts were consumed by fire.*

There were so many memories here, and she wandered from room to room recalling them all in vivid detail, trailing her hand over the polished pieces of furniture, and along the mantel and the window casements, where she had passed many moments quietly staring at the world beyond this room.

Each thing she touched helped to set fire to the memories in her mind, so they would be forever imprinted there, as warm and real as they had been when they were first made.

Her last stop was the kitchen, where she had bathed two nights ago in front of the fireplace, and Jamie had joined her there. He made love to her with the two of them squeezed in the copper tub, arms and legs going in every direction.

In the quiet hush of twilight, she caught the faint echo of their laughter as the water had sloshed over the edge and ended up on the floor.

Afterward, he washed her hair, combed it dry before the fire and made love to her again, this time on his plaid.

She walked to the door and, as she left the room, she took one last look and wondered how one said goodbye to memories.

"*Partir, c'est mourir un peu,*" she whispered. To leave is to die a little...

It was still bitterly cold five days later when they arrived at Monleigh Castle.

Jamie was in a foul humor, cursing the miserable weather, the temperamental nature of his horse Corrie, and most of all, Sophie's apparent indifference toward him and the way she had remained withdrawn for most of their journey.

His one positive feeling toward her was his admiration for the way she had endured the difficult journey without a single complaint. He still could not understand how a woman could sit a horse for as many hours as she had, and manage to keep her back ramrod stiff.

The ride from Danegæld had been a difficult one; especially when riding at the pace he set for them. Even the horses were close to being worn down. He knew she had been uncomfortable, for they had been pelted with freezing rain for hours. He did not miss the sight of her white knuckles while she held on to the pommel.

It was tedious riding along the narrow track that twisted and turned its way through the high mountain passes, where the snow was banked along the edge and made it difficult to see exactly where the trail gave way to nothing but thin air.

Danger waited at every turn, and yet she never uttered a word, balked or refused to go anywhere he led.

She was a lass with a stout heart, and he admired her for her strength.

When they came down a steep turn and saw the open moor ahead of them, she said, "I pray this is the last of the mountains. I long to see nothing but flat land."

He laughed. "Then ye willna be living in the Highlands, lass."

He saw the sad look on her face that his words

had put there, and he cursed himself for being such an insensitive lout. He wanted to say something to ease her discomfort, but the words seemed out of reach.

At last, she took the initiative.

"You know, we never talked about your family, aside from your telling me you had five brothers and one sister. Tell me more about them."

"Where should I start?"

"Since you are the earl, that means your father is dead. Why not start there?"

"Aye, my father is dead…ambushed by English dragoons. I was studying in Europe and had just left Italy the year before to study in France. I had barely finished my first year in Paris, when word arrived that both my uncle and my father were brought home with the blood of their wounds not yet dried."

"How long ago was that?"

"Ten years ago. I was nineteen."

And I was thirteen, she thought, and my father was still alive. "I wish you could have been spared that grief," she said. "The loss of a parent is a grievous wound that heals slowly. I understand why you hate the English."

He did not say anything, and she continued. "I am sorry you were not here when it happened," she said, "for I know it has added to your pain."

"Aye, I have always wished I had been here. The fact that I was not bothers me still."

He fell into silent contemplation after realizing she was the first, and only, person to ever indicate an understanding of how he felt about being denied this rite of separation. He should have been here.

"Yet it was your father who sent you to France to study, was it not?"

"Aye, when he caught me in the courtyard one day waving his sword around and shouting I would kill all the English single-handed, he tapped me on the noggin and he said, 'If ye learn to use this, then ye willna have so much need for this.' He touched the sword, then took it away from me, and said, 'Only the man with no brain must depend upon brawn.'"

"And you went to Italy."

"No, he sent me to Edinburgh the following year, and when I finished there I was sent to Italy, and then France."

"And your mother?"

"After my father's death, she married the Earl of Lanshire."

"Lanshire…it sounds English."

"It is English."

"Your mother is married to an Englishman?"

"Aye, only she is no longer my mother."

"Oh, Jamie, you cannot feel that way. No matter what she has done, she is still your mother."

"She has made her bed, now she must lie in it."

"You never see her or communicate with her?"

"None of us ever see her, or have anything to do with her. Her letters go into the fire, unopened."

"How did it happen?"

"After my father's death, she was so broken she said she had to go away for a while. She went to visit her aunt who lived in Kent. She met Lanshire. She never came back."

"Ah, she fell in love."

"The bastard is English."

And you are a Scot, I am French, and love does not respect borders, she thought. "Who are we to question love that can only be seen through the lovers' eyes?"

"Stay out of it. It is not your concern."

Before she could reply, he kicked Corrie and rode ahead, leaving Sophie to follow.

Later, when they were riding together, she said, "I still have some questions about your family."

"Ask them then, as long as they are not about my mother."

"But I want to know why she—"

He cut her off. "I would rather tell you about

the rest of my family. My brother Tavish you have met. The other four are Bran, Calum, Niall and Fraser. Arabella is my only sister. There are also various members of the Graham clan, all relations in one way or the other, who reside at Monleigh."

"Your mother never had more children?"

He did not answer at first. After a long spell of silence he said, "She bore that English bastard a pair of English daughters. Twins," he added, then said, "I will speak no more of it."

"You are fortunate to have such a large family," she said, thinking about her only sibling, the brother who was now the Comte de Toulouse, since her father had died.

She saw the spark of interest in his eyes, and she fully expected him to inquire as to the size of her own family, or if she had any recollection of them at all, but as quickly as it came, the spark faded, and instead, he said, "You might be interested to know we also have one of your countrymen nearby—a Frenchman who has lived in Scotland for many years now. His name is Vilain Rogeaux. He is quite a ladies' man, as you will soon discover."

Relief swept through her when he said the Frenchman had lived in Scotland for many years. Her only hope was that he did not keep up with what was going on in France. "It will be good to have someone to converse with in my own language," she replied. Then, knowing she was being a bit spiteful for doing so, she asked, "And your bride to be? Is she in residence here as well?"

"No, Gillian lives nearby."

"How inconvenient."

He laughed, knowing it was her nervousness that prompted her to react as she had, for he knew it was not Sophie's true nature to be ill disposed toward anyone.

She asked a few more questions and he answered them, but he refused to discuss the subject of his mother. At last she gave up, and they rode for almost an hour without either of them saying anything more.

For some time now, he had been aware of the way she seemed to grow more apprehensive as the gray walls and battlements of Monleigh Castle drew closer. When he saw it on the horizon, rising up like a massive volcano, wreathed in mist, as if it were ready to spew forth fire and brimstone, he felt glad to be so close.

He lifted his gaze to his home, where the massive walls rose steeply out of the rock that thrust straight up out of the North Sea. He felt pride in who he was, and what he had inherited by virtue of the Graham blood that coursed through his veins.

"Is that it?" she asked.

"Aye, I ken I am the first to welcome ye to Monleigh Castle, lass. 'Tis the home of the earls of Monleigh, but the eighth and present earl is the only one ye need to be concerned with."

"Well, when you see him, please tell the Eighth Earl of Monleigh that I think his castle is a place the newcomer looks upon with both awe and dread."

He supposed that to the first-time viewer, there was nothing friendly about it, for it was stark and somber if one looked at it without considering the warmth and love it harbored inside.

They arrived at the castle, and waited for the iron portcullis to lift slowly over the heavily carved arch of the gate.

He noticed the way her hands trembled. "It is not as inhospitable as it seems. No harm will come to ye. On that ye have my word."

"I daresay no one will be setting out the castle's finest gold and silver, either," she replied, not bothering to hide the bite of sarcasm.

His face was dark and impassive, but he tried to lighten her mood. "If it's gold and silver ye want, it might be arranged...if that sort of thing appeals to you."

She did not respond but merely lifted the reins, kicked her horse and rode forward through the gate and entered the courtyard ahead of him.

He did not miss the way her hand came up to wipe the smudges of travel from her face, or to tuck the wisps of hair back beneath the plaid covering her head. She was truly an exasperating lass, and more than once during their journey she had angered him to the point that he considered yanking her from her horse and making love to her on the spot, for there was little doubt in his mind that it would have made things better for both of them if he had.

He caught up with her and pulled out his handkerchief, which he offered to her.

She declined with the comment, "There is no one here I wish to impress. Let them see me at my worst. It will be in harmony with the way they will feel toward me soon enough."

"Have ye no optimism, lass?"

"Optimism? Pray, milord, what is that?"

He had never encountered a more stubborn, obstinate woman. That it was also the woman he desired above everything rankled him. How could he be so enamored with a woman whose every word carried with it the sting of an asp?

He watched her ride ahead of him accompanied

by her angry pride, and he had never observed royalty do it better. Sometimes, it was difficult for him to capture a picture in his mind of her as anything but an aristocrat, and for good reason. He would bet his life that she was not of low breeding. If she would only admit such it would simplify many things, but by this point he was beginning to doubt she ever would.

The men in the keep all turned to watch her ride by.

To say she caused a stir among them would be to understate things a bit. Several tried to outdo the other in rushing forward to help her dismount. She accepted their help graciously and was soon on the ground, although she was not, at first, too steady on her feet.

"Alert my family to my homecoming and tell them I have brought a visitor. And see to our horses."

There was a flurry of activity as men rushed to do the Earl of Monleigh's bidding. Jamie offered his arm to Sophie, but she declined. "I see no reason for us to present ourselves as anything other than what we are: lord and servant."

"You are not my servant, mistress, and I will warn you now not to use that phrase again."

Twilight was fast upon them, and the moment

they stepped into the darker interior of the castle, where torches flamed along passageways and candles guttered in sconces in the gathering rooms, they both had to wait a moment for their eyes to adjust.

A tall, graying woman hurried toward them, a ring of keys suspended from her belt. "Why did you not send word that you were coming?" she asked, her gaze going over Sophie as she spoke.

"I dismissed the servants at Danegæld upon my arrival, so there was no one to send." Jamie gave her a kiss on the cheek. "It is good to see you, Fenella. You are well?"

"Aye, I am as well as ever, God be praised. You have brought a guest, I see."

"Aye, this is Sophie. I will officially introduce her to everyone in the Great Hall." He glanced at Sophie. "This is Fenella. She is what you would call in France the *châtelaine,* for she is the keeper of the keys to all the rooms. Nothing goes on here that she does not know about."

It was the first time he had observed her around others, and he was greatly surprised, for Sophie greeted her politely, in a way that showed both consideration of others and good manners.

Her clothes might be dirty and her hair disheveled, but her manners were worthy of the English court. Even in her bedraggled state she commanded attention, and a quick glance at the men about said she certainly got it.

They entered the Great Hall and Jamie saw the way his sister's face lit up as she hurried to greet them.

"Jamie, you rogue! I thought you were never coming home," she said, laughing as Jamie caught her around the waist and swung her around.

"And how is my favorite sister?"

"Much better now that you have returned." With a glance at Sophie, she said, "Introduce me to your guest, please, for I am anxious to meet someone so lovely."

"My sister, Arabella," he said. "And this is our honored guest, Sophie."

Jamie put his arm around Arabella and the two of them walked a few paces in front of Sophie, who walked with Fenella. Obviously curious, Fenella asked a few polite questions, which made it impossible for Sophie to hear what Jamie and Arabella were talking about.

Me, more than likely, she thought.

By the time he got around to making the introductions everyone had gathered in the hall, which, thankfully, meant he only had to introduce Sophie one more time. He did not offer even a brief explanation as to who she was, or why he had brought her here, and he knew no one would dare raise the question.

He knew she was weary, so he did not prolong things, and after a short while said, "Sophie is exhausted from the journey."

Fenella nodded. "Shall I show her to her room, then?"

"Aye," Jamie said.

"I will accompany you," Arabella said.

"She has no baggage?" Fenella asked.

"No," he replied, and noticed the way Sophie's shoulders seemed to draw together at his reply.

He waited until the women had departed before he turned toward his brothers to greet each of them properly. Before they could ask, he began his story about the circumstances of how Tavish found her and brought her to Danegæld.

As he knew they would, his brothers had far too many questions.

Niall was the first. "She has been there with you all this time?"

"Aye, what was I supposed to do? Turn her out? She was near death when Tavish arrived, and in no condition to travel."

Fraser was next. "It was just the two of you… there…alone?"

"Aye, we were alone, and I will thank ye kindly to refrain from making any further comments as to that matter."

"Fortunate bastard," Niall said. "Why does nothing like that ever happen to me?"

They all laughed. Bran, Niall and Fraser all seemed jovial enough about it, and made various offers to take the lass off his hands.

Ignoring them, Jamie went on to explain Sophie's loss of memory and the fact that she had no knowledge of who she was.

Calum was not so accepting as the others. "Convenient, wouldn't you say?"

"What is that supposed to mean?" Fraser asked.

"Nothing. I was merely wondering how he was going to explain all of this to Gillian?"

"The same way I am explaining it to you," Jamie said.

"You cannot keep her here," Calum said. "To do so would be an insult to Gillian."

"Gillian is an insult to herself," Bran said. "I fancy I like having the lass here...much more in fact, than Gillian. I vow having a French lassie here will liven things up a bit."

Jamie scowled at his brother. "The lass is a guest at Monleigh, and she will stay here until she regains her memory, and in case she does not, then for as long as she likes, or as I deem it necessary."

"This will cause problems between you and Gillian," Calum said, obviously in a sulky mood over the way things were going.

"That is my worry," Jamie said, "and not yours. So you may leave the fretting over it to me. Now, let us have a glass of ale while you bring me up to date on what has transpired while I was away."

Sophie followed Arabella down a long corridor, listening to her gay chatter, which she found very comforting. She liked Arabella immediately, and was so glad to learn there would be a woman about who was close to her own age.

The only time Arabella eased up on her chatter was when they began to climb a winding staircase and, looking up, Sophie could see why, for the stairs in the tower seemed to go on forever.

Sophie began to wonder if she was to be imprisoned there, but they came to a door, stepped through it, and entered into another corridor that was part of a different wing of the castle.

"This is a rather roundabout way of getting here, but I thought you would prefer to come the long way and spare yourself the indignity of being stared at by all the male members of the clan."

Sophie immediately recognized a friend in Arabella, who seemed to accept her as an equal. "Thank you for being so considerate."

Arabella smiled. "Jamie said you lost everything when your ship went aground."

"Yes, although I don't remember what I had, so I have not had the unfortunate experience of grieving over my loss."

Arabella laughed. "That is a positive way of looking at it, I ken. Now, dinna ye worrit about having no clothes to wear. We are about the same size, and I have far too many clothes—a result of having nothing but brothers."

Sophie smiled. "Thank you for your offer. I must admit I had to borrow a few of your things at Danegæld. This is one of them, as you have probably noticed," Sophie said, indicating the gray wool dress she wore.

"Goodness, I did not recognize it, but then, I have not been to Danegæld for over a year now. You will have this room," Arabella said as she opened the door. "My room is across the hall. It will be such fun having you here. Having six brothers and no sister about can make it quite lonely sometimes." She took Sophie's hands in hers. "I am truly glad you are here, and I hope Jamie decides to make you our prisoner so you will be forced to remain here."

Sophie looked at Arabella's dark curls that framed the loveliest, sweetest face and wondered if she had any idea how close she had come to the truth.

"Dinner is usually served around eight o'-clock," she said, and when she turned toward the lamp she placed on the table, Sophie saw she had Jamie's mossy-green eyes. A second later, she was struck by the strong family resemblance between them, for it was obvious they were brother and sister.

Sophie gave her a tired smile, and said, "If you don't mind, I think I would prefer sleep to food."

"I know you must be tired. It is a hard ride from Danegæld, and my brothers always seem to forget that I am a girl when we make the trip. Do not get into bed until I send someone with a warming pan. The sheets can be frightfully cold in weather like this."

"You have been so very kind to me. I do not know how to thank you."

"You can thank me by remaining here." She laughed. "You see, I am worried already that you might one day leave."

"Not anytime soon, I fear, for my memory seems in no hurry to return." Sophie sat down. "I will wait here for the gown and the warm sheets...which sound wonderful, by the way. I've seen nothing but cold weather since I arrived here."

"Jamie said you almost froze to death before Tavish found you."

"I don't remember much about it save being cold and wet."

"You have no memory of who you are? At least that is what Jamie said."

"No, I have no memory of that as yet."

Sophie was wondering what else Jamie said. Surely, he did not mention their lovemaking.

"Dinna worry about it. You can make new memories here at Monleigh Castle."

"I hope I won't be here long enough to do that. I pray my memory will return soon and I can go home, or continue on my journey—wherever that was."

"You have no knowledge of where you were going before the ship wrecked?"

"No."

"The ship was bound for Norway. Did you know that?"

"Yes, Tavish told me."

Arabella's eyes lit up. "You better be glad it was Tavish who found you and not Calum. Calum is the moody one. He distrusts everyone and everything. Tavish is the charmer in the family. He loves to talk, especially to beautiful women. How did you like him?"

"I found him charming and considerate, with a mellow way."

A look of concern settled over her face. "Did Jamie treat you badly?"

"I don't think patience with women is what he is known for. I am sure he is a good chief."

Arabella smiled warmly. "Aye, it is good he has five brothers instead of five sisters."

They both laughed, and Arabella went on. "I have always wanted a sister. I do hope you will be with us for a long time. I will go in search for someone to warm your bed now."

"Thank you again."

"I took the liberty of having Fenella place a few things in your wardrobe so you will have something to wear until we can arrange for a dressmaker. There is a gown on the bed."

"Your kindness is overwhelming. I do hope we will be friends."

"We already are," Arabella said, and took her leave.

Sophie called after her. "If Jamie should inquire, please tell him I have already retired."

"Aye, I will tell him, although it will no' make

any difference to him. If he wants to speak with you, there is nothing to stop him from coming here."

Although Sophie was accustomed to Jamie's casual attitude toward entering her bedroom at Danegæld, she did not want to give that impression.

"He is an earl and such behavior would be unacceptable for him."

Arabella burst into a full-bodied laugh. "We are members of the peerage by birth, but we stuff all of the pomp that accompanies it in the nearest trunk, and only take it out for an occasional airing when there are other, more snobbish, gentry about. To the Grahams, Jamie is the chief of the clan and the laird of the castle, and that is far more important to them than his being the Earl of Monleigh."

"Very well. I will lock the door then."

Arabella smiled. "Aye, ye could do that of course, but it willna make any difference. Jamie would never let a little thing like a door keep him from going where he pleases."

Sophie dressed for bed, and once the friendly maid named Jean finished warming her bed, she immediately climbed into it. As she settled herself and closed her eyes, she wondered if she would be awakened later, as she often had been at Danegæld, by Jamie's lovemaking.

Twelve

I shall have mistresses.

—George II (1683-1760), German-born British monarch. *Memoirs of the Reign of George the Second* (John Hervey; 1848)

In his study, Jamie paused over the reading of a few letters and thought about Sophie, and his decision to keep a respectful distance between the two of them. It was not something he wanted to do, but something he deemed necessary, for he hoped it would give her time to adjust to her new surroundings.

In spite of his intent, it was not easy for him to avoid her, and he quickly learned his iron will was not as strong or unyielding as he thought. It was the Scot's way to set a stout heart to a steep hillside, but staying away from Sophie was proving to be more like climbing a craggy mountain: it was a constant battle.

Arabella was unaware that she was making the situation easier for him, for she and Sophie were together constantly. This made it difficult for him to get Sophie alone whenever his desire to be with her overrode his better judgment.

Strange though it was, it was during this time of abstinence that he realized his need to be with her was not born of lustful desires, but by more innocent intentions and purer motives. Simply put, he missed her.

He did not know Sophie had become a habit, as necessary to him as breathing, until he realized he felt the empty blank within only when she was not with him.

Instead of being a comfort, this realization left him on edge, because it did not fit within the boundaries of his plans, where he would marry a woman he did not love, and have mistresses to fill the emptiness. Because of this, he chose not to share these feelings with her.

He knew that having Arabella to confide in was good for Sophie, and it would ease her introduction into the Graham clan. He had much to attend to since his return, and was glad Arabella could fill the hours for Sophie that would have been quite lonely otherwise.

As for him, he tried to stay away from Sophie, as a way to protect her from gossip. To fill the void, he wrapped himself in his obligations and the duties that belonged on his shoulders, and he performed them faithfully, with late hours and devoted efficiency.

In spite of his good intentions, and devotion to his work, he had a feeling that those close to him saw beyond his concentrated efforts, and caught a glimpse of the turmoil going on inside him. Had he really fooled anyone? Was there one person at Monleigh Castle who thought him indifferent to her? Or did they realize that whenever he saw her, he noticed the French lass far more than a disinterested man would?

Seeing her occasionally throughout the day was not the same as spending time with her, and it left him frustrated and on edge. He missed the lack of restrictions he enjoyed at the lodge that enabled him to be with her, to go to her room freely, and to make love to her and sleep in the same bed with her each night.

When they were apart, days were too long, family conversation was too boring, and sleep was interrupted too often with dreams of her. He roared and growled like a starving fiend when he did not see her, and feasted his eyes upon her like a glutton when he did.

The rest of the time, it was pure hell. Such as now, when he was supposed to be doing his accounts, yet his mind was on Sophie and not on the calculation of numbers. About the time he managed to force his attention back to the figures before him, he heard the distractible sound of feminine laughter.

He paused, puzzled that it came from somewhere outside.

After he pushed back his chair and walked around the desk, he moved to the window where he could look out, and allowed his gaze to follow the direction of the sound.

Sophie and Arabella were bundled in their long capes, their hooded heads together as they took the fresh air in the garden. It was impossible to know what they talked about, but he had a good idea his name was mentioned frequently.

"What are you going to do with the French lass?"

Jamie turned and saw his brother walk into the room—Calum, the sensitive, rebellious and brooding brother with the countenance of a poet.

He had been expecting Calum to make an inquiry, and was surprised he had not done so before now.

Jamie remembered their boyhood, and the fear his parents harbored that the sickly and smallest of the Graham brothers would never live to reach maturity. Jamie had been the one to protect Calum, and consequently Calum was completely devoted to him, almost to the point of idolizing him—at least he was when they were younger.

Only now, it seemed he and Calum were always on opposite sides of every issue, especially if it was one that involved Gillian.

There were times when Jamie had difficulty understanding how it was that the two eldest brothers, born only a year apart, could be so different.

He turned to face Calum and looked straight into his luminous blue eyes. "I don't intend to do anything with her. The lass has no memory of her past. What would you have me do? Turn her out in the cold?"

"She canna stay here, Jamie…not when you consider your betrothal to Gillian. It does not look right, no matter what your intentions are. What is everyone supposed to think, with you bringing a beautiful lassie home and keeping her here? People will talk. You know they will."

Jamie scoffed at that. "Let them talk. You

should know by now that I am never swayed by public opinion."

"Think of Gillian," Calum said.

"Think what about Gillian?"

"The presence of another woman living under your roof will offend her."

"You would do better to let Gillian do her own thinking. If she has an issue with Sophie, she can come to me," Jamie said. "She doesna need to send you."

"And if Gillian decides to end things between you?"

Jamie shrugged. "Gillian will do what she deems necessary without any intervention from me...or you."

"You have known Gillian all your life, and yet you act as if you don't care for her at all," Calum said.

"You seem to care for her enough for both of us."

"I am concerned for her."

"And I am not in love with her, if that is what you mean. Not that it should come as any surprise to anyone. You were always closer to her than any of the rest of us were. Perhaps you should be the one to marry her. The two of you are much better suited."

Jamie did not know what prompted him to say

that and, once he had, he was surprised at Calum's reaction. Where Jamie expected him to angrily rebuke that statement, Calum said nothing. Not that he needed to deny it. The guilty look on his face said enough.

Jamie had never realized before now that Calum was in love with Gillian. Any other time he would have thrown back his head and laughed, then with a slap to his brother's back, he would have offered his congratulations with an announcement that he was going to end the betrothal between himself and Gillian in order to make way for his brother.

However, something held him back and he suppressed the urge. Perhaps it was Calum's sensitivity.

"I have always cared for Gillian, but I am the second brother, with no title to offer her. It is you she wants, and she will not tolerate the French lass being under your protection. It is an insult to her."

"It is only an insult if she tries to make it one. I daresay she would not consider it an insult if Sophie was a homely lass, or a portly matron."

"Have you bedded her?"

Jamie's face grew dark. "Back off, brother. You overstep the bounds of your position."

"You should have prepared Gillian by telling

her about the lass. Have you not considered the shock it will be when Gillian comes tonight, and discovers another woman living here? Try to see it from Gillian's perspective. That is all I am asking…that you be considerate of her feelings."

Jamie nodded. "As you should know brother, I am the epitome of consideration."

"You will get rid of the French lass, then?"

"No, but out of consideration of Gillian, I will be glad to tell her she is no longer welcome here."

With an angry oath, Calum turned to leave, and bumped into Bran who walked into the room at that moment.

"Och! I hope ye are no' as cross as ye look," Bran said when he saw Calum's grim expression. "Did ye have words with Jamie?"

"One does not have words with Jamie. Ye canna argue with him. If he misses you with his knife, he cuts ye down with his claymore."

Bran laughed. "I ken ye are angry…."

"Angry?" Calum repeated. "What I feel is far more than anger, but I haven't the words to explain it."

Bran laughed again and gave Calum a jolly slap on the back. "You are always armed with words, Calum. Now, cheer up, lad. I came to see if you wanted to ride over to Fergus Macfarlane's with me.

I hear that handsome niece of his is visiting from Glencoe. Seems she brought her sister with her."

After Calum and Bran were gone, Jamie turned back to the window for another glimpse of Sophie, but she and Arabella were no longer in the garden.

Only their footprints in the snow bore witness to the fact that they had been there at all.

He stared at their footprints, feeling something akin to desolation. He missed her, not only for the lovemaking, but also for the companionship. He shook his head, remembering the almost desolate feeling he had, the first morning he awoke in his bed at Monleigh and did not see the long brown braids lying on his pillow.

He wanted to see Sophie, and he recalled the intimate moments he had alone with her at Danegæld, and cursed the complications that made it impossible to be alone with her like that now. He knew his instinct had been right, for it was best to avoid her altogether, at least for a while, to give her time to adjust to her new surroundings and to allow the bond of friendship to develop between her and Arabella.

Being right did not help, because being right is not what he wanted. He wanted Sophie.

He missed her because she was so damn missable.

The dilemma he had created for himself was real, and not easily solved. He wanted Sophie, but it would be harmful for her if he gave her too much notice. He had feigned indifference toward her since their arrival, and no one seemed to think of his relationship with her as anything but a platonic one.

Unfortunately, Sophie was under the same assumption, for he had glimpsed the look of perplexed hurt upon her sweet face more than once.

It was only his desire to protect her that enabled him to maintain the distance between them, for he wanted to protect her from enmity, and it pained him deeply to think anyone would treat her with resentment, dislike, loathing or hatred.

Arabella took Sophie's hand. "Hurry. I have something to show you."

"What is it?" Sophie asked, as she practically ran up the stairs with Arabella.

"A surprise," Arabella replied, and walked ahead of her friend to enter Sophie's room.

Sophie gasped and came to a standstill, for sitting at the foot of her bed was the trunk she lost when the *Aegir* ran aground. She was so stunned to see it, she was speechless.

She could not think, at first, how the trunk could be here, but then she remembered Tavish saying something about everyone at Monleigh staying up half the night bringing in dead bodies. It was likely, therefore, that they probably found many trunks and other belongings as well.

She recalled that day in Paris, when her life was in so much turmoil, and tried to think about what she packed in the trunk. Think, Sophie, she told herself. What did you put in there that could be incriminating?

"Where did you find that?" Sophie asked, finally gaining her composure.

"It came from the ship you were on. Niall said it washed ashore. Several trunks were brought here. Most of them belonged to men. He said the clothing inside was very high quality and looked to be about your size."

"It obviously belonged to someone who died. I don't know that I relish wearing the clothes of a dead woman."

"Don't think about that. Come on. Let us open it. Perhaps there will be something you can wear tonight."

"After a bout with the sea, I doubt the things are wearable, anyway," Sophie said.

"Not true," Arabella said, "although that was my first thought as well. Niall said there was precious little damage done. Our laundress managed to salvage all but three items."

Sophie did not have a chance to say anything more, for Arabella was already throwing back the lid to the trunk. "Oh, my," she exclaimed. "Wait until you see what is in here."

A second later, she began pulling out the dresses, one by one, and tossing them onto the bed. "There is a fortune in clothes. Why, they must have come from the finest dressmakers in Paris. I don't think I have ever seen anything quite so fine. They are the clothes of royalty, I am certain, for they look fit for a queen."

Sophie wondered what Arabella would say if she told her the dark green gown had belonged to the Queen of France, and that she had given it to Sophie. Instead of saying that, Sophie merely sorted through the growing pile on the bed and said, "Yes, they are quite lovely."

"Don't you think they will fit?" Arabella asked.

Sophie picked up a mulberry gown and held it against her, checking the fit. "If not a perfect fit, it should be close," she said.

Arabella turned toward Sophie with a mischievous smile. "Perhaps it is my turn to borrow one of your dresses."

"You need not even ask," Sophie said, feeling

somewhat detached from what was going on. "I would be honored for you to take anything you wanted to wear, without asking."

"Oh, I could never do that," she said, then added impishly, "but I promise you I won't mind asking."

Arabella pulled out an ice-blue silk. "Oh, Sophie, this was made for you. It is almost the exact color of your eyes. You must wear this one tonight."

"Don't you think it is a little too formal for tonight?"

"No. It will be your first party. You should wear it so everyone will notice you. Here, put it on. I want to see you in it."

Sophie accepted the dress, for if there was one thing she learned about these Scots, it was that they did not understand the word *no.*

Moments later, she stood in front of the looking glass. How strange she felt. The last time she wore this dress was at court, shortly before her cousin, King Louis, announced her betrothal.

"Oh, it is a perfect fit." Arabella stopped and put her finger to the side of her face and tapped it a few times. "Oh, dear. There is one problem."

"What problem is that?"

"My feet!" she wailed. "My feet are larger than yours. What shall you do for shoes? I didn't see any in the trunk that would go with such a beauteous gown."

Sophie was pulling the dress over her head. "Look again," she said, her voice muffled under the yards of skirt. "There should be a pair of blue satin ones."

Arabella began digging through the trunk with ardent fervor. A moment later, she gave a cry of success and held up the blue satin shoes. "Here they are," she said as she turned toward Sophie.

Almost immediately, Arabella's expression changed. She looked at the blue satin shoes in her hand, and then at Sophie. Obviously puzzled, she asked, "How did you know they were in the trunk?"

Sophie wanted to kick herself. It was obvious she did not know much about subterfuge or being evasive. A mind like hers could not analyze the obvious. How could she have been so stupid? You must be more careful, she warned herself. Now, see what you can do to extract yourself from this bottomless hole you jumped into without looking. "That did not make much sense, did it? I…I meant to say there simply *had to be* a pair of blue satin ones. Can you imagine anyone having a dress so lovely as this one, and *not* having a pair of matching slippers? It simply is not done...at least not in Paris."

Arabella considered Sophie thoughtfully, seeming to weigh the truthfulness of her words according to her own criteria. Then she said, "Oh." But, to Sophie, even that one little word sounded a little forced and a little too uncertain, and Sophie was not at all convinced Arabella would not continue to think about it a while longer.

Arabella handed the shoes to Sophie, then she crossed her fingers and said, "For good luck. Oh, do try them on. I am most anxious to see if they fit."

Something gave Sophie pause. It occurred to her a moment later, what that was. "There is something here that is not right. Jamie loaned me a pair of your slippers to wear at Danegæld, yet you said your feet are larger than mine. I do not understand how that can be."

Arabella did not have to think upon that at all. "Oh, I think they were probably a pair of old shoes. Probably some that I wore when my feet were smaller."

Sophie was still reluctant to try the slippers on. They would fit perfectly, of course, and she feared that would only serve to make Arabella more suspicious, or at least bear witness to the fact that she had lied.

"Oh, do try them on, Sophie. What are you waiting for? I am dying to see them on you."

Reluctantly, Sophie put the shoes on.

Arabella studied them for a moment. "Do you know what I think?"

"No, what?"

"I think this is your trunk and these are your clothes inside."

Sophie was terrified. To be found out so easily. She was caught off guard and had no reply floating around in the giant vacuum of her mind. She did not know how spies did it. And Jamie suspected her of being one? She wanted to laugh.

If he only knew.

She was wondering how she could go about persuading Arabella not to say anything, and was no more than a hair's breadth away from giving Arabella a full confession, when Arabella miraculously saved Sophie with her next statement.

"I think you must have had some premonition about the shoes. It's like you remember, but you don't remember that you remember what you remember."

Sophie's eyes crossed.

"It's all stored in your brain somewhere, along with all your knowledge, only it leaks out bits at a time, like water dripping from the roof after a rain. Do you understand what I am saying?"

"Yes, you are saying that when I lose enough drips, I will eventually regress to an idiot."

They both laughed, and Arabella said, "That didn't come out right, did it?"

"No," Sophie said, smiling, and suppressing the urge to hug Arabella. "But, I understood what you were trying to say."

"I am very glad you understand, because I'm not all that positive that I do," Arabella said. "I do believe this is all so exciting…just think, we have found your very own trunk. Oh, let's do look some more."

Sophie frowned. "Why don't we eat first? I am famished. We can unpack later."

"All right," Arabella said. "I find I am a bit hungry as well. Let us go eat, and when we return, we can finish this. Who knows? Perhaps we will find something to tell us who you really are."

That was Sophie's greatest fear, and the smile on her face disappeared. She suffered no delusions of self-righteousness, for she was fully aware of her guilt, which was accompanied by feelings of shame and regret—shame for having lies and deception; regret at knowing the truth would eventually be known.

Thirteen

So stately his form, and so lovely her face,
That never a hall such a galliard did grace;
While her mother did fret, and her father did
fume
And the bridegroom stood dangling his bon-
net and plume;
And the bride-maidens whisper'd, "'twere
better by far
To have match'd our fair cousin with young
Lochinvar."

—Sir Walter Scott (1771-1832), Scottish novelist. *Marmion: A Tale of Flodden Field,*
Canto V (1808)

It was an hour later when they returned to Sophie's room.

For a moment, the two of them stood looking at the huge trunk without saying anything.

After a few more seconds passed, Sophie said, "I suppose we might as well tackle this now."

"I do hope we find something in it that might jar your memory," Arabella said.

"Yes, so I can be saved from a life of idiocy."

Arabella smiled with a mischievous light in her eyes. "You will never allow me to forget that, will you?"

Sophie returned her smile. "Would you, if the situation were reversed?"

Arabella gave her an impish smile. "Heavens no—and you are right about unpacking the trunk. I should have realized it myself. I will forget riding for now, so I can help you."

"You don't need to help me. I would feel much better if I did not deprive you of your ride," she said as she watched Arabella head for the trunk. "Truly, I can manage this by myself."

"I would like to help," Arabella said as she reached into the trunk.

They worked quietly for half an hour when Arabella turned to Sophie and said, "Och! 'Tis a keepsake. Look, is this no' a lovely miniature?"

Sophie felt the color drain from her face. Blast! She had forgotten about the small painting. She made an effort to hide any hint of surprise or irritation in her voice. "Here, let me see it," she said.

"Do you know who it is?" Arabella asked, and handed it to Sophie.

Sophie pretended to be studying the portrait for a while, and then shook her head. "No, I do not recognize it, nor do I have the feeling I have seen it before."

"Or at least you dinna remember having seen it before," Arabella said. She gave the miniature another look. "Whoever the man is, he must be someone very important. His clothes are very fine, his horse blooded, and there is a regal air about him. Perhaps he is someone in your family."

"No, it couldn't be," Sophie said. "His clothing is far too fine for anyone in my family, I think."

"Jamie said he didna believe you were a maid. No one else does, either, for that matter."

"And you? What do you think, Arabella?"

"I do not believe it, either," she said. "Not that I mean to doubt you. It is only when I look at the clothes we removed from the trunk that I realize those are not the tatters of a maid, but the finery of a very genteel lady."

"We sometimes believe the things we want to

believe and not what is true. Is it not a very common practice for a servant to be rewarded with gifts of clothing? Besides, we only *think* this was my trunk. We have no proof."

Arabella's attention was still on the miniature. "Hmm... Och, I am sorry. I was only thinking that perhaps Jamie would recognize who this is."

Sophie felt the rapid acceleration of her heart. She was no better at deception than she was at lying. "There is no need to bother him," she said.

"Och! Jamie willna consider it a bother. I can tell he likes you, so he will be happy to help in any way he can."

Sophie tried a different approach. "If the face in the portrait does not mean anything to me, I daresay the name will not, either."

Arabella dropped the miniature into her pocket. "Probably not, but it will not hurt to try. We must not leave any leads unexplored."

Sophie felt the panic grip her throat like fingers closing around her neck, squeezing slowly until she could not breathe. "No!"

Arabella jumped. Her expression was one of startled surprise, although it was the question that loomed in the depths of her eyes that had Sophie worried.

"I'm sorry," Sophie said. "This is so nerve-racking for me. My nerves are all on edge. I know I sound snappish. Truly, it is not the way I feel in my heart. You have been nothing but kind to me. I think I need time to sort through all of this on my own before I seek help. I know you want to help by finding out the identity of the man in the portrait, and that you mean well, but the moment you mention it to Jamie, the man in him will want to take charge. I shudder to think of all the questions he would ask. I am not up to that right now." She put her hand on Arabella's arm. "I do hope you understand."

Arabella's expression softened. "Of course I do. I am sorry I rushed in and took charge of things like I did...." She smiled. "I mean, like *Jamie* would...without giving you the consideration, or the opportunity to make your own decisions. It was thoughtless of me."

She put her hand into her pocket, withdrew the miniature and handed it back to Sophie. "Here. You keep it until you decide who it is, or if you want me to show it to Jamie."

Sophie dropped it back into the trunk and shut the lid, but she knew this was not necessarily the end of it. Her first impulse had been to hurl it out the window and watch it disappear into the thunderous waves pounding on the rocks below the castle. But she decided she should not, for its disappearance might make Arabella more suspicious. Besides, she hated to part with it. Her grandfather gave it to her father and he, in turn, had given it to Sophie.

Sophie's mind spun backward to a day that was still vivid in her mind. It was during the time of her father's illness when his condition had gradually deteriorated over a period of several months. Throughout his illness, all of Sophie's thoughts were on her father and she went to his apartments each day to visit and read to him.

One afternoon as she was about to open the book and read another chapter, he took the miniature from his bedside table. "My father had several of these painted," he said, "one for each of his children. They are scrupulous copies of the large portrait that hangs at Versailles, and done by the original artist."

Sophie looked at the picture of the Sun King. She knew he was her grandfather, but he had died before she was born, so she had no memory of him. Yet, she loved him because her father loved him.

"I want you to have this."

"But, Papa, it is your favorite. I cannot take it."

"Sophie, my darling daughter, I am dying. I

want you to have it, so I must give it to you now. Once I am gone, the vultures will descend upon the châteaux, and you, with your kind and gentle ways, will be pushed aside by those driven by greed. Put it in a safe place and tell no one you have it…at least not for a few years. Promise me."

"I promise."

He placed it in her hand and as she gazed at it, he said, "Remember, Sophie, no matter what happens in life, always hold your head up proudly. The blood of the Bourbons flows in your veins."

"I will, Papa."

He studied the face in the painting as if for the last time. "Louis XIV. He was the greatest king France has ever known, but he was also a devoted father to his many children, both legitimate and illegitimate. You should be proud to call him grandfather."

"I am, but I am more proud to call you Papa."

He caressed her cheek. "I know I will enjoy heaven for I have already been blessed with the presence of one of its angels."

It was the last time Sophie saw her father, for he died that night in his sleep.

True to her word, she never mentioned having the portrait and, after a while, those driven by greed, who fulfilled her father's prophecy, ceased to search for it. Yet Sophie never mentioned it.

To this day, no one knew she had it.

Now it seemed that was all about to change.

In the Great Hall, Jamie was talking with his neighbor, Vilain Rogeaux, who was the first to arrive for a festive evening of dinner and dancing. He was wondering how Sophie would take to this fellow citizen of France. Handsome, slim, elegantly blond, Vilain was educated, polished, well bred and flirtatious. He had a definite eye for the lassies.

The two of them had conversed about generalities for a time, and Jamie was about to tell him about Sophie when Gillian interrupted them.

"There you are," she said, siding up to Jamie. "I have been looking everywhere for you." She nodded at Vilain. "And how are you, my dear Vilain?"

"Much better now that my eyes have feasted upon you in that lovely gown."

"It is the latest thing from France," she said, giving him a better glimpse as she turned around. "I knew you would like it."

"Exquisite taste as always," he said, taking her proffered hand and kissing it.

Gillian trailed her closed fan seductively down Vilain's arm. "I want a dance, Vilain."

"Anything your heart desires, *cherie,*" Vilain said. "Would you like something to drink?"

"A perfect gentleman as always," she said, and with a sultry smile she added, "but I do not care for anything just yet."

"Then I will leave the two of you to visit," Vilain said, and with a bow, he excused himself.

Jamie knew Vilain's departure signaled the end of Gillian's pleasant disposition and he was right. "I only learned of your return, although I understand you arrived several days ago."

He turned to her. "You are looking lovely this evening, as Vilain said."

"Obviously I am not lovely enough for you to take the time to pay me a visit, or at least send a note to let me know you were back."

"There were pressing matters I needed to attend to first. I knew I would see you tonight."

"Your pressing matter wouldn't be the French hussy you brought here, would it?"

"Jealousy does not become you, Gillian. The lass needs our help, not criticism. Now, if you will wait here, I will get something to drink, and when I return, I will do my best to make amends."

"You might start by playing the role of the doting fiancé for a change."

"I never dote. You should know that. As for the other, is that what you think I am? Your fiancé?"

"We've been talking about marriage long enough that you should be by default, but obviously you do not feel that way. Perhaps it is just as well. You do not seem to have the inclination or the time to be a fiancé to anyone. You obviously have taken a fancy to that whore."

Jamie's face grew dark. "Say something like that again, and I will have someone escort you home. I am going for that drink now and, by the time I return, I expect you to either be gone, or to have made the decision to behave yourself." He gave her a brief nod. "I shall return anon."

As he departed, Jamie was tempted to have Calum take Gillian home, anyway, for he was not only furious over her underhanded comment, but he also feared she would soon set her sights on Sophie, and that meant she would waste no time in digging her spiteful talons into Sophie's tender flesh.

He was halfway across the room when a hush seemed to come over the hall. He saw Sophie enter with Arabella. As he stared along with the rest of the room, the moment seemed frozen in time.

He had never seen her wearing the clothes of a lady before, and it was obvious to him that she had a natural instinct for wearing them—and the knowledge that clothes possess the power to sway.

Ice blue was her color, for it brought out the mystique of the enigmatic woman she was. His gaze went to the low cut of the gown, and the breasts that were well exposed. The décolletage was barely enough to be called modest, and not a whit more.

He watched her walk farther into the room, and found her grace as alluring as her heart-stopping beauty.

A slow glance around him said he was not the only man in the room to feel this way.

When Sophie entered the Great Hall with Arabella she was taken completely by surprise. She had not expected to be greeted by a room full of people. She popped her fan open with a flick of her wrist and used it to cover her lips as she leaned toward Arabella. "I had no idea this was such a large gathering," she whispered. "You should have warned me."

"Why? You could not possibly look any better than you do. Can you not see that everyone in the room is looking at you?"

"That was not my intention."

Arabella smiled. "I know, and that is part of your allure. Come, let us find Jamie. I want to watch his face when he sees you."

They strolled past the fireplace where the piled logs burned brightly, making the room pleasantly warm. Candlelight was everywhere: on the tables, on the candelabras high overhead and in the torches burning from their brackets on the gray stone walls.

"Here comes Jamie now," Arabella said. "I knew he would find you the minute you entered the hall." She let her gaze continue around the room. "I wonder where… Oh, my, there she is, on the other side of the room."

"Who?" Sophie asked.

"Gillian. She has already noticed Jamie is coming this way, and she is looking none too happy for it. If you don't mind, I think I will retreat before the fighting breaks out."

Before Sophie could respond, Arabella bolted.

A moment later, Jamie joined Sophie.

He kissed her hand, and Sophie noticed he held it as long as he could and still be considered polite.

"Och, lass," he purred. "I have missed seeing you."

She blanched, for her first thought was that he was making reference to the fact that he missed seeing her sans clothing, and she wondered if there was anything private or sacred with him. The thought left as quickly as it came, for she knew Jamie would never stoop so low. She almost felt guilty for even considering it.

"I trust Arabella has been treating you well," he said.

"Very well, milord. Arabella is the perfect hostess. Obviously that is something she did not learn from you."

"Things are not always as they seem. I thought it would be best for you if I kept my distance."

Sophie did not have the opportunity to reply, for out of the corner of her eye she caught sight of a flame-haired woman coming toward them with a look of determination on her face and fire in her eyes. Sophie also noticed she was wearing an exquisite green gown that she recognized as the latest design from Paris. The emeralds and diamonds at her throat were almost blinding as they reflected the light of so many candles.

In spite of her finery, there was something about the way she sailed toward them that reminded Sophie of a French brigantine, with her sails full of wind.

Jamie noticed her, too, but said nothing, and Sophie was tempted to shove him into the path of the stalking woman, for there was little doubt that this was the infamous Gillian, to whom Jamie had betrothed himself. Sophie had to fight the impulse to turn to him and ask "Why?" for she could tell this was not the woman for him. This woman would not love a man. She would devour him.

One glance at Gillian and Sophie found it easy to harden her heart toward Jamie. She was a fool to let him talk her into coming here. At least he had been right to keep away from her. She would make it easier for him in the future.

She would have turned away at that very moment, but she was curious to see how he would handle this. The scoundrel deserved nothing more than her complete indifference, which he would soon receive.

Gillian smiled at Jamie and slipped her arm possessively through his. "Oh, here you are," she said, as if she had accidentally stumbled upon him.

Jamie did not give her an opportunity to say anything, for he immediately introduced them in a manner that one would only expect to witness at court: formal and impersonal.

"Sophie? Just Sophie?" Gillian turned to Jamie. "She has no last name?"

"She cannot recall her past," he said.

Gillian's brows rose. Her gaze swept over Sophie. "How convenient."

Sophie smiled with practiced ease beneath the woman's scrutiny. She thought it a shame that a woman with such fine features and such a pretty face found it necessary to be so waspish. Sophie saw immediately that her first impression had been right. This woman would never be Jamie's equal, no matter how many Paris gowns and fine jewels she wore.

Sophie always thought it something to be pitied whenever she happened upon a woman who thought the only way she could hold on to a man was by playing the watchdog.

However, Sophie also saw Gillian as a formidable foe, and one to be dealt with carefully. She must never let her guard down around her. Gillian's talons were firmly implanted in James Graham's flesh, and she would not let go of the Earl of Monleigh without a fight.

Pity she did not know Sophie had no interest or intentions in that regard.

"A pleasure to meet you," Gillian said. "Do you speak English?"

"I can converse in English, French, Spanish, Italian and Latin. Which one would you prefer?"

"I will give it some thought," Gillian said, making it a point to look over Sophie's dress. "You were fortunate to find such a lovely dress to borrow. I don't remember seeing Arabella in it."

Of course, Sophie could not tell her the dress was her own. Instead, she adjusted the lace at her sleeve to hide a smile of amusement.

It was apparent that Gillian had already decided that Sophie was not a threat as far as Jamie's affections were concerned, and that made her think this French girl could easily be swept aside. Little did she know that Sophie was not the kind of woman to flee the field in the face of battle. Nor was she the kind of woman who would back down—borrowed dress or not.

Curtly dismissing Sophie, Gillian turned to Jamie. "Come, dance with me."

Vilain Rogeaux joined the group at that moment. "I could not wait a moment longer to meet your beautiful guest," he said as he turned to Sophie. "I knew you were French, *mademoiselle,* the moment you entered the room."

Sophie thanked him for the compliment.

Vilain kissed Sophie's hand. "I am Vilain Rogeaux, and I am completely at your disposal."

Jamie stepped between Sophie and Vilain before formally introducing him to Sophie.

"It is a pleasure to discover a fellow countryman in our midst," Vilain said. "There are times when I do sorely miss having the opportunity to converse in French. Would you care to dance, *mademoiselle?*"

"*Merci, monsieur,* but it would be terribly rude of me, since Mistress Gillian has already expressed a desire to dance. Pray, do ask her for no one else has."

Vilain seemed at a loss for words, but only for a moment, and then he recovered. "Of course. How remiss of me," he said, with a knowing gleam in his eyes and a smile that stretched over his shapely lips.

"You are very kind," Sophie said, "for truly, I could not enjoy myself knowing the gentlemen in the room were being so neglectful in asking someone as lovely as Gillian to dance at least once."

Sophie smiled at Gillian and saw the hatred in her narrowed yellow eyes, before she accepted Vilain's proffered arm and let him lead her to the dance floor.

Jamie was amused; Sophie could see it in his slow grin and in the way his eyes seemed to laugh at her.

She smiled sweetly and gave one of the buttons on his doublet a thump. "I do hope I haven't ruined your evening, milord."

Arabella found Sophie standing with her back to the fire, talking to Arabella's brother Bran, who was telling Sophie about his solo appearance at the French court two years ago.

"Goodness," Arabella said to Sophie, "what did you do to Gillian? She is positively fuming. When Vilain asked her if she would like to dance again, she told him to 'Go begging.'"

Sophie smiled and wished she had witnessed that send-off. "She came at me, daggers drawn, so I parried."

Arabella laughed. "I have never seen anyone get the best of Gillian. I am so glad you are here. I hope you never leave." She took Sophie's arm. "Come, Bran. Let us find a seat at the table before all the good places near the fire are taken."

As it turned out Bran, Niall and Fraser sat with them and the five of them talked and laughed, not caring that almost everyone in the room watched them with interest and discussed them with fascination.

Sophie took an instant liking to Jamie's brothers, at least the three who had joined them. She had already sensed that his other brother, Calum, did not approve of her and had chosen to keep his distance.

Arabella had confessed it was because he was close to Gillian and feared Sophie would come between them.

As Sophie watched Jamie seat Gillian, she saw

a look of relief pass over Calum's worried face, for it was Gillian and not her who was seated between Calum and Jamie.

After that, Sophie made it a point not to observe them overmuch, but she did take note of the fact that there was not nearly as much laughter coming from their quarter. It wasn't long until she dismissed them completely, for it looked to her as if they were all three bored, and Jamie looked fed up to the back teeth.

She had always heard the Scots were a dour lot, solemn, slow to smile and even slower to laugh, but Sophie found it quite easy to fall into conversation with the clansmen around her, and just as easy to join in their gay laughter.

Unlike those at court, there was a true sense of kinship among the Graham clan, and everyone was accepted as an equal, regardless of their position. She made note of the fact that no one used Jamie's title when addressing him but, instead, called him by his given name. It was a surprising discovery to learn that social correctness was seldom exhibited by these clannish Grahams.

She had to accustom herself to these laconic Scots.

When Niall asked her to dance, Arabella leaned close and whispered in her ear. "Have a care," she said, "for he has requested a wild and indiscreet country frolic, much like 'Gagliarda,' a wanton galliard played in triple time. I ken he means to provoke Jamie by the doing of it."

"The galliard is also popular in France, but I have never seen it danced," Sophie replied.

Bran gave Arabella a nudge. "Let her be. It would take more than a lass dancing to get the best of Jamie."

Sophie smiled at Niall and gave him her hand as the music began. From the table she could hear Bran singing:

> Four and twenty Lasses went over Trench-
> more Lee,
> And all of them were Mow'd, unless it were
> two or three
> Then up with Aley, Aley, up with jumping
> Joan,
> In came wanton Willy, and then the game
> went on.
> The piper he struck up, and merrily he did
> play,
> The shaking of the sheets and eke the Irish
> hay:
> Then up with Aley, Aley, up with Priss and
> Prue;

In came wanton Willy, amongst the Jovial
crew.
Now with this jovial Wedding, I do conclude
my Song,
And wish that Trenchmore Lasses, they may
live merry and long:
Then up with Aley, Aley, up with the merry
train:
We will all be merry, if e're we meet again.

Arabella was right. It was a wanton, lusty dance, and for the first few bars Sophie had to watch his steps, but before long she had a feel for the rhythm of the song and the steps.

Niall was the perfect partner, for when she erred he only laughed and spun her around faster, apparently not minding that she threw in a step or two of her own.

Across the room, the green-eyed bug bit Gillian. "My, they do make a lively couple, do they not?" she said.

Jamie kept his solemn gaze on the dancers and did not reply.

Sophie laughed as Niall whirled her with such speed that her skirts lifted from the floor, and she was sure everyone could see her blue slippers.

It was at this point that Sophie realized no other dancers had joined them. In France, this was not the sort of dance one did at family gatherings, or in the presence of their guests.

But Sophie knew Niall would not have requested the tune or asked her to dance if it would truly embarrass or anger his brother, and she so desperately needed to be young and carefree. If only for one night, she wanted to laugh and enjoy herself. She wanted to forget who she was, and why she was here, and leave caution stomped beneath their lively feet.

When the music ended, as wildly as it started, with a final climax of increasing volume and tempo, Niall put his hands around Sophie's waist and lifted her above his head and spun her around before lowering her, laughing and gasping for breath, to the floor.

"If I had known ye were a lass of such spirit, I'd no' have asked ye to dance."

"And why is that?"

"Because I ken my brother will be in a sulk and looking for a way to pin my ears back for the doing of it. Still, I wouldna trade the experience for a hundred dances with any other lass. 'Tis a pity Jamie met you first."

She scoffed and did her best to imitate his Scots

brogue. "And why would ye be saying a thing like that, Niall Graham, wi' yer brither betrothed to marry the fair Gillian?"

"I'll not be betting my best horse on that race," he said. "Gillian isn't the right woman for Jamie and he knows it."

"Is that a fact?"

The look in his gaze was light and teasing, yet his tone was serious. "Aye. You are better suited to him."

"Give me one reason you would think that."

"You give a man room to breathe, and yet you are not as shy and modest as the average maid," he said. "'Tis something that would please my brother."

"Then I shall work on acquiring more maidenly reserve," she said, "and hang your brother."

Niall threw back his head and laughed, then he grabbed her and spun her around once more before he led her back to the table. She did not miss the openmouthed stares the Grahams directed at them as they threaded their way through the tables.

She was making good use of her fan when the music of a more sedate song began, and Sophie asked Arabella if she intended to dance.

"Not for a while. I always eat too much at these gatherings," she replied, "and now my laces are too tight."

"Dinna fret," Fraser said, whipping out his knife. "I can cut them with my dirk and ease yer suffering."

"And what will ye be doing about my humiliation when my dress falls off, ye big lout?" Arabella asked, and everyone laughed.

More wine was poured and Sophie, feeling warm, comfortable and uninhibited, stole a glance in Jamie's direction. She saw his dark head bent next to Gillian's red one, as if he was listening intently to something she said, with his face close enough to her bosom to see down to her toes.

Niall followed her gaze and put his arm around her, and gave her a kiss on the cheek. "I hate to see a lassie pine, so if it's a braw lad ye be looking for, I don't think you can do any better than me."

Bran cuffed him on the head. "She isn't looking for a braw lad, but a man, so that leaves you out. Now, if it is a man you are needing…" His chest, she noticed, expanded greatly at this point. "You need look no further than me."

Fraser, who had been studying her for some time, asked, "How was your time at Danegæld with Jamie?"

Sophie laughed. "Cold. It took a week for me to get warm. I did find the hunting lodge quite accommodating. I would love to see it in the summertime."

"And Jamie? How was he toward you, lass?"

"He never seemed to forget he was the chief of the Grahams and laird of the castle, and he had a poor memory for recalling I was neither a Scot nor a Graham."

The sparkle in Fraser's eyes told her that he approved of her, even before he said, "I've been waiting a long time to see a lass with the fire to match his."

"I doubt my fire is of any interest to your brother, for he seems to go out of his way to dampen it whenever he has the chance," she said. "I don't think he is aware I'm in the room. He is otherwise occupied, in case you have not noticed."

"Oh, he is aware all right. It's just that Jamie is most observant when he appears the least interested."

Someone was playing the pipes, a lively tune, but not as lively as the galliard. A few couples got up to dance. Niall took her by the arm and pulled her to her feet. "Come on, lass, and I'll teach ye how to dance the Highland reel."

Fraser grabbed Arabella and followed them. "We'll make it a foursome reel."

Sophie laughed through almost the entire dance, and found the circular figure of the reel to be quite beautiful, the gliding steps easy to learn, although everyone seemed to be doing different ones—and that was part of the magic of it all.

So, she simply threw caution to the wind and joined in the fun.

It was much later, when exhaustion set in, that Sophie realized Scots danced until they were worn out. Having almost reached that point, she realized she needed to reserve enough energy to walk back to her room.

She left the dancing and returned to the table and her glass of wine.

Only once did she venture forth with enough daring to glance at Jamie. He must have been watching her with his cool, moss-colored eyes evaluating and forming comparisons, for quite some time. Even with his face shadowed there was something powerful and moving about him, and she could see the qualities he possessed marked him different from all the other men in the room.

Damne...damne...damne, she whispered in French.

How dare he be so utterly desirable.

Whenever she looked at him, she saw he was clear-headed and responsive, and even when joining in the merrymaking, he was watchful and ready to deal with whatever happened. She was glad she had had the time with him at Danegæld, for it was there that she came to know the real Jamie, and saw he could relax.

He just rarely did it.

She knew it did not serve her well to continue her observation of him. Jamie was as lost to her as yesterday.

For the rest of the evening she was content to laugh and clap from her chair, save for one time when Fraser would not take no for an answer and pulled her back out to dance with him and the others.

Once the dance was over she returned to her chair and watched while the others danced until they could dance no longer. When the celebrating was over she felt an odd sort of euphoric sadness, and realized that she would never know if it was Jamie or the wine that prompted it.

Fourteen

There's a snake hidden in the grass.
—Virgil (70-19 B.C.), Roman poet

When Vilain Rogeaux returned from his afternoon ride his butler announced he had a visitor waiting in the parlor. "He said his name is Mirren MacDougal. He claims he is in the service of William Arthur Wentworth, the Duke of Rockingham. He said he was certain you would be familiar with the duke."

Vilain nodded. "I will change clothes, and then I will see him in the library."

Vilain wondered why a Scot would be in the employ of the illustrious duke, for he knew Rockingham to be a shrewd Machiavellian, an effective secret agent and a spymaster for the crown. He had heard, not too long ago, that there was some sort of falling out between King George and Rockingham but, at the time, Vilain had not been all that interested in something that went on in England.

After changing clothes, Vilain went below stairs to see what Mr. MacDougal had to say.

He did not care for MacDougal's sort the moment he walked through the library door and saw him standing near a map of the world. However, Vilain had learned not to let his first impressions interfere with what was at hand.

"Please, have a seat," he said, and indicated the chair on the opposite side of the desk. "I must admit I am surprised to learn a Scot is in the employ of the Duke of Rockingham, and that he has requested a moment of my time. I am somewhat puzzled by the purpose of this visit. You are aware that I am French and not a Scot?"

"Aye. I heard that ye were a native of France, and have lived in Scotland for the past ten years or so."

"That is correct. Now, how may I be of service?"

"Do you know the Duke of Rockingham?"

"I know *of* him."

"And do you know that he was betrothed to a cousin of the King of France?"

"No, I did not."

"The lass has disappeared and I have been hired to find her."

"I'm sorry, but I fail to understand why you have come to me," Vilain said.

"The duke has learned that his betrothed fled France on a ship, the *Aegir*, which was bound for Norway. During the great storm a month ago the *Aegir* ran aground on the rocks beneath Monleigh Castle."

It was starting to come together now, but Vilain did not let on. "Yes, I remember. Everyone was lost. Belongings and bits of the ship washed ashore for two weeks after the tragic event."

"The duke feels his betrothed did not die along with the others, since hers was the only body that was not found. He has hired me to contact everyone within a sizable radius of the shipwreck, to see if anyone has any knowledge of the lass."

"Do you have a name?"

"The name she used was Sophie d'Alembert."

Vilain nodded. "The name means nothing to me. So, tell me, what is it that you would like me to do?"

"The Duke of Rockingham is offering a sizable reward for any information about the survival of his betrothed, or information concerning her whereabouts. The King of France has also offered a large reward."

"I see. Well, I do thank you for sharing this with me. If I should come across any information how should I get word to you?"

"You can send it to me at the Black Bull Inn. I will be staying there from time to time."

After MacDougal left, Vilain thought back over the events of the past few days. There was little doubt in his mind that the Sophie with no last name, who was brought to Monleigh Castle by James Graham was Sophie d'Alembert. He was not familiar with the name d'Alembert, but it was perfectly possible that the family could be related to Louis XV. Bourbon blood could be very important.

Vilain decided that before letting anyone know of Sophie's identity and her whereabouts, he needed to find out just how badly the King of France wanted her. It had been Vilain's dream, since his exile by the king ten years ago, to return to France and reclaim his home and confiscated lands.

Question was, would the king be willing to restore these things in exchange for Sophie?

He decided to accept the Grahams' invitation to dinner tonight.

* * *

There was more dancing in the Great Hall after dinner, but Sophie did not feel the same joy and enthusiasm that she felt when she danced a few days ago.

"Are you certain you don't want to stay and dance some more?" Bran asked. "I could easily dance with you all evening."

"I would like to, Bran, but I think I danced and drank too much the other night. Tonight I am very tired. I think I shall retire early."

"You could drink a glass of wine and watch us dance," Arabella said.

"Thank you, no. Perhaps tomorrow."

"Good night, then," Arabella said, and kissed her on the cheek. "Shall I check on you when I come to bed?"

"Let me walk you to your room," Fraser offered.

"Thank you, Fraser, but there is no need. I have learned my way about and shall have no trouble finding my room tonight. All I need is sleep and tomorrow I shall be fully recovered."

Sophie said good-night to each of Jamie's brothers save Calum, who, as always, seemed content to sit some distance away and watch her through suspicious eyes.

Often she would see him with Gillian, their heads together and deep in conversation. They reminded her of a couple of spies, and perhaps they were, for nothing seemed to escape their notice.

Faith, if she did not know better, she would swear there was something going on between Calum and Gillian. With their matched glares and brooding natures, they seem better suited to each other than Jamie and Gillian ever could.

Still, it was none of her business what went on here, and the sooner she could come up with a plan to leave, the better.

She knew Rockingham would have men looking for her, and more than likely King Louis would have a reward on her head. She would have to keep moving. The thing that held her up was money—that, and the fact she had no particular destination in mind. She would have to find a way to sell some of her belongings, and as for a destination, France and England were out, and so was Norway.

Perhaps she could go to Italy, or America.

Whatever she did she knew she could not confide in Jamie, although she was beginning to think he would not care. He had been terribly distant toward her since their arrival. The only bright spot she could recall was a letter from Tavish, which was so jovial and pleasant she found herself wishing he was here. She had written him back almost immediately, for she had long wanted to thank him for saving her life.

As for Jamie, she had not seen him since early afternoon, and that was from her bedroom window as she watched him ride into the courtyard with a group of men, his plaid flying behind him as he brought Corrie to a sliding stop.

He had thrown one leg over the saddle and dropped to the ground, and she wondered as to the cause of his rush.

Gillian, probably…

Sophie left the Great Hall and, as she glanced through a window she saw it was not snowing. She decided to take the shortcut to her bedroom wing, which meant she would go up the stairs and cross over the battlements to the opposite wing, then down the stairs to the floor her room was on.

She lifted her hood to cover her hair and pulled the cape closely about her as she neared the top of the stairs, for the cold air was penetrating. Once she climbed the last of the stairs, she pushed the heavy door open and stepped outside.

Inside the Great Hall, Vilain Rogeaux leaned against the stone wall beneath a tapestry of Robert the Bruce, depicting the fight against the English. He observed Gillian as she watched Jamie leave the hall through the same door Sophie had taken only minutes earlier.

He did not miss the way Gillian's eyes closed to narrow slits, dark and seething like the eyes of a sorceress, and he wondered if it was born of ordinary female jealousy, or if there was something between Jamie and Sophie that gave her cause and fueled her hatred.

He thought about the interesting conversation he'd had with Mirren MacDougal, and the letter he had dispatched earlier that day to King Louis. Still, he would make no decisions on any of it until he heard back from the king.

In his mind, he had been presented with a golden opportunity and he would use it to his full advantage.

His mind conjured up the lovely image of Sophie, with her angel's face and lovely eyes. He had to admit she had a certain *je ne sais quoi,* that mysterious, indefinable quality that makes a woman more desirable. Even before he discovered she was a cousin to the King of France, he thought the little *mademoiselle* was in possession of possibly the loveliest face he had ever gazed upon.

One only had to take a glance at the mottled skin of Gillian's angry face to see the truth of those words.

With an amused smile, he pushed away from the wall and walked toward Gillian, who knocked over her wine, and then slipped into a jealous rage.

It was a beautiful evening with a huge, hump-backed moon, and stillness all around. Overhead the clouds were riding on the wind and racing beneath the stars. Sophie put her hands on the wall above the portals and looked out over the North Sea. She loved the smell of the sea and she inhaled deeply, listening, as she did, to the thunderous sound of the waves hurling themselves against the rocks below.

She hoped the fresh air would stop the headache that was beginning to pound at her temples. She turned her face into the wind, and felt inside as wild as the elements.

A vision of Jamie rose up before her, and she saw him the way he had looked to her the last time they made love at Danegæld, when she sat upon the bed and watched him walk toward her. He had stopped close enough that she could reach out and touch him, but instead, she watched him remove his shirt. He was about to drop his kilt, but paused when he saw the way she was looking at him.

She purposefully let her gaze drop. Will you satisfy a woman's curiosity, sir? Is anything worn beneath that kilt?

No, it's all brand-new, lass.

She laughed. I love knowing there is nothing but you underneath that kilt, she said, and began to slide her hands up his powerful thighs until she came to the place where he was long and hard and so ready for her that he closed his eyes and gasped when she took him in her hand.

She should not remember such as this, for she felt a corresponding need for him that shot straight to her womb, and she was overcome with the desire to have his child—not for the selfish reasons she considered earlier, but because his child would be a part of him she would always have.

Even so she felt the loss of joy, for she realized if she were with child, she could never tell him of it, for she knew the kind of man he was—a man who would want his son or daughter in his life, to love, to nurture and to see into adulthood. If he had any inkling she carried his child he would never let her leave, and she would spend the rest of her life loving him yet at the same time, be an outcast, forced to endure the knowledge that it would never be her that he came home to each night.

Do not be so foolish as to think he cares, she

thought. He may want to make love to you, but that does not mean he wants you to bear his children. He has chosen another for that purpose.

She felt the splash of a tear upon her hand, and then another, and another. She chided herself and wiped her face, turning her face to the wind again, and inhaling deeply, three times.

Sophie, you must not cry, she admonished. If someone should see you…well, they would begin to wonder, and a wondering mind can formulate all sorts of wrong ideas.

She realized it had started to snow again and she watched, mesmerized, as the fat flakes did a slow, graceful dance upon their descent. She put out her cupped palms to catch them, but they melted away the moment they touched her hand.

"How sad that something so beautiful cannot last as long as the ripple of an oar upon the water," she said, not caring she spoke audibly until she heard the click of the door. She turned quickly, and saw Jamie himself standing a few feet away.

"Some things were never meant to last, and sometimes we are too foolish to hold on to the things that were," he said. "It doesna have to be that way, lass."

"For you, perhaps, but it is different for a

woman. We have no power, no authority and no control. Fate can place us in circumstances beyond our power to change, and we are like marionettes who must move when the string is pulled."

He knew what troubled her, and it pained him to think that after what they had shared she still refused to tell him of the circumstances that brought her here. "And if I said I was an indulgent sort, that nothing can be as black as you paint it, could you trust me then?"

"Sometimes the dispensation of leniency can be a way to invoke control."

He took her in his arms. "I have never seen a lass who needed help more than ye do. Let me help you."

She looked down at her hands. "No one can help me now, I fear. I am beyond rescuing."

He caught her by the chin and lifted her face so the moonlight enabled him to see she was close to tears, for already they pooled like diamonds in her beautiful eyes. He was puzzled and he could not understand how one so young could be so deeply mired in a predicament that it could turn her into such a fatalist.

"It would help if you could talk about it," he said.

She shook her head. "No, it would not. Can you not see there is no reason to discuss it?"

"And so you will simply give up and take the

coward's way out?" He knew his voice was edged with antagonism, and that it was reflected in the cold expression that settled over his face, turning his features hard. "Tell me now how you came to be in Scotland."

They had talked around the issue so many times that she was caught off guard by his direct question, and had no ready answer.

Not that it mattered, for he saw immediately in her face that she would not tell him and, if she did address his question and give him an answer, it would be a lie.

He took her face in his hands and brought it closer to his own. The moment his mouth covered hers his hands slipped beneath her cloak so he could hold her pressed tightly against him.

He kissed her deeply, showing her with his tongue what he would like to do to her with another part of his body. He felt the heat in her burst into flame, and he remembered how she was always like dry kindling, ready to catch fire whenever he touched her. With a groan, he pushed her back against the embrasure and dropped his hands to cup her buttocks and lift her against him.

He did not kiss to seduce. He was far beyond that now.

Mastery was what he was after and he meant to

show her she belonged to him, and that any reluctance on her part would not be tolerated. He wanted to delve into the very soul of her, to place his mark there, branding her for life, and ruining her for all time for the touch of any other.

He felt her hands slide beneath his doublet and he could not help the response that made him press himself hard against her. He wanted her to the point of insanity. The thought of making love to her again drove him past all caution. He wanted her enough to take her here, on the battlements, in the middle of falling snow.

He broke the kiss but moved his mouth mere inches from hers.

Her lips were soft, wet and swollen with his kiss, and he traced the fleshy part of her lower lip with his thumb. Her breathing was heavy and labored and he saw the glazed expression of intense desire glowing like hot coals in her eyes.

His hand slipped hungrily downward until he could touch her and feel her pressing against his palm. He tugged her skirts upward until he found her leg and then followed it, going higher still, until he found the damp place he searched for, and knew so well.

"You have no idea what it is like to want you. I think of nothing else."

"Please," she whispered. "Touch me, Jamie. Touch me until I cannot bear the agony any longer, and then touch me again, and again until I shatter."

She was all warm, smooth flesh, open to him, and he was about to press on, needing no real encouragement from her, for he had enough for both of them. His hand was right where he wanted it to be, when he heard the hinges of the door rattle as if someone was about to open it.

He dropped her skirts back in place and did not realize her hands were beneath his velvet doublet until she hastily withdrew them. The sudden action dislodged the snow collected on his shoulders, and it showered down upon her.

Standing there as she was, with snowflakes on her lashes, in wide-eyed surprise, she had never looked so lovely, and his desire for her pounded against his temples with each unsteady beat of his heart.

She stepped a few feet away from him and turned her gaze to the North Sea, her breathing still bearing the telltale signs of passion, ragged and uneven. "I wonder how I survived in that cold water."

"You must have found something large enough to lay down on, because you would not have survived being submerged in the water for very long. Fortunately for you, the storm blew in with a fairly mild temperature compared to what it could have been."

"I seem to remember being in the water now, but I don't remember much after that."

He lifted his hand and followed the line of her throat with his finger. "I have not seen you wear your medallion of late. Have you lost it?"

"No, I have not felt the urge to wear it lately."

The door scraped against the snow and opened, and Gillian stepped onto the battlements, followed by Vilain.

"We came to find you, to thank you for your hospitality and to bid you good evening," Vilain said.

Sophie saw the muscle work in Jamie's jaw.

He nodded curtly, never taking his gaze from Gillian's face, as if he knew who it was that wanted to search them out and why, and it had nothing to do with thanks or bidding them good-night.

Even before she looked at her, Sophie could feel Gillian studying every detail about her. "You have been standing out here in the cold for a long time. I am surprised to find you are not chilled to the bone. You must have found a warm place to stand," she said.

Oh, yes, I had my hands under Jamie's kilt, Sophie was tempted to say, but instead she said, "It must be the fur lining my cape, for I am not cold in the least."

Sophie saw the possessive way Gillian slipped her arm through Jamie's. Take him, she thought, with my blessings. She vowed then, that if she ever had a man of her own she would *not* be possessive.

Not ever.

When Sophie saw the flash of anger in Jamie's eyes and his dark scowl, she wondered if being searched out by a woman, no matter how beautiful, was something he was not inclined to endure.

Poor woman, she did not understand that a man like Jamie was not one to submit to a woman's domination, nor was he one who would respond well to being the sole object of her slavish affections.

It was some small consolation to see the way Jamie's expression turned thunderously dark when Vilain offered Sophie his arm and said, "I would hate to see you turn your lovely ankle. It would be best if you let me walk you back inside."

She did not look back to see Jamie's reaction when she smiled at Vilain and slipped hers arm through his.

Sophie could not have been more surprised when Jamie extracted himself from Gillian's hold long enough to take Sophie's other hand. He lifted it to his lips. "I look forward to visiting with you at a later time, so we might finish our conversation."

As he released her hand, he pressed something into it.

"I am happy to know my chatter did not bore you," she said, and dropped the object into the pocket of her cloak.

Sophie saw the possessive look in Jamie's eyes, and wondered if it was because he did not want to leave her, or because he did not want to leave her with Vilain.

Regardless, it hurt to see him walk through the door with Gillian on his arm.

She understood how a horse must feel when he wins the race and the silver trophy is given to the rider.

Fifteen

She knew treachery,
Rapine, deceit, and lust, and ills enow
To be a woman.
—John Donne (1572-1631), English metaphysical poet and divine.
The Progress of the Soul (1601)

After they were gone, Vilain turned to Sophie. "Are you cold, *mademoiselle?*" he asked, his eyes as cool as his words. "Shall we go inside?"

She started to say she was going to her room, but decided she did not want to be alone just now, so she replied, "Yes, I think it is time we rejoined the others."

"Excellent," he said, and gave her a warm smile.

"I must tell you how good it feels to speak my native tongue with a Frenchwoman. I did not realize how very much I missed it until I heard you speak. I had hoped to find some time to visit with you. I am always hungry for news of France, but I am even more interested to hear what brought you to Scotland."

"I daresay you would be bored, *monsieur,* for my reasons for wanting to travel would sound like they were fresh from the schoolroom to someone with your educated polish."

Before he could respond, Sophie began to ask him question after question which he could not refuse to answer without appearing rude. However, she was thankful to see they were at last approaching the Great Hall, for she was running out of questions. "I have enjoyed talking with you, *monsieur...*"

"Please, do call me Vilain. We are, after all, countrymen."

She saw he was about to ask her something, so she said quickly, "I can tell you are a man who came to Scotland but left his heart in France. Tell me, Vilain, why did you leave France and come to Scotland?"

She saw immediately that she had found the vulnerable spot in his armor.

Just then they stepped into the Great Hall and Vilain preferred to leave rather than answer her question, for he kissed her hand and said, "Almost all the guests have departed. Although I would love to stay and talk, I make it a rule to never be the last to leave when I am a guest in another's home. Therefore I must make haste. I bid you adieu, Sophie. Until next time."

Sophie said good-night, but she did not watch his departure, rather letting her gaze rest on Jamie Graham. He was standing on the opposite side of the room, laughing heartily at something Gillian said.

Sophie turned away and decided she must have misjudged his feelings on the battlement, for he did not look put out in the least with Gillian's possessiveness.

Obviously the intimacy they shared before the appearance of Gillian and Vilain meant nothing to him. She was nothing more than a dalliance.

What comes easily is easily forgotten.

It was one of life's hard-earned lessons, that a woman who chooses to be the mistress of a rich and powerful man will be provided for, but she will never be loved.

About to return to her room, she put her hand in her pocket and felt the piece of metal Jamie had pressed into her palm.

She withdrew her hand, opened her palm and saw the gold medallion she had ripped from her neck that day at Danegæld and flung into the pond. She searched her mind for what Jamie had said earlier, and her reply to him.

"I have not seen you wear your medallion of late. Have you lost it?"

"No, I have not felt the urge to wear it lately."

She folded her hand over the medallion and slipped it back into her pocket. So, he had tricked her, and in so doing, caught her in a lie.

She wondered if he would even believe her now, if she threw caution aside and told him the truth.

It's a little late for that, she reminded herself. Do not forget you could be carrying his child, and if that is true you cannot remain here. She would not complicate things for him any longer than necessary.

She saw Arabella sitting close to the fireplace, talking quietly with her brothers. Jamie was still by the door, and Sophie, not wanting to pass by him, went to join Arabella.

It was much later when Sophie decided to return to her room. She looked out the window and saw the wind was howling fiercely, blowing across the North Sea. She knew it would drive drifts of snow in deep piles along the battlements.

"Dinna take the shortcut, lass," Fraser said. "You would never make it and more than likely ye could end up back in the sea."

"Very well. I will take the long way then. *Bon soir.*"

"Good night," they replied in unison.

She swore softly in French. To take the long way meant she had to pass close to Jamie's apartments. She prayed she would not see him. Her one encounter with him earlier had weakened her.

Even now she could still feel the slow, curling knot of desire deep in her loins, and she knew it would take very little effort on his part to have her panting in his arms.

She hurried from the hall.

The wind whistled through the windows in great drafts and the torches sputtered, but the strong walls of the ancient fortress rose up as solid as a mountain, stopping the massive force of each wave the sea sent crashing against it. She supposed this fortress had seen many such storms and had survived them all.

She could only hope she could do as well.

In her room at last, Sophie sat by the fire in her gown and robe. She stared hypnotically at the flames, the taste of Jamie still on her tongue, the scent of his skin upon hers. She knew she was being foolish to give thoughts of him so much of her time, but memories of him were all she would have left before long. I might as well practice, she thought.

She was surprised to hear a soft knock at her door.

It must be Arabella, she thought as she rose to her feet. Arabella had remained behind in the hall after Sophie left. It was not uncommon for her to stop by for a late-night talk.

Sophie opened the door and was stunned, as well as humiliated, to see Jamie standing boldly in front of her, for anyone who should pass by to see.

"What do you want?" she whispered.

The green eyes were soft and heavy with desire. Oh, she knew what he wanted.

"I came to see you, lass."

She stared at him as if not comprehending what he said, then gave herself a mental shake. "I'm sorry you went to all the trouble to come here, but I am expecting someone else."

She moved to shut the door but he put his foot in the way. "God's blood! You are the most obstinate wench I have ever encountered. There is no give to ye, lass. Ye are too tightly laced for a man to get a hold on ye. Whom are you expecting? If it's one of my men, his blood will be on your hands."

"Thank you for the compliment. Arabella said she might stop by."

The sight of his knowing smile irked her and she moved to close the door.

He shoved it open with his foot and stepped into her chamber. He closed the door behind him. "That is the second lie you have told me today. I warn you, mistress, not to try for another."

"Warn all you like, but I make my own choices." Sophie did not know why it pleased her immensely to know she had angered him. It not only pleased her, but enough so that she found herself wishing he would stay that way. It was easier to resist him when he was being the laird of the castle.

"What has happened to you?" he asked. "Two hours ago you were melting against me like warmed butter."

She decided against telling him how he was two hours ago. "I would think you gentleman enough not to mention that, but since you asked, I have realized the error of my ways. I am wiser now."

"I am gentleman enough to know that your response was an honest one, unlike your words."

"Is that what you came here for? To bandy words with me?"

"Ye were eager enough to see me earlier, and responsive enough that I have thought of naught else since I left you, but I'm beginning to wonder why I bothered to give you so much thought."

He excelled at choosing the right words to infuriate her. "Do you think that is all I live for…to be in your thoughts? It is precious little comfort on a cold night to wrap myself in the knowledge that you are thinking about me. You think about your horse, but I daresay you do not expect him to grovel at your feet. Moreover, in case you are interested, I rarely give you a thought at all. I find my days filled with so many activities that your memory hardly surfaces."

"I should have finished what I started up on the battlements," he said, "for that is obviously what angered you."

"I am not angry. And, if finishing what you started was such a big issue, I could have finished it myself the moment I arrived back in my room."

She did not realize what she had said until the slow, stretching smile eased itself across his face. "Well now, although I am pleased to know you are a self-sufficient lass, I am also disheartened to know I can be so easily replaced. I thought it best to leave you alone, but now I can see I should have come sooner. I cannot bear the thought of a lass such as ye being forced to pleasure herself."

"Please leave."

He stepped closer and she backed up until she bumped against the bedpost. Only a few feet separated them now.

"Stay away from me."

"You know I cannot."

"Go visit your betrothed. It's her bed you should be warming, not mine."

"It's you I want."

"All right, you have told me, and I thank you for the compliment. You cannot know how comforting it is to know. Now leave."

For a moment she regretted her words, for he looked as though he might grab her and shake her until her teeth rattled together. She knew he was angry.

That was why she did not understand, and she gave him a puzzled look, when he began to remove his socks and shoes. Her eyes grew wider as he unbuckled his belt and tossed it on the chair.

"What are you doing?"

"Undressing, as you can see."

"I want you out of my room. You cannot sleep here."

"I'm the laird of this castle. I can sleep anywhere I choose, and with anyone I choose—including a maid." He took a step, unbuttoned his shirt and dropped it on top of the belt. He took another step and let his kilt fall to the floor.

Her gaze dropped lower in spite of her determination not to look. He was erect and so hard the knowledge of it brought a tightness to her throat and a corresponding tightness farther down.

Her defiance deserted her, and she stood mutely while he loosened the buttons of her robe, slipped it from her shoulders and let it fall to the floor.

"I came here to give us both something, and I willna be leaving without the doing of it." His arms went around her and he drew her against him.

She could feel him, hot and hard, pressed against her belly. Her gown slid down her body to join the robe on the floor. Backed against the bedpost, she could not move away for his body was so close she was pinned there.

She could feel his heart pounding with a wild rhythm that matched the tempo of her own. His hands were in her hair and he turned her head so as to give him access to her mouth. He was too close for her to see the expression in his eyes.

"I will never have enough of you," he said. "Never."

He turned their bodies and pressed her back against the bed, her feet still on the floor as he parted her legs.

She closed her eyes, wanting the feel of him coming into her.

Her eyes flew open in shock when she realized that was not what he intended at all.

Mon dieu, not with his mouth. She tried to close her legs, but his arms were strong, and he was determined. After those first few seconds she no longer wanted to resist him and found herself opening to him completely, as he lured her deeper and deeper into the world of insatiable greed.

His hands were on her breasts, thumbs on her nipples, and still he kissed her, his tongue going deeper until she writhed in agony, begging him to end her torture.

At last, she felt the spiraling coil and knew she would at last find her release, but he lifted his head and watched her as she lay open to him, her breath coming in short pants.

She could not speak. She could not move. She could only lie there, with her legs spread, feeling as though he could read all she was thinking by looking at her eyes, and still he did not touch her.

Her breathing was almost back to normal when he lowered his head. She pulled her legs together, and he began to place kisses along her stomach and down one leg, then up the other.

By the time he reached the juncture of her thighs, she was insane with wanting him again, and she dug her fingers in his hair and pulled him hard against her.

He seemed to lose control after that, kissing her hard and fast until she panted. She was mindless now and completely out of control. He brought her to her shattering release, and again, and then one last time, before he moved up her body. He covered her mouth with a groaning kiss, he drove himself into her, and they went over the edge together.

Exhausted, she fell asleep in his arms, surrounded by his presence, and the scent of their lovemaking.

She had no knowledge of how long she slept, but when she awoke, she saw he was dressed and sitting on the bed beside her, one hand caressing her breast until the nipple was hard and protruding.

He lowered his head and tasted her, swirling and drawing her into his mouth.

Suddenly he stopped and she saw his eyes were already dilated, and heavy with desire. His hand slid slowly over her belly, and lower, until she felt her legs open to him.

"It is never enough, is it? This yearning for ye…even when I take ye again and again, I know it will never be enough."

She said nothing, but lay there watching him.

He studied her face for a moment, leaned forward and kissed her gently on the mouth. "Do not ever tell me that you don't want me, lass. I will not tolerate another lie."

Sixteen

When my love swears that she is made of truth,
I do believe her, though I know she lies.
—William Shakespeare (1564-1616), English poet and playwright. Sonnet 138 (1609)

Jamie lay abed, enduring another wakeful night. He longed for the sweet spirit of sleep that sheltered a man like a cloak, but neither poppy nor mandragora, nor any other somniferous calmative would usher him into the twilight of drowsy sleep.

For a few hours' slumber he would gladly entertain the supernatural soliciting of battalions of phantoms, or the terrors of nightmares galore. Yet the repose of the night would not come to him to set his soul at rest.

It seemed eons ago that he had gone to Sophie's room to settle things between them, so they could move beyond suspicion and distrust.

He began to doubt he would ever get enough of her if she slept in his bed and he took her each night for the rest of his life. He realized now that the first time he saw her something in him branded her as his. He did not realize it at the time, of course, and now that he had, things were much more complicated.

He was no longer plagued by the thought that she might be an English spy, but neither did he trust her completely. He knew she still withheld information from him and that she remembered far more than she admitted.

Question was, how could he convince her of his feelings for her—at least enough to make her want to tell him the truth?

He hated to be the one to doubt her, but too many things had happened, and too many slips on her part had reinforced the belief that she suffered no loss of memory, except the loss she imposed upon herself because it was easier than telling the truth.

Unable to fathom what she could be hiding, he

hoped she would come to care for him sufficiently so that she would, of her own accord, trust him and reveal what secrets she kept.

Did she not understand that by refusing to confide in him she was forcing him to play the game of seduce and conquer? Could she not see that there was a tender side of him, one capable of loving her the way she wanted, and deserved, to be loved? Was she unable to recognize a heart able to love one woman for all time, or a man who would court her until the day he died?

He had never wooed a woman and he knew naught about it, but for her he was willing to learn that, and all the other silly little things a woman needed from her mate.

Time was unbalanced. The moon was out of phase. His heart melted and emotions poured out of him like water. No matter how much he desired her or cared for her, he could not allow her lies and deception to continue indefinitely.

This was the wedge driven between them, the block that that kept them apart. He had declared that he would tolerate no lies, and yet she had done the opposite and lied to him three times.

He could not allow her to lie to him again. If she did, it would be over.

Trapped in a labyrinth, he stood between the icy

shadows of inescapable duty and fealty to his clan. He tried to cope with the paradox of being the Earl of Monleigh and Chief of Clan Graham, and honoring the obligation and responsibility he owed the woman he loved.

In the quietness of thought, the weight of loyalty and desire settled over him. The leader in him clamored for a solution, and the man within searched for one as simple as the rod of reproof to an errant child.

Duty came before devotion, and he knew his task would not be an easy one.

His heart must be of marble, impartial and pitiless. If she lied once more, God help him, he would have to end it. It would tear his heart to tatters to send her from him. He did not want to lose her, but he would have to let her go.

Sleep...hypnotic and mesmeric come to me and, on the morrow, I will deal with the sweeping out of shadows.

In the fog-shrouded mist of early morning Jamie went hunting, accompanied by a few men and his brothers Bran and Fraser. They rode out of the castle hoping to stalk a red deer somewhere in the desolate hills.

Infinitely silent, infinitely gray, the Highlands

were melancholy today, and Jamie felt the saturated weight of them. There were too many mountains, too many streams, too many questions from his brothers, and too many decisions awaiting his return.

The fog was gone by the time they killed two stags. Jamie sent some of the men to carry one stag to the village, to give to the clansmen there. The rest of his clansmen carried the other one back to Monleigh Castle.

"Why did you send the men on with the stag?" Fraser asked, since it was rare for Jamie to do this, because he always preferred to ride with his men.

"I wanted to talk to the two of you."

Bran and Fraser exchanged looks.

"Aye," Bran said. "I have been wondering when you would get around to realizing ye are going to have to address yer problem with the lasses. You canna court two women at the same time and have any peace of mind."

"I have figured that out for myself."

"Weel then, what will ye be doing about it?" Fraser asked.

"I will speak with Gillian."

Fraser nodded. "You intend to cry off?"

"I hope to give her the opportunity to end things between us…before it gets to that point."

"And if she doesna choose to do so?" Fraser asked.

"Then I will end it."

"You have no official betrothal agreement between you," Bran said, "so ye dinna have to fash yerself over the doing of it. I ken Gillian already knows where yer heart lies."

"Aye, there is no' a betrothal, but I ken the right thing to do is to tell her I have no intention of marrying her. Once that is said, I will offer her my apologies."

Bran snorted at that. "Och! Yer apologies, is it? Ye can save yer breath, brother. She will no' be wanting yer apologies. 'Tis yer hide she will be after."

Jamie nodded. "Aye, I understand that, and I am willing to let her extract her pound of flesh...but no more."

"Are you going to tell her of your intentions to marry Sophie?" Fraser asked.

Jamie grimaced. "That would be premature since I have not, as yet, decided what to do about Sophie."

"Gillian won't believe that," Bran said.

Fraser agreed. "Gillian only believes what she wants to believe."

"Not everything hangs upon Gillian," Jamie

replied. "What she chooses to believe or disbelieve is not my main concern."

Fraser's face was grim. "Then I would sleep with one eye open from now on, if I were you. She will be angry enough to cut your heart out and eat it for breakfast."

Bran laughed and spurred his horse. As he rode off, he called back over his shoulder, "I will pray for you, brother."

"A prayer wouldn't be a bad idea," Fraser agreed. "Och, I wouldn't want to be wearing yer trews."

"Aye, they are becoming a wee bit tight," Jamie said, and the two of them spurred their horses and rode at a gallop to catch up with Bran.

Jamie was never one to let something that needed to be done hang over his head, so he rode over to Gillian's home the next afternoon.

"I was thinking bad thoughts about you and now you are here," she said, when she walked into the room and saw him waiting for her.

"Yes, I am here. I want to talk to you."

She ignored that. "You dinna come when I want to see you, and then you show up when I dinna expect it. No wonder I am always in a state of confusion when it comes to you." She sat down and indicated a chair for him. "Do sit down, Jamie. We can be civil to each other, at least."

He nodded and sat down.

"Would you care for something to drink?"

"No."

Something about the way her eyes narrowed when she looked at him told Jamie she had an idea why he was here. "This isn't a social call, is it?"

"No, it isn't."

"I thought not." She smoothed her skirts and shifted her position in the chair. "So, what bad news have you brought me? Let me see if I can guess. You want to cry off and end our betrothal."

"We were never officially betrothed, Gillian, and you know that."

"A mere technicality, but if you push the point…"

"There was never anything legal drawn up if you recall," he said.

"No, but God's blood, Jamie, everyone has known we would marry since we were children. Our families have never considered anything else."

"I know. It is as if everyone had everything all arranged for us without ever considering how we felt about it."

"I never had a problem with it. You were always the one who—"

"I accept the blame," he said. "The fault is mine."

"Yes, it is all yours. You should have told me before now. Why didn't you?"

"I never had any real plans to marry anyone, and then after I became the earl it was apparent that marriage was expected of me. I let things go, hoping that I might come to love you… something beyond my feelings for you as a childhood friend. Later, when those feelings did not emerge, I thought that perhaps we could marry in order to provide me with an heir, and then we would each be free to indulge ourselves elsewhere. Before long that also lost its appeal."

"I would have agreed to that. You know I would. It is still not too late."

"Gillian, I dinna think ye love me any more than I love you. Like me, it has been a part of your life for so long you simply let it carry you along, to see where it would all end up. We are not suited. You deserve more. And so do I."

"Like your French paramour?"

"I had hoped we could handle this betwixt ourselves without malice and without casting stones about. However, if you choose anger and vindictiveness I will warn ye that I will not tolerate it."

"So, you warn me, and that is it?"

"Aye, that is it, at least for now. You will need time to settle into all of this. If you decide to accept it in a manner becoming a lady then I am proud to continue to call you my friend, and the gates of Monleigh will always be open to you."

"And if I do not?"

He stood. "I would not choose that option if I were you."

"Get out!" she screamed.

"As you wish," he said, and turned away.

"You have ruined my life, you bastard. It may take me a long time, but I will find a way to make you sorry."

Arabella was on her way to her chamber when she passed by Jamie's study and heard the rattle and shuffling of papers, followed by loud bellowing. "God's eyeballs! How can anyone be expected to handle things by correspondence, when they canna read it? I seem to be the only man in the Highlands with a legible hand."

"Do you want me to try?"

Arabella recognized Niall's voice.

"Aye," Jamie said, "see if you can decipher that chicken scratching. I have work to do. I do not have time to waste on that."

"I will work on it and bring it back when I finish," Niall said.

Jamie grunted but said nothing more.

Niall almost ran into Arabella when he left. "I wouldn't go in there just yet, if I were you," he whispered.

"He will be nice to me," Arabella said.

"You are a saucy wench today. Want to help me with this?" He thumped the papers under his arm.

She glanced down at the stack of papers. "No, I don't think so. That sort of thing gives me a headache."

"Why not? You should be good at this. You speak three languages."

"And I know how to say no in all of them. Enjoy your day," she said, and rose up on her toes to plant a kiss on his cheek.

Although the door was still open, she knocked lightly and stepped into the room. "I'm not bothering you, am I?"

Jamie looked up, gave her a half smile and jabbed the quill into the inkstand. "Today, everyone is bothering me, and I can tell you that there is nothing more irritating than to find yourself feeling generally angry at the world without having anyone or any specific cause to blame it on."

She laughed. "Then I shall try to cheer you up."

"Just seeing you here brings me cheer. Sit down and I will try to hold back my tendency to grumble."

She came closer and glanced down at the letter. "I dinna have difficulty reading that."

"That's my handwriting. I am writing a letter to my banker in Edinburgh. I'm authorizing the draft for two horses I'm buying."

"Oh, who are they for?"

"One is for Sophie."

"And the other one?"

"I couldn't give Sophie a new horse without giving one to you, now could I?"

"Oh, Jamie. Thank you," she said, and for the second time that day, she planted a kiss on her brother's cheek.

"I will ask you not to tell Sophie."

Arabella smiled and sat down near his desk. "Of course not."

"So, tell me, are you here for a purpose, or simply stopping by on your way elsewhere?"

"Actually, I did not come here purposefully. I happened to hear your rampage as I passed by, so I thought I would see if there was anything I could do to make your day more pleasant."

"You have already done that by coming in here."

"I know this is a change of subject, but do you think Sophie likes us?"

He was surprised by her question, and it required him to think a moment about his answer. "Well, I suppose she likes us well enough. Why do you ask?"

"Because I like her so very much, and I am so very happy to have another female my own age around here. I very much want her to stay. Do you think she will?"

"Until she regains her memory she isn't going anywhere."

Arabella expelled a slow breath of relief and smiled. "I am glad I asked you. I feel much better now."

"If it's that big a relief, I am glad you did, too. Was there anything else you wanted to know?"

She picked up the silver letter opener and twirled it in her hands. "No."

Jamie nodded and went back to his letter.

Arabella leaned back in the chair and let her gaze travel around the room. She loved Jamie's study with its rich wood paneling, the leather chairs and the books that lined the walls. She remembered with fondness how often she hid under his desk when she was a child and Fenella was looking for her. The rich leather smells in the room comforted her still.

She continued her visual inspection of the room until she paused to linger upon a small oil painting, and wondered why it never caught her attention before now.

"Oh, my!" she exclaimed, and leaped to her feet.

Jamie put his pen down. "Arabella, what are you about?"

"That's the same painting Sophie had in her trunk." She stepped closer to examine it in detail. The shared characteristics, the uncanny resemblance was remarkable, but each was slightly different from the other. A subtle difference in the color of a coat, the detail of the face—and she was able to distinguish that they were two different portraits.

By this time Jamie had come to stand beside her. He studied the painting. "If she had a painting of King James in her trunk, then it could mean that she is a supporter of Bonnie Prince Charlie and sympathetic to the Jacobean cause."

Arabella felt wretched for she heard the excitement, and the hope, in Jamie's voice, and she knew he saw this as a link, and a way that might lead them to knowing who Sophie was.

"I am sorry, Jamie. I made a mistake. Although the two paintings are remarkably similar, with many qualities in common, they are not the same." She sighed. "Like you, I was so in hopes that it would be a clue."

"Tell me about the painting in the trunk."

Arabella went on to relate to Jamie how she had found the miniature, unable to remember a time when her brother had seemed as interested in anything she had to say as he was now.

"You are certain she showed no sign of recognition when she saw it?" he asked.

"She did not seem to, but sometimes it is difficult to judge her reactions."

Jamie nodded in agreement. "What did this man look like?"

"His clothes were a bit old-fashioned, but he was dressed well and sitting on a blooded horse. Perhaps he is a famous French general. There was an air of authority about him."

"I will have a look at it and see if I recognize him."

They talked on for a while and, at some point, Arabella mentioned the beautiful clothes in Sophie's trunk. "I should love to go to a dressmaker in Paris. Sophie's clothes are like nothing we have in Scotland. The women there are very fortunate."

Still in her talkative mood, she continued to tell Jamie about the unpacking of Sophie's trunk that day and finding the blue gown and how perfectly it fit her. "I thought it was uncanny how she knew there were blue satin slippers inside to match, and that's when I suspected that it was truly her trunk."

Jamie was pulling the plume of the pen slowly through his fingers. "Aye, very uncanny."

"Well, I am disappointed not to recognize the man in the portrait. I was hoping it might help Sophie's memory if she knew who he was. I don't suppose we will ever know who he is."

"Don't give up so easily. You said his clothing and bearing were of someone important. It is also highly probable that he is French, since you said you found the miniature in Sophie's trunk. So, you see, we know two things already. All is not hopeless."

Arabella glanced at the clock on the mantel and realized she had to change for dinner. "You are always so understanding," she said.

He smiled. "Only when it comes to you."

She stood and blew him a kiss. "I must be off or I shall not have time to change before dinner."

After Arabella's departure Jamie looked thoughtfully off into space; his mind was not on Arabella's departure, or his letter to Edinburgh, but on the information she had shared with him.

He tried to put that out of his mind and forced himself to focus on the letter he had been writing, although he had difficulty moving his thoughts from the miniature and putting them back on the purchase of horses.

After several abortive attempts, he realized he would not be able to concentrate on much of anything until he dealt with what troubled him.

Jamie thought about Sophie, and wondered what kind of battles she could be fighting. The only thing he wanted was the truth, then she would have his heart, and his hand to protect her if need be.

He sorted through the jumble in his head for a time, and tried to make it into some logical sequence, then decided it was time to pay Sophie a visit.

He went straight to her room and knocked on her door.

Surprise stole all the color from her face the moment she opened the door and saw him standing there. Her hand came up to her chest. "Goodness, I was not expecting it to be you. I was about to change for dinner."

"A common occurrence about this time of day," he said. "Arabella told me about the miniature in your trunk. May I see it?"

"I really need to dress."

Jamie stepped into the room. "Dress then, and I will look for it."

That he angered her was evident by her snappish tone. "If it's that important to you, I'll get it myself."

He remained silent as he watched while she opened the trunk and searched for the miniature. A few moments later she closed the trunk and he saw she had something tightly enclosed in her fist.

She crossed the room and almost slapped it into his hand. "Here. Is this what you wanted? I doubt it will be of any value to you. As you can see, it is quite small and the features are difficult to see."

He studied the painting. Arabella had been right. It was very similar to the one in his study, but not so much so that he would assume the same person painted it. He continued to examine it, even as he spoke. "Is there nothing about this that is familiar to you?"

"No, nothing."

He dropped it into the pocket of his doublet.

"What are you doing?"

"If you don't mind, I would like to keep it for a while."

"I assumed that you would."

Jamie nodded. "I will see you at dinner then. Pardon the intrusion, mistress."

She followed him to the door. "Think nothing of it. I find I am becoming quite accustomed to it," she said, and slammed the door.

The next morning impatience ate at Jamie as he drew on his boots, and when his man attempted to help he waved him away. When the second boot was on, he grabbed his doublet from the hook on the wall and buckled his sword on his way out of the room.

It was still dark when he started down the stairs, and the great castle was alive with the sounds of his men shouting and rattling their equipment as they tried to dress in the clammy cold of the early morning hour.

Torches were blazing by the time he walked into the Great Hall, and already many of his men were dressed and milling about, talking and laughing softly among themselves. He paused to speak with several of them, giving new instructions, or making changes in the tasks each would fulfill this day.

"Will ye be joining us to break the fast, Jamie?" Lachlan asked.

"Not this morning, lads, but that doesna mean ye can be forgetting to warm yer knives so ye willna be using so much butter."

The men laughed and Simon called out, "Aye, and we will no' be using the silver trenchers, either."

"Where are you going this braw morning?" Archibald asked as Jamie passed by.

"I thought I would pay a visit to my neighbor, Vilain."

"I didna ken ye were as good a friend of that Frenchman as that," Archibald said.

Jamie smiled and clapped him on the back. "Weel, ye ken now," he said, and left the men the way he liked them, laughing and in good spirits.

Half an hour later Jamie swung into the saddle and spurred Corrie through the gates. He splashed through the shallow water that spilled over the stone bridge, and rode away from Monleigh Castle and into the perpetual mist.

Before long the wind began to blow in from the north, driving a light dusting of snow along the track ahead of him, and Jamie knew the snow would begin to fall before nightfall, but by then he would have his business with Rogeaux completed, and would be safely ensconced back within the protective walls of Monleigh.

A half hour later he rode into Vilain's courtyard and tossed his reins at the groom at the same time he threw a leg over the saddle and slid to the ground. "Dinna stable him," he said, when the groom appeared. "I will be leaving soon."

He did not have to wait long for Vilain to greet him.

"It must be something important to bring you here so early in the morning. Not bad news, I hope."

Jamie withdrew the miniature. "I came to solicit your help in identifying the man in this portrait."

He handed the miniature to Vilain. "Would you happen to know who he is?"

Vilain took one glance at the man mounted on the white horse. *"Roi Soleil,"* he whispered, and then said more loudly, "It is Louis XIV, the Sun King. I know this painting quite well. The artist was Adam Frans van der Meulen. It was either painted at the Battle of Fleurus during the War of the Grand Alliance, or at the time of the War of the Spanish Succession. The original hangs at Versailles. Where did you get this one?"

"It was in some of the belongings that my men fished out of the water after the Norwegian ship ran aground."

"Hmm, it is a bit odd that it was found in such a place."

"Why would you think that?"

Vilain rubbed his thumb over the portrait, then turned it over to examine the back. "This sort of portrait, especially when it is royalty, is usually given to family members, or to very close friends of high standing. I was not aware there was someone of such import on that vessel." He handed it back to Jamie.

Jamie took the miniature and returned it to his pocket. "We may never solve the mystery of whose it was, or how it got here," he said.

"No, there are any number of explanations," Vilain said.

Jamie agreed. "Aye, it could have been stolen, or given away."

Vilain laughed. "Quite true, for that brings to mind my own dear mother. She was a childhood friend of Queen Mary Louise of the Netherlands, who gifted her with a miniature painted on ivory, but after a falling-out between the two of them, my mother gave the queen's miniature to her maid."

When Jamie arrived back at Monleigh Castle, he was about to go in search of Sophie when he caught a glimpse of her skirts going around the corner.

He went after her, hearing the sound of her footsteps going up the stairs. He caught up with her before she reached the first landing, and put out his hand and took her by the arm.

She turned to face him. "Have a care. If I lose my balance, I could fall all the way back down."

"I wouldna let such as that happen to ye, lass."

"Was this a chance meeting or were you following me?"

"I caught sight of you when I returned and, since I wanted a word with you, I followed you."

"Why do you need to see me?"

"I wanted to return your miniature." He removed it from the pocket of his doublet and handed it back to her.

She took in the sight of his doublet, and the way his hand rested upon the hilt of his sword. "I have not seen you about today. Were you out?"

"Aye, I left early."

He saw the way she dropped her gaze to the miniature, then back to look to him, her expression guarded. "Thank you for returning it." She slipped it into her pocket. "You did not keep it very long."

"It did not take me long to discover the man in your miniature is Louis XIV, the Sun King. Does that jar anything in your mind? Does the name stand out at all?"

"I know he was a king of France, of course."

"Nothing more?"

"No, nothing. And you? Did you discover something more? Some reason why he should be important to me?"

"No, but I did learn something interesting."

"Oh? Then share it. Please do."

She was calm and unflappable, and he had to admire her levelheadedness, her self-control. She was not easily perturbed. He would hand her that much. "I learned this type of miniature is usually given only to family members, or to very close friends. I cannot help but wonder, which one are you?"

She made a valiant attempt to look nonchalant, just as she endeavored to keep the tremor out of her voice, but she was unsuccessful on both counts. "I...of course I am neither one."

"You are sure of that?"

"Of course I am. How could I be a family member, or even the kind of friend the king would favor with such a miniature? I was not even born when Louis XIV died. I find it a bit preposterous to think it possible that he could have bequeathed it to me."

"There could be other ways," he said.

"Possibly," she said, and smiled at him. "But we will never know, will we? Now, give me your arm and walk me to dinner."

Seventeen

Is there, in human-form, that bears a heart
A wretch! a villain! lost to love and truth!
That can, with studied, sly, ensnaring art,
Betray sweet Jenny's unsuspecting youth?

—Robert Burns (1759-1796), Scottish poet and songwriter. "The Cotter's Saturday Night" (1786)

Vilain ran his long, slender fingers through his hair. That one move would have signaled, had there been anyone else in the room, his tremendous frustration.

"Merde!" he cursed, when he reached the end of the dispatch from Louis XV.

He cursed again, more loudly this time, and

tossed the letter onto the desk. He poured himself a glass of brandy and began to pace the room. Damn the French king…damn Louis, and damn his Bourbon blood.

He walked to the window, turned and thought a minute, trying to understand what the letter did not say.

Was this a fine net of stratagem the king had set to ensnare him?

Or was it nothing more than a ruse, and that French bastard was trying to deceive him?

Why else would he blandly give instructions for Vilain to take Sophie to England and hand her over to the Duke of Rockingham?

He finished the brandy, poured another one and tried to remember what else the king had said, and when he could not he snatched the letter from the desk and found the words he searched for.

Once I receive word from the Duke of Rockingham that Sophie de Bourbon is safely in the duke's hands, I will forgive all my former grievances against you and restore your title and lands.

Something about all of this did not sit well with Vilain. He was uneasy about involving himself in the intrigue of kings. It was a good way to end up dead.

As for the Duke of Rockingham, he had the reputation of being the doer of dark deeds. He was a man whose intelligence matched his ruthlessness. At one point, King George had become so fed up with him that he had given Rockingham a diplomatic post, and sent him to French court.

That must have been where he met Sophie.

He tossed down the rest of his drink. He did not really care how Rockingham met Sophie, but one thing was certain: it was not a love match.

Vilain had another brandy. He was feeling better about all of this. If the brandy held out, he might even go so far as to feel jovial.

He wondered why Rockingham wanted Sophie so desperately, and tried to imagine what might have happened that could have put Rockingham in such good standing with King Louis, for it was well known that the French had no feelings of attachment when it came to the English.

By the time Vilain had his fourth...or was it his fifth...brandy, he decided the best approach was to extract himself from the entire matter. He had an uneasy feeling that the King of France wanted him to hand Sophie over to Rockingham and, once he did, King Louis had no intention of restoring Vilain's property.

It was just as well. Vilain had already lost his appetite for playing the game of kings. Besides, he liked Sophie, and the thought of handing her over to Rockingham sickened him.

He thought of another reason to keep Sophie here, for he knew James Graham cared more for her than he let show. That would soon begin to cause trouble between him and Gillian.

Vilain planned to be there when Gillian needed a shoulder to cry on—and when she did, he would offer his.

Tomorrow, he would go to Monleigh Castle and tell James Graham what he knew. That left him feeling better, for James Graham was the kind of man one wanted as a friend and not as an enemy.

He stretched out on the sofa in his study and finished his brandy. What he needed was a woman. He thought of Gillian Macara and her fine red hair, pining away for Jamie Graham, who would never marry her. Especially now that he had Sophie. Vilain thought about how he would like to tell Gillian that, but she would not believe him.

What a waste. Such a fine-looking woman, with the most delectable body…

He looked down at the tightness in his groin and thought this was a fine time to be aroused.

Vilain was about to unfasten his breeches and

relieve himself when his butler knocked at the door and announced, "Mistress Gillian Macara is waiting here to see you."

Opportunity dumped in his lap! And what was he, but an opportunist?

Gillian was warming her hands in front of the fire when Vilain entered the room. "I did not expect to be greeted by so lovely a sight on a day like this. What brings you here, Gillian?"

"Och! It was a long, cold ride over here, Vilain. Can ye no' offer a lady something to warm her?"

"Would you be needing something to drink, or someone to warm you?"

She smiled and removed her cape. "Something to drink…first."

She was wearing a dark blue riding suit with a nipped waist that drew attention to the shapely curves of her breasts. His gaze dropped past the feminine swell of hips, and unbelievably long legs.

Vilain had to take a deep breath before he could manage to say, "Brandy?"

She nodded. "That is one thing I love about the French. I could almost fall in love with a man who supplied me with brandy."

Vilain laughed and poured her a large glass. "Then you have found the right Frenchman, for I have a cellar full of it. Shall we go down and test the truth of your words?" He placed the drink in her hand and allowed his hand to remain on the glass, touching hers long enough for her to notice.

Her smile warmed him more than the brandy. "I like a woman who knows what she wants and goes after it."

She tasted the brandy. "You are never subtle, are you?"

He laughed. "I am French. I have no morals. Subtlety is for the schoolroom. If I want a woman, I tell her." He paused, and gave her a questioning smile. "But you have not told me why you rode all the way over here in the snow."

"To see you."

"And James Graham?"

"He is pursuing other interests."

"It is just as well. He is not the man for you. The two of you would have never suited. I have wondered over the years what held you to him. I always took you for a smart woman, and yet when it comes to affairs of the heart you always seem to leave your brains at home."

"I did not come here to be rebuked and reprimanded. However, you are right so I cannot be angry with you for speaking the truth. I suppose some of us learn faster than others. At least I have realized I have been going down the wrong road—I have decided to change directions."

He refilled both their glasses. "I might warn you that I had several of these before you came. You might want to consider leaving before I have another one."

"Why?"

"Because you are a damn beautiful woman and I have wondered for years what it would be like to bed you, and I am fast losing all my courtly manners. Drink does that to a man. Take now, for instance. When I look at you, I do not see you sitting there comfortably, with your dress tucked around your ankles and your maidenly high collar. I see you with nothing on, and all your beautiful red hair let down to your waist, with the light of the fire bringing the color to life. I see your breasts, high and firm, with your nipples puckered, and I want to roll them between my fingers until they are hard and I take them in my mouth."

He could hear her labored breathing. "You should not say such to me."

"No, I shouldn't, any more than you should sit here and listen to it, but you are listening, and I have given you fair warning. Would you like me to ring for William to have your horse brought around?"

"No, I find myself intrigued, and fear I would prefer to hear the rest of what you see when you look at me."

"I see your skin, smooth and white over lush hips I long to caress. I see the way your soft stomach draws my eye lower to the shadow of desire, and I see it matches your fiery hair. I see you lick your lips when I look at you, and I imagine you parting your legs with an invitation I am helpless to ignore."

"And if I did give you such an invitation? What would you do?"

"I would go to the door and lock it like this." He crossed the room and the *click* of the door was strangely loud. "And then I would remove my clothes, and I would spend the rest of the night showing you what you have ignored for the ten years you have been pining for James Graham."

"Then show me."

Gillian was mesmerized. She had never seen a man who was more open and honest, and so terribly arousing because of it. She might not be a virgin, but never had she watched a man undress in a way that made her want to be as boldly forward as he.

She was lost in his words, and wondered why she had never noticed before what a godlike creature he was, with his dark blue eyes, his golden head and the heart-stopping accent that made her shiver.

He was tall and slender and...she dropped her gaze down to see what he had to offer, and smiled.

Now, here was the fantasy lover she had dreamed about but never expected to find. His body was beautiful, and well endowed, and he had made it known how much he desired her.

He had not touched her yet, but already she liked this French way of seduction.

Truly, it was a very long night and she did not remember falling to sleep at all.

When Gillian awoke the next morning she was in Vilain's bed, but he was not in the room.

She lay there for a while, thinking back over the wild lovemaking that had lasted almost all night. Then she pouted because she was hungry for more and Vilain was gone.

She dressed and went downstairs to look for him, but found no one about. She was fast allowing herself to be in a fine temper and, if she saw him, she would let him know it.

She yanked on her gloves and picked up her cape. That fool butler of his was nowhere to be found, so she decided to go to the stables herself and have her horse saddled.

She had almost reached the front door when she heard voices, and thinking she would not only find Vilain but also his butler, she followed the sound until she came to the library.

The door was ajar and she paused, clearly hearing Vilain's voice, but the other voice was not that of Angus.

She listened, curiously wondering with whom he was talking, being hesitant to interrupt him until she knew.

"I was told by someone who has been to Monleigh recently that there was a French lass there… one who has lost her memory. Have ye any knowledge of such a lass?"

"A French lass? Why, no, I have neither seen nor heard of anyone such as you describe. I was there only two nights ago for dinner and dancing. I am certain I would have recognized a French *mademoiselle,* if she had been in the room."

"Perhaps if she has no memory she would have remained above stairs."

"It is possible, I suppose. You said the Duke of Rockingham was betrothed to her?"

"Aye. And he is most anxious to find his lass."

"To be sure," Vilain said. "I will keep her in mind and alert you if I learn anything. You said her name was Sophie, I believe."

"Aye, she boarded the ship under the name of Sophie Victoire d'Alembert, although her real name is Sophie Marie Victoire de Bourbon. Her mother's maiden name was d'Alembert, so I suppose she was using that so no one would recognize her."

Gillian wanted to look but she was afraid they might see her, so she remained where she was and listened to Vilain's reply. Her heart hammered with the powerful words she heard.

She moved her ear closer to the door.

Vilain was speaking. "Yes, a name like de Bourbon would certainly get her noticed. The family goes back over five hundred years to Louis I. They have provided France with many of its kings."

"It is the same family, then, for I was told she is the daughter of Louis-Alexandre de Bourbon, Comte de Toulouse, duc de Danville, duc de Penthièvre, duc de Châteauvillain, and duc de Rambouillet. He is..."

Vilain whistled. "The son of Louis XIV, *Roi Soleil*...the Sun King."

"Aye, the Sun King is her grandfather, but it is my understanding that her father was an illegitimate son of the king. I learned later that King Louis legitimized all of his illegitimate children."

Gillian held her breath, unable to believe she was privy to hear such. She knew she should leave.

Things like this could get one murdered, but she had to hear what Vilain had to say next.

"Yes, that is true," he said. "Louis was a devoted father. He did legitimize them...all of them."

"I would like to ask you to make a few inquiries as to whether anyone has seen the lass. Since you are known in the area, you can ask such questions without arousing all the suspicion my investigation would bring forth."

"And if I learn anything?"

"Just leave word for Mirren MacDougal at the Black Bull Inn."

Gillian trembled with anticipation. At last she had the perfect way to be rid of that French hussy, for there was little doubt in her mind that Jamie had bedded the wench. Gillian knew she could not afford to let him become too enamored with Sophie, or her hopes of being the Countess of Monleigh would be destroyed. Of course he would be angry at her, Gillian knew, but he would be angrier at Sophie for her lies and deceit. After a while, he would come to his senses.

With Sophie out of the way, everything would be as it had been before.

She knew she had to be away from here quickly so she turned away and went quietly down the hall and back up the stairs.

When Vilain entered the room half an hour later Gillian was lying naked on top of the bed, her legs spread the way Vilain liked them.

He began removing his clothes. "Ah *chéri*, you know the way to get a rise out of a man."

"Prove it," she said.

Simon McIver, the proprietor of the Black Bull Inn, was drying tankards when the noise in the room suddenly dropped.

He looked up to see the cause—a woman in a long black cape, with the hood over her head, walked into the tavern.

"I have a message for Mirren MacDougal. Is he here?"

"Aye, ye can leave yer message here and I will see that he gets it."

"This is an unwritten message, meant to be delivered to MacDougal in person. Will you summon him?"

Simon put the tankard down. "Aye, ye can have yerself a seat over there to wait."

"I prefer to wait outside. Tell him I am in the coach."

She was gone before the innkeeper could raise a speculative brow or direct another question her way.

Ten minutes later, Mirren MacDougal tapped

on the door of the coach. The door opened and a woman's voice said, "Mr. MacDougal, do come inside. I have some information that you will find most useful."

Captain Robinson, of the Black Watch, listened intently to what Mirrin MacDougal had to say. When MacDougal finished, the captain had a few questions.

"You mean this woman named Gillian is betrothed to Monleigh?"

"Aye."

The captain knitted his dark brows into a thoughtful frown. He folded his slender fingers with the well-manicured nails and rested his chin upon them. "Hmm... One would think she would fear Monleigh's wrath. When he learns she was the one who betrayed him and the French lass, she will be anything but dear to him."

"The way she feels, it would be better to have Monleigh angry than not to have him at all."

The captain nodded. "Aah... So he is smitten with the French lass?"

"Aye. Quite smitten, according to his fiancée," MacDougal replied.

Captain Robinson smiled. "It is always nice to experience a little pleasure while doing business."

"Aye, but how will you wrest the lass from Monleigh? 'Tis no easy task, ye ken."

"We will confront him, of course, and give him the opportunity to turn her over to us, with a friendly reminder that it is, after all, his duty as a member of the aristocracy."

MacDougal thought about that for a moment. "And if he refuses?"

"Then we have no choice but to arrest him."

"But he is the Earl of Monleigh."

"If he refuses to hand over the fiancée of the Duke of Rockingham, that makes him an enemy of the crown. Need I remind you that an enemy of the King of England has no rights?"

MacDougal shook his head. "No, you needn't remind me. How will you go about this?"

"Leave that to me," Robinson said. He opened a drawer, withdrew a small pouch, and tossed it to MacDougal.

The *clink* of money could be heard when Mirren caught it in one hand.

"Your thirty pieces of silver," Captain Robinson said.

Eighteen

If she be false, O! then heaven mocks itself.
I'll not believe it.
—William Shakespeare (1564-1616), English poet and playwright. *Othello* (1602-1604), Act 3, Scene 3

Jamie was in the midst of settling himself in bed when two glossy ravens perched upon the battlements.

Uneasiness settled about him at the sight of such a bad sign for, according to folklore, it was an ill omen to see two ravens, and he silently recited the admonition in verse.

To see one raven is lucky, 'tis true

But it's certain misfortune to light upon two
And meeting with three is the devil!

Were they the heralds of some misfortune that was to come, or an indication of something fated to end badly? Only time would prove the answer.

The ravens remained there until dawn and then, with great flapping of wings and a croaking cry, they flew away.

Upon arising, Jamie was in a state of uneasy calm, unable to shake the feeling that closed in around him—that this was not going to be an ordinary day. In spite of trying, he could not shake the presentiment of coming misfortune, although it was not clearly based on anything but the two ravens.

Deciding to put the ill omen out of his mind he dressed, not in his customary clothing, but in a white linen shirt and his plaid. His finest basket-hilted broadsword hung suspended from a tooled baldric with silver trim. Even the ever-present dirk he usually wore was replaced by one with intricate knotwork carving on the haft.

Today promised to be a long one. He might as well face it well dressed.

Unlike the Lowlands, where the land was

arable, the fishing good and trade with England plentiful, life in the Highlands was hard, physically and mentally. The land was rugged and remote, and the soil was poor, requiring the members of his clan to depend largely upon fishing and cattle.

The severe weather and bad harvests of the past year had driven many Highlanders to emigrate elsewhere, and Jamie still regretted the fact that many of those who left were members of his own clan.

Yesterday he had inspected the eroded hillsides where, due to overgrazing, much of the land was reverting to rough pasture, bracken and rush. Today he would ride out to inspect the lower slopes of damp grasslands and flush bogs that dotted the lower slopes.

Last night he had placed Fraser and Calum in charge of seeing that the cattle were moved from the higher plateaus of the mountains to the lower glens. Only moments ago Niall had reported his concern about the farms, which were barely scraping a living from the miserable Highland soil.

He had promised Calum that tonight they would go over the crops they planned to plant in the spring.

As if his mind was not preoccupied enough,

Jamie kept having visions of his bachelorhood dwindling away before his open eyes. Soon the bards would be composing ballads of how the mighty Chief of the Clan Graham, after loving all the lasses, had given his heart to only one, for today he intended to ask Sophie to marry him.

He tied his hair back in a queue, put on his jacket and declared himself ready to face the day. He hoped that by nightfall things would be looking much better—after Sophie said yes.

He was about to leave his room when Bran knocked on the door and entered.

He did not greet Jamie in his usual jovial manner. His face was grimly set, his lips tight, as if he tried to hold back his words. "A regiment of the Black Watch was spotted a few miles from here," he said. "What do you suppose those English-loving bastards want?"

"Spying is their primary occupation, is it not?"

Bran nodded. "Aye, that along with arresting anyone they wish and turning them over to the English."

"Keep an eye on them, but stay out of sight. It could be nothing more than a patrol, or an advance group ahead of General Wade's road builders."

"Or, they could be here to quash the tribal fighting between the Crowders and the McCrackens," Bran said.

"Aye, that too."

Out of the corner of her eye, Sophie saw Jamie come down the stairs like an immense black shadow, dwarfing everything around him. To her he seemed as tall and powerful as the towers of the castle, and everything about him was dark and hard as granite.

Her gaze fell on the claymore at his side, a cold and dangerous reminder of what he was capable of, and of the danger that seemed commonplace to the Grahams.

She was about to greet him when Arabella came rushing around the corner. "Jamie, come quickly… into the library. Wallace Graham has brought a woman and her five daughters to see you. He says the woman is a witch and has caused his cow to stop giving milk."

With an oath uttered in Gaelic Jamie headed toward the library with great, long strides, with Arabella practically running behind him to keep up.

Although Sophie was curious and would have liked to witness what was going on in the library, she did not feel it was her place to intrude upon a situation such as this, so she sat down on the bottom stair, chin resting in her hands, to wait.

Half an hour later, Arabella joined her.

"What happened to the woman and the children?"

"Jamie had one of the men take them back home."

"He didn't accuse her of being a witch, then."

"Of course not. The last witch was hung in 1727, but of course that doesn't mean people don't still believe in them."

"What caused the cow to stop giving milk?"

Arabella laughed. "The woman's husband was arrested by the English, and she has no money. So, she was getting up very early each morning to milk her neighbor's cow, so her children would have something to eat."

"So, how did Jamie settle things?"

"He paid the man for his cow and gave it to the woman so she can feed her children, and Angus Graham can buy himself a new cow."

Sophie smiled. Chiefs, she decided, were busy lads.

Arabella went to her room and Sophie was about to do the same when Jamie reappeared and invited her to ride out with him.

"Where are you going?"

"To look over the glens."

By the time she changed into her riding clothes

Jamie had a fine chestnut mare saddled for her. She accepted his boost into the sidesaddle and drew the sides of her cloak together, careful to see that it covered her skirts.

A few feet away Jamie mounted Corrie and spurred him to a trot. Sophie watched him for a moment, then touched her whip to the mare's flanks and rode after him.

The wind on her face was cold, but the sun was out and her black cape did a good job of absorbing much of its warmth. She was glad when they left the narrow track through the mountains and entered the moor, for then she could ride beside him, instead of following behind.

They rode along a burn to the place where it curved into a pool in a shallow fall. Bushes of heather grew in clumps between the gray rocks.

"In the summer the flowers here smell like honey," he told her, and she felt a sadness deep inside knowing she would not be here when the flowers returned in the spring.

They rode past ancient forts, standing stones and cairns into a glen where history seemed to stand still. She stopped her horse and looked around as Jamie told her this was a sacred place, where eight thousand years of history lay crumbling. They dismounted and led their horses over the hummocky ground with its jutting outcrops of rock, interspersed with patches of heather.

They did not stop until they reached a large stone and Sophie inquired about the carving of a rod, crescent moon and what looked to be spectacles.

"No one knows what they stand for. The knowledge has died out," he said, and she was reminded of the days when men walked the earth, imbuing each stone and tree with a living spirit, only to vanish and leave nothing but his ancient stones and strange markings behind, as witness that he had ever existed at all.

They walked on for a while and stopped by a stone cairn. Jamie was about to help her mount when she stepped on a stone and turned her ankle.

She looked down, prepared to kick the stone away, then paused and, leaning over, picked it up. "It looks like a small teapot," she said.

He took it and looked it over. "It's an ancient stone lamp," he said, and handed it back to her. "It's probably lain there for thousands of years, right where someone dropped it. Bring it with you if you like."

She started to take it with her but had a second thought. "No, somehow it doesn't seem right to move it."

He flashed her a grin. "Are ye afraid it will carry some sort of curse? You aren't superstitious, are you?"

"No," she said, and felt a cold chill ripple down her neck. "At least not very superstitious."

He laughed and put out his hand to take the lamp. "Very well, we will leave it here."

He put the lamp back in its resting place and turned back to her. "Seems like I finally have ye all to myself."

His words were exciting, and the spark of fire in his eyes caused a ripple of desire to pass through her. She felt paralyzed, unable to move. Tightness gripped her throat. Something strange seemed to settle over her, hungry and impatient.

He must have felt it, too, for his arms came around her.

She leaned back against one of the stones and lifted her face to his, waiting for the kiss she hoped would come, and she was not disappointed.

It had been so long since she had kissed him, and she was swept away with a sense of urgency. His mouth was hot and his hunger matched hers, and she wanted him now, right here, at this very spot, not caring that they were completely out in the open, in the middle of the day.

Weak from his kisses, she began to slide down

the length of the stone until she was sitting down. She saw Jamie had already dropped his claymore beside them on the ground.

He dropped down beside her. His hands gripped her hair as if holding her for the kiss that followed: raw, sensual and earthy—a kiss as barbaric as his ancestors, and she knew their mating would be primitive and frantic. She clung to him, arching against him as he slipped her clothes off.

She whimpered when the cool air washed over her, and groaned with satisfaction when he covered her warmly with his heat, the hard length of him cradled against her belly, then moving lower, teasing her with each grinding stroke of his hips until she could stand it no longer and captured him in her hand.

The heat, the size, the heady sense of power it gave her to hold him thus, to see the beauty in a face she loved, even when the beloved tanned features were gripped with aching desire, startled her.

It was an exhilarating feeling: a light-headedness that came upon her like too much wine—intoxicating and so powerful.

She realized at that moment that she liked the heady feeling—the daring of making love to him here, in the open, and the reckless spirit, the threat of danger that always hovered close beside him.

Her desire for him stabbed at her until she cried out, wanting, needing to satisfy an insatiable craving that gripped her in its jaws and would not let go, until she heard herself begging.... "Please, Jamie...please..."

He went over the edge at the sound of her whisper. She lifted her hips to meet his entry, taking all of him and giving all she had to give in return. At last he was where she wanted him to be, kissing her, touching her, whispering what he wanted to do to her, leaving her screaming for more and telling him not to stop.

"I could never stop. You have been mine, a part of me since the beginning. You don't know what it's like to touch you, to feel you open like a flower, welcoming me home. Every time I make love to you, I die a little inside...slow and painless until I realize I'm halfway to heaven."

His words wrapped around her and she wondered if the magic of it was because of the place they were in, if there was still some lingering presence from long ago, when the gods came down and copulated with the inhabitants of the earth.

Too powerful, she thought. He had cast a spell over her that was both mystical and erotic. And still he teased her, bringing her to the edge until she arched against him, ready to be swept away, then withdrawing, almost leaving her completely until she clutched at him and whispered, "No, don't leave."

"Never," he growled.

She felt the grind of his hips against hers, circling, pressing, faster and faster until she was out of control before she shattered exquisitely.

She lay in his arms for a time, until her heart stopped slamming against her chest and her breathing returned to normal. She still had that strange feeling. "There is something about this place," she said. "Did you feel it?"

"Aye, like we were in a place of timelessness and joined to the past."

She rolled over onto her elbows and looked down into his face. "Yes, that's how it felt...as if coupling was the one unchanging thread that connected us to the past, that would connect us to the future. They were lovers, and so are we, and those who come after us. It remains constant." She smiled and kissed him full upon the mouth. "Do you think it would have been the same if I had made love to primitive man in a wolf pelt?"

"Och! I hope not."

Something about the almost petulant way he said that struck her as hilarious and she began to laugh.

He rolled on top of her and pinned her arms down on each side of her head. "If it's primitive ye want, lass, I dinna mind granting yer wish."

And he did.

Jamie Graham, she learned, was a man of his word.

Later, when she opened her eyes and saw him standing over her, she asked, "Where did you find the strength to stand?"

"It takes practice."

"Practice?" She grabbed a clump of grass and threw it at him. "Boastful braggart."

She watched him fasten his clothing, and when he finished, she stood, and found she felt as wobbly as a colt. He smiled down at her and held out his hand. "Come, lass."

She placed her hand in his and felt the warmth as his leather gauntlet closed around it and he drew her into his arms. "Are you sure you want to leave this place, or do you want to go for a third time?"

"I don't think I could bear it if you had any more practice. I ache all over."

"I will give you a nice warm bath when we are home."

She smiled and thumped him on the arm. " 'Unarm, Eros!' " she said, wondering if he read Shakespeare.

"'The long day's task is done, and we must sleep,'" he said, finishing the quote, and she knew he had not only read Shakespeare at some time in his life, but he knew it well enough to recite it.

"I always discover something new about you that I did not know before," she said. "I had no idea you could quote Shakespeare."

"I have a lot of secrets you do not know about. And you? Do you harbor secrets in that heart so pure, sweet Sophie?"

Even before he said those words her heart was beating erratically, for she had come a hair's breadth away from saying, "I, too, have secrets." Yet, she did not make that declaration when she answered him, but simply blanketed it with a generality. "I suppose everyone has a secret or two. It is part of being human, I think...to hold back a little part of ourselves, lest we become as transparent as glass and harmed by those who would use it against us."

"Is that what you fear? That someone will do you harm?"

"I was simply caught up in one of my clouds of conviction," she replied, "nothing more."

The horses had wandered off as they grazed so arm in arm, Sophie and Jamie walked up the rocky hillside together to follow them.

When they reached them at last, he lifted her into the saddle, and she looked down upon the handsome features of the man who had become such a part of her life in a very short period. She fought the urge to lean forward and kiss him, and to tell him the words that burned in her heart: *Je t'aime... I love you...*

He put his hand on her thigh and let it rest there for a moment, unaware that it burned a memory of this day into her flesh.

As they rode away she turned back, to look one last time upon this place where the ancients once roamed, and thought that one day they, like this moment, will slip away, quiet as a vapor.

Arabella was waiting for them when they arrived. "I wanted to warn you," she whispered. "Gillian is here. She has been waiting for you the better part of the afternoon. She is up to something, for she looks as smug as the cat what ate the cream and got away with it. She said she wanted to see you the moment you returned. She said it was urgent."

Sophie started up the stairs, but Jamie caught her by the arm. "Come with me. I want you with me."

"No. You go alone. She did not come here to speak with me."

Nineteen

For I have sworn thee fair, and thought thee
bright,
Who art as black as hell, as dark as night.
—William Shakespeare (1564-1616), English
poet and playwright. Sonnet 147

If Gillian was surprised to see Sophie with Jamie she did not let on, remaining serene and unruffled in her chair by the low-burning fire in the library. She closed the book she had been reading, held it out in front of her and, without taking her gaze from Sophie's face, she said, "I am reading an interesting book on the Bourbon kings. Have you read it?"

Jamie knew by the look in Gillian's eyes that

she had tasted the aromatic wine of vengeance, and she was here to wreak some sort of havoc, but what she was up to was not clear at this point.

The impending chaos lacked definite shape, as a shadow is indistinct. He only saw a foggy outline, indistinct and not fully understood. What was clear was Gillian would choose whatever way she could, henceforth to cause most offence.

What he did understand was that she did not address him, but Sophie, and that is what prompted him to turn to Sophie with a quizzical look. "Do you know what this is about? Is there something you want to tell me, Sophie?"

Sophie, lovely Sophie with the angel's face and the downcast eyes. His heart had questions and no answers, and she would not look at him. Why so shy, my lovely lass? he wanted to ask her. What are you hiding, love?

Suddenly, he did not need to ask those questions for he knew he had been deceived by the one he trusted above even his own instinct. He recalled something...yes, what was it she said when they were riding?

"I suppose everyone has a secret or two. It is part of being human, I think...to hold back a little part of ourselves, lest we become as transparent as glass and harmed by those who would use it against us."

Deception, that fatal poison to truth.

He glanced back at Gillian with a questioning look. What game did she play? he wondered. Did she use vengeance, a woman's weapon, or was she here to oil the lethal wheels of gossip?

Her smile was like a knife hidden in the sleeve. A sickness of heart gripped him, for he knew now that in some way Gillian would use whatever truth she had come upon to entrap and destroy.

And through it all, sweet Sophie said nothing.

Gillian, gaining strength and confidence from Sophie's silence, said, "Well then, perhaps you are not familiar with the family."

Jamie's head snapped around. He spoke irritably. "I doubt you rode all the way over here and waited for us for over two hours to play guessing games. What is your point, Gillian?"

She rose and tossed the book on the table. "My point, dearest James, is this. Sophie d'Alembert is the name she traveled under when she fled France on the *Aegir,* but that is not her real name. It was your mother's maiden name...d'Alembert...was it not?"

Sophie still did not speak.

"Shall I go on?" Gillian asked, not waiting for a reply. "Her true name is Sophie Victoire de Bourbon. She is the daughter of Louis-Alexandre de

Bourbon, Comte de Toulouse, duc de Danville, duc de Penthièvre, duc de Châteauvillain, duc de Rambouillet. Her father was made an Admiral of France at the age of five, and later he became the Grand Admiral of France. You must be thinking, as I did, that this all sounds rather far-fetched—but it really is not, you see—not when he was the third son of the King of France. And that would make Sophie the granddaughter of Louis XIV, the King of France, otherwise known as the Sun King. Of course, her excellent bloodline is tainted somewhat by the fact that her father was an illegitimate son of the king, by his mistress Françoise-Athenaise de Rochechouart-Mortemart. However, I would not wish to be accused of being unjust, so with all fairness, I will say he was later legitimized by his father, the king."

He turned to Sophie, wanting…needing her to say it was not true, that his faith and trust in her had not been misplaced. Sophie, so good at what she did. She had cut his throat and he had not even noticed.

Sophie wanted to banish the look on his face from her memory, for she knew it would haunt her for the rest of her days. She did not think he could have looked so wounded had she taken his sword and run him through.

And then, before her eyes, the look of stunned hurt changed to one of intense, seething fury. "Tell me now, lass, that you have no knowledge of the facts she reported. Tell me now that she lies, and I will believe you...but it had better be the truth. Does she lie?" he shouted.

He knew the answer already, for it was written on her face, and the tears of abject sorrow bore witness.

She had deceived him. But to what gain?

Gillian, he thought, so fair and so foul. With nothing more than a cold glance in her direction he let the intensity of his fury come down upon her. "Get out. Leave here now, and do not darken this door again."

"I did it for you, Jamie. I didn't want her to play you for the fool any longer."

"You did it for yourself, out of malice, or a jealous rage, because I ended things between us."

Gillian tossed her head back. "Hardly jealousy, since Vilain has proved to be such a satisfactory lover."

Silence descended upon the room and settled on those in it...betrothed, betrayer and betrayed.

Footsteps sounded outside the door as someone approached.

The door opened and Calum stepped into the

room. His face registered surprise. "Oh, I beg pardon, I did not know anyone was in here."

"Get her out of here, Calum. Now!"

Calum looked from Jamie to Sophie to Gillian in confusion, until Gillian said, "I was leaving, anyway. I have finished what I came here to do."

Calum, obviously still puzzled by all of this, was wise to recognize it was not the time to ask questions and, with a nod, he took Gillian by the arm.

Jamie followed them to the door. "Find someone to guard this door," he said, "and tell him no one enters this room for any reason."

Jamie closed the door, turned the key and turned back to Sophie. She could have been a marble statue. Sophie…as tempting as a saint, as black-hearted as the devil, and even now, after learning the truth, he still wanted her.

"I'm sorry," she said so softly he almost did not hear her. "You cannot possibly know just how sorry I am."

"The time for apology is as lost as the time for telling the truth. I do not want your apologies. It's too late, and this goes much deeper than that."

"Please listen to me, to what I have to say."

He waved his hand to silence her, and let her know her honesty would give him no comfort. "I have begged you for the truth for weeks and you coldly refused. Why should I listen to more of your lies now?"

"I never meant for it to go this far, Jamie. Truly, I did not. I had hoped to find a place to start my life over before the French or the English found me, or before you discovered my identity. I never intended to hurt you or to play you false. I never meant to place you and your family in jeopardy, or ruin the future you had planned."

"Words…nothing but words. I want to know why," he said, his own words hollow and broken. "Why did you pretend you did not know who you were?"

"I was afraid."

"Afraid? By God's teeth, woman, what were you afraid of? Me? Have I done anything but try to help you?"

"I did not know you well enough to know that when I first came here. I was desperately afraid you would turn me over to the English once you discovered who I was."

"I am a Highlander. I don't hand anyone over to the damn bloody English."

"Well, I did not know that, and not everyone in Scotland feels that way. It was common knowledge in France that the Scottish nobility—even in the Highlands—held beliefs more in line with the English than the Gaelic-speaking clans. And what about you?—telling me that the Black Watch was drawn almost entirely from the Lowlands, where hatred of anyone who spoke Gaelic ran deep."

"And later…when you came to know me, when you knew I would never hand you over to anyone? Why didn't you tell me then?"

"By then it was already too late. I knew you could never forgive me for deceiving you. You were going to marry Gillian. You had made me your mistress. You were a peer of the realm. If you discovered that I was the king's granddaughter, you would have been forced to marry me."

"And would that have been so bad?"

It was the softness in his voice, the raw pain in his eyes that was her undoing. She could not bear to look at him, to see the anguish in his eyes. Be angry with me. Strike me. Lock me in the dungeon. Do anything but look at me like that, she thought. To see you thus, breaks my heart.

I cannot bear this, she thought.

She turned away from him because she could not stand to see the pain she had inflicted, although there was precious little comfort in it for her. There was no way to escape her shame. She wished with all her heart the floor of the castle would open beneath her feet and she would disappear.

He grabbed her by the arm and spun her around. "Damn your lying eyes. Do not turn away from me. I asked you a question, and by all that is holy I will have my answer. Would that have been so bad?"

"Yes," she shouted. "Yes, it would have been bad. Do you think I wanted to be the one who ruined your future? What kind of life would it have been for you to be married to a woman you were forced to marry, a woman you did not love. How do you think I would have felt, knowing I would spend the rest of my life with a man who was in love with another woman?"

"I was never in love with Gillian."

"Well, how was I supposed to know that? You never mentioned it, and you certainly made it clear to me…on more than one occasion, I might add, that you planned to marry her."

She paused, put her hands to her head and began to shake it. "This is all so pointless. The fault is mine. I have ruined everything for both of us. If Gillian knows who I am, that means the English know. They will come here looking for me. I cannot stay here any longer. I must leave."

She made a move to turn away, but he yanked her back against him.

"You are no longer in control of what happens to you. You relinquished that right when you set out to deceive me. You are not going anywhere," he said, his voice cold and sharp as icicles.

"But the English—"

"Damn the English, and damn you. I have no right to call myself a man if I cannot hold off a band of puny Lowlanders who serve the bloody English crown."

"You cannot keep me here. It isn't safe for either of us."

He ignored her. "You will remain here, as my prisoner, until I decide what to do with you."

"You cannot hold me here against my will." She twisted away from his grip and made a dash for the door, but he caught her before she was halfway there.

She fought him, trying to free herself. "Let me go. Please. You do not understand what will happen. They will find me here and take me to England, and I will be forced to marry Rockingham. I would rather die than accept such a fate."

He released her. "Rockingham?" He almost spat the word out. "You were to wed that bastard the Duke of Rockingham?"

She rubbed her wrist. "It was none of my doing, I assure you. I was running away when the ship ran aground. I was going to Norway. I was nothing more than a pawn. My betrothal was arranged between my cousin, King Louis, and Rockingham. I was not informed of what negotiations took place, but I do know there were advantages for both sides."

"Your words fall on ears that will not listen, lass. There is nothing you can say. Your lies have taught me well. I do not believe you."

"What are you going to do with me?"

"I told you. You are my prisoner. You will be confined to your chamber. You will be kept under guard, night and day. You will remain here until you are too old to walk across the room, much less leave. And you will give yourself to me willingly…when I choose…where I choose…and for as long as I desire it."

"I would rather die."

"That, too, can be arranged."

She was wild-eyed and so beautiful he ached; yet her lies tore at his heart. He knew he could never trust her again.

There was nothing quiet about her desperation as she began to fight him, to beg and plead for her freedom. He knew she was desperate, although it did not soften him, and he easily subdued her.

He held both of her hands in one of his and,

with the other, he turned the lock and opened the door.

Bran was standing guard outside the door and Jamie shoved Sophie toward him. “Take her to her room and lock her in. Stay outside the door until I send someone to relieve you. No one is to enter, save me. Not even you. Understood?”

“Aye,” Bran said, and, without asking why, he led Sophie away.

Sophie refused the evening meal when it was bought to her by the guard—a man she had seen a few times and knew only by his given name, Colin.

“I will leave it on the table, then.”

She waved him away. “Take it back. I do not want it. If you leave it, I’ll throw it through the window.”

Colin removed the tray and did not say anything.

After he was gone, Sophie began to pace the floor. She went to the window and looked out. No escape there, she thought, for there was nothing but a sheer drop, straight down into the sea.

When it was too dark to see, she lit a lamp and removed her dress, and clad only in her shift she went to her bed and lay down. She purposefully tried not to think about anything that happened today. Her mind needed to be free of clutter, so she could decide on a way to leave, to plan some avenue of escape.

And still, thoughts of Jamie crept into her consciousness. She heaped every vile word she could think of upon his head—using the full resources of her vocabulary, in five languages. When that did not seem to relieve the anguish, the frustration and the disappointment over his treatment of her, she did what any young woman her age would have done.

She cried.

But even crying has to come to an end and, when it did, she drifted off to sleep.

She refused breakfast the next morning, and lunch, and dinner.

When the next day came around, she refused food again.

The fourth day she did the same.

Jamie was out most of the day, and when he returned, it was already dark. He went into the kitchen, to see if there was any dinner left.

Maude, the cook, was putting the last of the kitchen in order for the night, but when Jamie asked if he might have a piece of bread, she included with it a bowl of soup.

"I'm glad there was some soup left," he said, when he finished the last of it.

"There wouldn't have been if yer lass had eaten her dinner."

"I have no lass," he said.

"Aye, 'tis true enough, for she willna be alive much longer."

"What are you talking about, old woman?"

"The French lass," she said. "She has not eaten a bite since ye locked her in her room. She said she wouldn't eat anything that belonged to you."

"She will...if she gets hungry enough."

"I wouldn't be so sure of that, if I were you." Maude cleared the last utensils from the table. "Tomorrow will be the sixth day she's been locked in her room, and she hasn't eaten a bite since she's been there."

Damn her stubborn pride. If she thinks this will soften me toward her she is mistaken, he thought. She will not break me.

He did not consider that it might be Sophie who would break.

He returned to his room, undressed and went to bed.

An hour later, he was still awake. He folded his hands behind his head and watched the shadows from the fireplace dancing in place on the ceiling.

He kept seeing images of Sophie's face, her long hair, and the feel of it, silken and cool, when wrapped around him in the heat of lovemaking.

"Damn you," he said. He left his bed, grabbed his shirt and kilt and dressed as he walked to the door.

Five minutes later, he approached the door to Sophie's room and said to the guard, "Unlock the door and lock it after I enter."

He had seen men possessed of an utter absence of hope, and knew it could be born of a sense of futility or defeat. In Sophie, he saw both the spirit of hopelessness and the belief that her continued efforts to save herself would only end in failure.

She stared at him with empty eyes, showing no recognition, and giving no response when he spoke to her.

He sent for the doctor, and waited with her until he arrived.

Jamie had known Dr. Macrae all of his life, but that did not earn him the right to be present while Dr. Macrae examined Sophie. "I will speak with ye when I have finished," Macrae said.

Jamie did not return below stairs, but waited outside the door for almost an hour before Dr. Macrae stepped out to have a word with him. "She suffers from a despondency that arises from her inability to believe anything can save her. Ye cannot hold her prisoner any longer, Jamie. She is like a trapped animal. She will not eat in a captive state."

Sophie stood at the open window, feeling so weak she had to brace herself against it. She turned her face into the cold wind.

A thin, wispy fog was the only reminder that a thunderstorm had passed over the castle on its blustery way down the coast. Overhead, the moon found a clearing, and the moonlight seemed to shatter into a million tiny fragments that floated upon the surface of the water.

Two days ago, she had wondered how things could get much worse. This morning she found out, after another wave of nausea hit her and she realized this had been happening with some regularity for the past few weeks. The tender breasts, the bouts of nausea…how could she have missed the signs?

Until Dr. Macrae told her, why did it never occur to her that she might be with child?

She thought of the way she had used her unborn child to persuade Dr. Macrae not to tell Jamie. The doctor tried to persuade her by saying it was his duty to tell Jamie. In the end, it had been Sophie's threat to continue her refusal of food that won the doctor's concession.

"Very well," Dr. Macrae said, "as long as you stay healthy, I will remain mute."

That night, she ate a little barley soup and a few bites of bread.

When she finished her meal she went to her desk, still weak and sickened by nausea, yet she managed to rummage through the drawers until she found what she was looking for—a silver letter opener.

She carried it back to bed with her. If the opportunity arose for escape, she would take it.

She slipped the letter opener under her pillow and laid her head upon it. For quite some time she did not move as she tried to think about escape, but it was difficult to think with a clear mind when her heart beat so painfully in her chest.

Jamie, she knew, had a right to feel betrayed. She recognized he had a right to be angry. True, she had lied to him, but she expected that he would have been somewhat understanding.

It was his inability to forgive her that hurt.

With him, there was no middle ground and no halfway point. It was all or nothing, and nothing was what she was going to get—no compassion, no understanding, no sympathy, and certainly not one ounce of feeling.

She finally realized what it was about all of this that hurt her most. How could he have made love to her so many times, so tenderly and with so much feeling, and then turn so cold?

How could she have misjudged him so?

She thought he cared for her, but the truth was, she was nothing more than a receptacle for the fruit of his passion, and now she carried the proof of that in her womb.

He has used you, Sophie, without love, without marriage, without feeling. You will have to accept that fact and, in time, you will overcome the pain and the hurt.

Tears gathered. Her nose burned. I loved him, she thought, and slammed her fists against the pillow. I loved him.

I love him still....

She was almost asleep when she heard the door open and someone stepped into the room.

She did not care who it was.

The door closed. The lock clicked back into place. She lay quiet and subdued, waiting.

Even with her eyes closed she could tell that whoever it was carried a candle. The light behind her lids grew brighter as the footsteps came closer, and closer still.

Sophie slowly opened her eyes and saw Jamie

standing beside the bed, watching her with inscrutable eyes.

Not knowing what he intended caused the sleepy feeling to vanish, and replaced it with a cold, empty sobriety.

Her hand inched forward, under the pillow and a little farther, until it closed around the silver letter opener.

"Are you unwell?" His hand was warm and solid on her forehead.

She turned her head away. "I have no fever, if that is what you are asking."

"I sent for the doctor as soon as Maude told me you were refusing your meals."

"If that is why you came, you can leave. The doctor was here. I ate some soup."

"Yes, I know."

"Then why are you here?"

He stroked her cheek with the back of his fingers.

She turned her head away. "No. We are done with that. There is nothing between us now but anger and distrust. I hope that your anger toward me has subsided enough that you realize I cannot remain here. You are an earl...a man of breeding and honor. It is not right for you to keep me as your prisoner. You have to let me go."

"Aye, I have told myself the same thing, time and again."

Careful to keep the letter opener under cover she struggled to sit up, but she was too weak to do so. She saw the way he looked at her, and it was obvious he could see through the thinness of her shift. She drew the sheet up with one hand and clutched it beneath her chin.

"Why hide it? I have seen everything, and often enough that I have committed it to memory."

"Then leer at your memory and stop looking at me."

"I have already tried that, lass, to no avail."

Everything seemed to jerk to a standstill, as if time had suddenly careered into a stone wall.

The ticking of the clock on the mantel faded away.

Tick... Tick... Tick...

After a few seconds, tension began to gather like prickly points of icicles stabbing at her nerves. For a single panic-stricken moment her only emotion was an instinctive urge to hurt him as he had hurt her...continued to hurt her.

Sophie found it difficult to breathe or move, for she was paralyzed with the thought that he intended to make love to her—that he actually thought she could toss aside all the things he had said and done, and make love with him.

As if they could so easily go back and pick things up where they had left them. It wasn't that easy. At least, not for her.

"I would rather jump out that window to my death than have you touch me now," she said, in spite of the awareness of him that throbbed in her blood until she wanted him to love her, and keep on loving her, until they both forgot all the reasons why they were now compelled to hurt each other.

"It is a theory worth testing," he said. "Shall we find the truth of it, then?"

With a twisting move she broke free of the bed and faced him, her long gown wrapped around her legs, the letter opener gleaming in the light of the candle.

She held the letter opener tightly, the sharp point not more than two feet from his chest. "Open that door and tell everyone to stay away from me."

"You couldn't run fast enough or far enough that I would not get you in the end. Not that it matters. You will never leave here, lass. Not even if you kill me." He started toward her.

"I can meet that challenge easy enough," she said.

When she saw his look of disbelief, she added, "I mean it."

"Aye, I ken ye do, lass. However, I grow weary

of this game where neither of us wins. I want you in my bed. You want to run away. We cannot have it both ways, lass. One of us has to lose."

"I don't intend to lose. I am leaving here. Tonight."

"Then I will make it easy for you. I'm going to keep walking until you run me through."

He took a step toward her. Her hand began to tremble. "Get out of the way. I don't want to do this, but I will."

"I know."

"I'm warning you."

He took another step, and another, until he was mere inches away.

"I will use it. I have nothing to lose at this point."

"Neither have I," he said softly. "I have already lost the only thing that meant anything to me."

"We have that in common, at least."

"Use the knife, lass. Use it, or yield."

His voice was infuriatingly soft and calm, the way he would speak to a skittish horse, gentle and soothing. She watched him warily.

"Strike now, Sophie, or throw down the knife."

She lunged at him, and instantly realized what she had done. This was the man she loved, the father of her unborn child. How could she have sunk this low? Even if he intended to kill her, she could not inflict any more pain than she already had upon him.

At the last moment she twisted her arm to change the course and felt the tip scrape across his flesh.

She dropped the opener and it hit the floor with a clatter. A thin red line of blood oozed from the scratch across his stomach to ooze through the fabric of his shirt. Her startled gaze settled upon his face and she felt herself yanked into his arms as his mouth crushed down upon her pale, cold lips.

The room whirled about them and she felt the floor lift up beneath her feet, then with a sensation of spinning faster and faster they were swept into the center of an emotional hurricane. He lifted her into his arms and laid her down on the bed. With one rip he tore her gown off. A second later his shirt and kilt fell to the floor.

His mouth slammed against hers and she answered his kiss with a raging desire of her own, their hunger for each other matched as she pulled him to lie over her, his hips slipping into the warm cove between her legs when she moved them apart to accommodate him.

A wanton fire of throbbing passion rose over

them in molten waves, burning and sweeping them over the edge of a volcano. He loved her, as she needed to be loved, as she wanted to be loved—with abandon and a tender sort of savagery that laid her defenses to waste.

Even when the wanton burn of fire had passed, and nothing remained but the smoldering reminder of what had happened between them, he still did not withdraw, but remained joined with her. "As long as I am in you, you are part of me and cannot leave."

Tears welled in her eyes. She wanted to tell him she could easier cut out her own heart than to leave him. The agony of not knowing what to do cut to the core of her, and left her torn and hurting inside, where he could not see.

She lifted her hand to caress the cheek, the face that would always haunt her dreams, and wound her fingers into the soft skeins of his long hair. If only they could be this way forever, for when they made love there was no distrust, no lies, no pain, only the deep aching want, the need to mate, the love she felt for him that would never end.

He said nothing, and she knew he was thinking about her deception and his inability to forgive her. She knew he was trapped in a web he had spun for himself. He had no choice, really.

If he could not forgive her, he had to let her go.

She made a move to get up. His hand shot out and caught her by the wrist, but more gently than before. "Where are you going?"

"To put on my dress…to pack my things…to make arrangements for my departure."

"What happened between us changes nothing. I will never let you go."

"You can't keep me here, because you will never be able to trust me or forgive me. No good will come of this. You will continue to distrust me until I come to hate you, and then we will destroy each other. Is that what you want? It would be easier for both of us if I went willingly, and of my own accord, to Rockingham."

"Do not try to reason with me. I have no reason left. You are in my blood. Even though I know I should, I can't let you go." Swearing softly, he pulled her back and kissed her with a wild sort of desperation that broke her heart.

He wanted her, but his pride got in the way.

He took her again, swiftly, urgently, as if driven by devils he could not control. Somehow, she knew it would be done between them this time. When lust is spent, and when something is over, it's best done quickly.

A trembling, sweet agony gripped her and left

her clinging tightly to him, sated and trembling in his arms.

They lay together for a long time, still and silent, as if by not speaking they could prolong the inevitable.

At last, unable to bear it any longer, she said, "You know it is ended between us."

"In any event, that would not change anything," he said.

She felt the tightening of his jaw, then the pressure of his lips against her hair. His voice was ragged: half plea, half anger, "Try to understand…"

Her heart felt as cold and heavy as a stone.

"I understand," she said. "I understand nothing has changed. Everything will go on as before… you with your freedom to take a wife, while I will be kept as your paramour."

Twenty

O you gods!
Why do you make us love your goodly gifts
And snatch them straight away?
—William Shakespeare (1564-1616), English poet and playwright. *Pericles* (1606-1608), Act 3, Scene 1

It had been a week since Gillian's visit, and one piece of the puzzle had not yet fallen into place.

The one question that he could not answer was how did Gillian find out about Sophie?

After much thought, he decided it had to be Vilain. Gillian has certainly inferred he had bedded her. There was only one way to find out. He would go to Vilain and ask him in person.

The ring of his spurs on the stone steps of the turret had barely died away by the time Jamie mounted his horse.

Niall was watching him closely, worried for his brother's apparent lack of concern. "Do ye think it's safe to be riding out without any of yer men to accompany ye?" Niall asked. "There might be patrols about. Why dinna ye let me go with ye, at least?"

"I have committed no crime," Jamie said, and hearing the portcullis rise, he wheeled his horse to ride through the gate. "Therefore, I have nothing to worry about."

"As if that will make a difference to the English," Niall said, but Jamie was already through the gate and cantering down away from Monleigh.

Niall continued to watch him as Corrie broke into a full gallop and his brother disappeared from sight.

It was bitterly cold from the bite of snow in the wind blowing down from the mountains. It was early still, and the mist so heavy it was hardly discernable from rain. Jamie rode down the side of a rock-strewn mountain, the narrow trail wide enough for only one horse.

Before long the trail began to widen some as he turned his horse to round an outcropping of stone that opened onto the moor. He found himself surrounded by at least two dozen Highlanders wearing the dark plaid of the Black Watch, ready to betray their countrymen whenever they could.

Jamie sat astride his horse, facing Captain Robinson. He was not so naïve to think they had come upon each other by accident. He knew they were here because of Sophie. Because someone in their midst had betrayed him.

"Lord Monleigh, I believe?"

"I think you knew who I was before you stopped me."

"I am Captain Robinson of the Black Watch. I apologize for stopping you like this. We were on our way to see you."

"About what?"

"I understand you have a French lass under your protection. She goes by the name of Sophie d'Alembert, though her real name is—"

"I know who she is," Jamie said. "I doubt you rode out here to tell me that."

"No, your lordship, I have come to tell you Mademoiselle d'Alembert must be taken to England so that she may be reunited with her betrothed, the Duke of Rockingham."

"Mademoiselle d'Alembert does not wish to be reunited with the illustrious duke."

Captain Robinson nodded. "Be that as it may, she has been officially betrothed by her cousin, the King of France, and that is something neither of us has the power to undo. You must hand her over to us."

"The lass stays at Monleigh Castle, under my protection," Jamie said, never taking his gaze from Robinson's face.

"You are being very foolish, Lord Monleigh, and you risk much."

"Be that as it may, but the lass stays at Monleigh where the might of the Grahams will protect her, down to the last man."

"My God! We did not come here to start a war with the Grahams."

"The choice is yours."

"If you refuse to hand the lady over then I have no choice but to arrest you. Your sword, please."

Jamie looked around the circle of the twenty or so men who surrounded him with their swords drawn. With a nod at the captain he unsheathed his sword and handed it over to Captain Robinson.

"Bind him," Robinson said.

There was a moment of uneasy silence as each of the members of the Black Watch looked at one another, as if reluctant to be the one who would bind the hands of the powerful Earl of Monleigh.

Jamie saw the captain raise the sword he had

just surrendered to him and a moment later everything went black.

Captain Robinson looked at Monleigh's body lying on the ground. "I said, bind him! Now, if you please...unless you wish to join him."

Vilain had also risen early that morning and, after his horse was saddled, he rode toward Monleigh Castle. He had ridden less than half a league when he saw the open moor ahead of him, through the thinning trees.

Vilain recognized the gray stallion that belonged to James Graham galloping toward him, although they were still far away. He was almost to the edge of the trees when he saw the Black Watch ride out and surround the Earl of Monleigh.

Vilain stopped and dismounted. Hidden in the screen of trees, he watched silently as the Captain of the Black Watch struck Jamie on the side of his head with the flat side of his sword, and Jamie toppled from the saddle. By the time he regained consciousness he had been gagged, bound and tied across his saddle.

Without moving, Vilain listened to the ring of hoofs glancing against stone, the jingle of stirrups and the rattle of bridles as the Chief of the Clan Graham was led away.

Vilain remained safely hidden behind the trees until they were completely out of sight, then he mounted and urged his horse to a full gallop as he rode toward the Earl of Monleigh's home.

He splashed across a narrow burn then up the steep track until he slowed to a canter and rode through the gates of Monleigh.

Once he was inside, he broke the news to Jamie's brothers that the Chief of the Grahams and the laird of the castle had been arrested and taken away.

Niall broke the news to Sophie.

"I don't understand why they arrested him. I'm the one they want."

"They knew Jamie would never hand ye over, lass."

"What will you do now?"

"We will find where they have taken him, and then we will try to arrange for his release."

"They will not set him free. You know that. You have no choice but to take me there and arrange to exchange the two of us."

Fraser whistled. "Jamie would never sanction that."

No, but Calum would, Sophie thought, and suddenly an idea came to her. "Jamie is in no bargaining position at the moment. His life is in danger. You do agree on that point, at least, do you not?"

"Aye." They seemed to speak in unison.

She knew they were not going to involve a woman in their manly business, and she chose not to waste the effort it would take to even try to convince them. "Please let me know what you decide to do."

Niall nodded. "I will keep you informed."

After Niall was gone, Sophie spent the afternoon sewing with Arabella. With pricked fingers, Arabella embroidered the top for a stool, while Sophie stitched a cushion. It was a way to stay busy, and eased some of the tension that hung over the castle, stormlike, dark and ominous.

Later, dissatisfied with the progress of her cushion and her fingers throbbing from too many pinpricks, Sophie went above stairs and took dinner in her room.

When Arabella stopped by later they sat in the soft candlelight and talked quietly well into the night.

Once Arabella was gone, and Sophie had assured herself that everyone else had retired for the night, she dressed and left her room to make her way quietly below stairs. The hall was dim, but she could make out the door to Calum's room.

She knocked softly.

Calum had not yet dressed for bed for he opened the door almost immediately, still in his clothes. He was obviously surprised to see her. The surprised look soon gave way to one of intense dislike. Not that it surprised her. She had known since her first day at Monleigh that Calum neither liked nor approved of her.

His voice was cynical. "You have wandered into the wrong room, haven't you? Jamie's is further down the hall, although it will no' do you any good to go there. He isn't here."

"Yes, I know about Jamie. I have come here because I know of a way to free him. I must speak with you."

She recognized that look. It was the same look of distrust she had seen often enough on Jamie's face. It must be a Graham family trait, she thought. When in doubt, frown, look grim and distrust everyone in sight.

In spite of his dislike and distrust, he did open the door wider and stepped back, allowing her to enter his room.

His face was quite grave, and she wondered what disdain and scorn he would heap upon her, for she thought of him as a man who would be ceaseless in his reproach.

"I don't suppose it will tarnish your reputation any further if someone sees you come in here," he said.

Although his disdain was not amiss, her cheeks burned at the reference to her loss of both reputation and status. "No. I have moved beyond both reproach and redemption now."

"Before you say what you have to tell me, I want to know why you came to me instead of one of my brothers."

"You were the one who made your dislike known from the beginning. Therefore, it seemed logical that you would be the one most likely to go along with my plan."

Something that lay between admiration and respect flickered in his eyes. "Then perhaps I should tell you that recent events have persuaded me to alter, somewhat, my initial opinion of you," he said.

Well, if that wasn't the unexpected spark that kindled a fire, she thought. He caught her unprepared, and it left her with a sort of false balance. How could she not respect his forthright honesty without changing her own persuasions of him?

She discerned Calum was a man who was mentally faithful to himself, and how could she fault that? He had no use for the oily art of glib remarks, nor did he wear the mask of piety to hide the ugly features behind it. In spite of his blunt honesty, she found herself valuing his regard.

"I wish I had more time to pursue that," she said, "but it is good news come too late. We must focus on Jamie now and, if we are successful, I will not be around to enjoy your change of heart."

His interest obviously piqued, he asked, "All right, tell me of this plan of yours."

"I want to give myself over to the English—in exchange for Jamie—but I need your help. I do not know where they have taken him, or how to get there. There is also the small matter of my distrust of the English. With me being a woman, the odds of betrayal are even greater. Were I to arrange the exchange, I fear they would end up keeping both of us. I need you to negotiate with them and arrange the exchange."

"I am humbled by your courage," he said, "and I bow to your charity, for it is apparent you love my brother. It's my guess they have taken him to Inverness."

"Can you take me there?"

"Aye, I could take you, but Jamie would have my hide if I did that."

"Jamie won't have any hide left if you don't take me. You know he is too stubborn to tell them what they want to know. He would die first, and we both know they would be more than happy to oblige."

He remained thoughtful for a moment. "Aye, I will take you. 'Tis better to have an angry brother than a dead one, I ken."

It was at that moment that Sophie experienced an epiphany that would forever change the way she viewed this man, for she understood that the supreme measure of a man was not where he stood in times of peace and leisure, but where he stood in times of conflict and controversy.

Twenty-One

An honorable imprisonment...as is due to one who is in treaty for ransom.

—Sir Walter Scott (1771-1832),
Scottish novelist. *Ivanhoe* (1819)

Because the roads in the Highlands were nothing more than cattle tracks, Calum had arranged passage for them aboard a ship that would take them to Inverness, which lay at the southwestern end of Moray Firth, on the banks of the River Ness.

They docked at New Quay, which was sometimes called Citadel Quay, and soon wound their way through the medieval streets of Inverness, until they arrived at Bunchrew House, where Calum arranged for a room for Sophie.

"You must remain in the room until I return," he said. "I have arranged for the proprietor to bring you your meals. Do not open the door to anyone else."

"Except you."

For a moment, Calum looked at her warily, then he almost smiled. "Except me," he said, and Sophie felt they had crossed an important milestone.

"Where will you go first?"

"I thought I should start at Inverness Castle, to see what I can find out. I hope that they will be able to tell me where he is. I'll be back as soon as I can."

He opened the door and was about to depart when she called out to him.

"Calum, wait!"

He turned back to her and Sophie said, "If you can arrange it, I would like to see him. As a favor to me, please do not tell Jamie the purpose for our visit—at least not until I am gone. Just let him think we came to see him."

"Aye, I will see what I can do, but first I must learn where they have taken him."

When Calum returned he brought the news that Jamie had been at Inverness Castle, and had been transferred several days ago to Fort Augustus, some sixty miles from Inverness, at the foot of Ben Nevis.

They departed for Fort Augustus early the next morning, several hours before the sun was up. The journey took longer than she had anticipated due to all the climbing, with the last ten miles being what she could only call brutal.

When, at last, they began their descent into Fort Augustus it was a slow journey due to the strong headwinds.

As he had in Inverness, Calum placed her in a small inn and went to find Jamie and make arrangements for her to see him.

Jamie was lying down in a room barely large enough to accommodate the small bed. His sole light was a small rectangular window set high in the wall near the ceiling. It was the only connection to the world outside.

He heard the tread of feet and the sound of voices as someone approached. A moment later the small pass-through in the door was opened and a guard said, "You have a visitor."

Jamie eased his broken body off the bed, wincing as the raw flesh chafed against the manacle around one ankle. His meals had been vile and few, and his weakness caused him to sway unsteadily the moment he stood. He had to brace himself with one bruised arm against the wall.

One eye was swollen shut and the other he was only able to open a little, but it was enough that he could see where he was going.

He limped toward the door. The chain scraped the floor with a rattle with each step. When he reached the tiny opening he could see the guard's mouth moving, and then the words penetrated through the ringing in his ears.

"You have three minutes. No more."

He looked through the tiny opening in the door. Sophie...she looked exhausted, and her lovely features were grim and drawn. His gaze swept lower. "You have lost weight, lass. I would hate to think ye were grieving for me."

"Why would I be grieving for someone who cannot stand the sight of me?" she said.

He tried to open his eye a bit more, to see her more clearly, but her features were blurred. "What are you doing here? Who brought you?" he asked, for he had already vowed someone would pay a dear price for bringing her here. He would kill the bastard who told her where he was.

"I haven't much time...only three minutes, and I prefer to use it to tell you what I came here to say. Do not say anything. Only listen. I am sorry for everything that has happened since I came into your life. Please believe that I never intended for any harm to come to you or your family. I owe you so much...." Her voice cracked and she paused. "I am sorry. I hate tears."

He had never wanted to hold her and comfort her any more than he did now. She looked small, desolate and exhausted. He knew how she must have worried about him, and how she would have blamed herself for what happened.

"What I said is true," she said. "I do owe you a tremendous debt. I pray I can pay some of my indebtedness with a small gift. Perhaps then you can find it in your heart to forgive me."

"Sophie..."

She shook her head, not wanting to give him an opportunity to tell her what he needed to say. "How I envy God, for he can be with you always, while I cannot." Her voice broke for the second time.

She never appeared so strong, yet fragile, or so very far away. He had seen a great deal of suffering in his life—after all, he was a Scot—but he had never seen such anguish as he saw in her eyes before she turned away.

"Sophie...for the love of God, wait a moment."

"Time's up," the guard said, and shut the window.

* * *

The visit with Jamie subdued her, and Sophie was quiet during the ride back to the inn. She would never be able to erase the memory of his poor face, swollen and bruised, with a dozen cuts where the blood had dried to a thin crust. She knew the rest of him probably looked even worse, and was glad she had been spared the seeing of it.

Calum, sitting beside her, did not have much to say, either, but he did manage to ask, "Are you certain you want to do this? Once the exchange is made you will be on your way to England, and into the clutches of Rockingham. There will be no way any of us can help you once that happens."

"It is not what I want to do, but what I must do. It was my deception that pulled Jamie and the whole Graham clan into the fray. I alone bear the responsibility of getting him arrested. It is therefore fitting, I think, that I be the one to set things right."

"You're a lass. You shouldn't be involved."

She had decided at first not to tell Calum about the condition of Jamie's poor face, but thought better of it. This was because they had allowed only one of them to see him, and so Calum had arranged for that person to be her. "I cannot let him stay there a moment longer. You did not see his face, Calum. It was nothing but bruises, cuts and grotesque swellings. One eye was completely swollen shut, and the other not much better. His lips were raw and caked with dried blood. I dare not imagine what the rest of him has endured. He has been manacled like an animal. I heard the chain rattle when he walked. We have to get him out of there, and unless you have a better plan we go with mine."

"Jamie willna see it that way."

"Then you shall have to persuade him to see things differently."

"Aye, if he dinna kill me first."

"He willna," she said, trying to lighten his mood with her terrible attempt at mimicking his Scots burr. "He may be angry, but he will not do bodily harm to his own brother. Besides, none of this is your fault."

"The fault lies with Gillian and the traitors in the *Am Freiceadan Dubh,* who had their bloody hands in the middle of Jamie's arrest."

"I am not familiar with that name."

"It means the Black Watch. They are so called because of the dark tartan they wear. Unlike the scarlet coats of the British, the dark tartan makes it easier to spy on unsuspecting Highlanders, who would never believe they could be betrayed by their own countrymen."

"Yes, Jamie told me once that they were mostly Lowlanders, but some were Highlanders who chose to serve the English rather than their own country."

"They are the pick of the Highlanders, for they are the sons of some of the more powerful aristocracy. They bear the taint of being loyal to the bastard who sits upon the throne of England. Black is the color of their hearts, and watch is what they do, ye ken?"

She nodded. "Yes, I knew they were traitorous spies…"

"…who watch the Highlanders, arrest them, kill them or turn them in. We are no' allowed to carry weapons in the Highlands and when we are caught and they find a weapon, it is all the reason they need to arrest us."

"What do you mean you are not allowed to carry weapons? You carry them all the time."

It was the first real smile she had seen on Calum's grim face. "Weel, ye ken it was like this…after they put down the uprising in 1715, the clans were told to turn in their weapons. Some did, and the rest imported a shipload of worn-out muskets and swords from Holland. They surrendered those and kept their own."

Sophie fell quiet. She was thinking about Jamie

and the vigorous Celtic stock he was descended from. She remembered her first impressions of this land with no roads and an abundance of moor and bog—a land peopled by savage, warring tribes who spoke the most outlandish gibberish they called a language, and adhered to customs and dress that went beyond human understanding.

She recalled the vision of Jamie when he let his plaid drop, affording her an ample view of his well-muscled buttocks and a glimpse of what lay on the opposite side, and decided there were some things one did not have to understand to enjoy. It was his wildness, his love of country, and the way of life they tried to hold on to that made him the man he was.

The loyalty these Highlanders had for one another and their land deserved admiration, especially considering that Scotland was a small country of barren soil, few people and a rugged life, yet any one of them would gladly spill his blood for his wee bit o' wild scenery and romantic ruins.

Was this, too, something handed down through their Celtic blood, from their brooding, reflective ancestors?

They were a law unto themselves: men who lived by a strict code, filled with integrity. They had no king and no legal system—nothing but the chief of their clan, a mighty, claymore-wielding arm, and a spirit that would not die.

God only knew the British had tried to break that spirit, for they had built chains of fortresses, put in garrisons and even tried to murder an entire clan in order to tame the Highlanders and bring them to yoke.

Nothing worked until they began to recruit independent companies from the clans loyal to the crown—men who spoke Gaelic and knew the countryside and raised their arms against their own countrymen.

It shamed her to think she had been as deceptive as they.

The next morning Sophie looked at the scarlet coat of Major Charles Penworthy, of His Majesty's 10th Dragoons.

"I welcome you to Fort Augustus, *mademoiselle*. I regret any hardships you had to endure during your trip here. Rest assured, the Duke of Rockingham has made arrangements for the rest of your journey that are, shall we say, much more appropriate for a woman of your class and breeding."

Her heart hammered. She was here, in the same

garrison where Jamie had been, only now he was on his way back to Monleigh Castle with Calum. Never had she ever felt so alone. She knew the men here were falling over themselves to treat her well, now that they understood who she was, and who she was to wed. Little ease did these superficial things give her.

Dread crept in through her every pore.

She had a feeling that her trip to the home of the Duke of Rockingham would be the most pleasant part of it all, for once she was in his clutches she knew he would not simply kiss her hand and say, "My dear, all is forgiven."

Twenty-Two

> Let me remind you what the wary fox said once upon a time to the sick lion: "Because those footprints scare me, all directed your way, none coming back."
>
> —Horace (65-8 B.C.), Roman poet.
> *Epistles* (c.20 B.C.)

Those who knew the Duke of Rockingham said the diamond ring on his little finger was as ostentatious as the duke himself. And so was his palatial home.

Nothing could have prepared Sophie for the stunning sight of Swifford Castle, or its surrounding two thousand acres of parkland. And when one added the farmland, woods and moorland, the size of the duke's holdings rivaled that of the king's.

As for being palatial, it came close to holding its own against the beauty of Versailles.

The ducal carriage drove over a picturesque stone bridge, where graceful swans floated aimlessly and ducks paddled among the reeds along the water's edge. The carriage continued on down a graveled lane and through an opening in the woods where a copper weeping willow stood alone in the middle of a meadow, dripping tears from its branches, and she wondered if it cried for her.

Enchanting, fairy-tale towers rose over the treetops, giving no hint that within the gothic towers lay lavish, even opulent interiors, rich with priceless paintings, stained glass, marble, gilding and elaborately carved furnishings, and a man with a heart as hard and cold as stone.

Once the carriage arrived and she alighted, Sophie was led into the house through the south corridor into an enormous hall adorned with scenes from the time of the Emperor Augustus. The floors were marble, imported, she was told, from Italy. An obvious way to display his wealth, Sophie was certain.

A butler with a thin, pinched nose met her at the

door and promptly gave her over to the care of the sour-faced woman standing beside him. "Mrs. Crabb will escort you to your apartments."

With a kind of haughty effrontery, Mrs. Crabb was one of those people who could, with one look, show disapproval and be insulting at the same time. "This way," she said.

Sophie fell in line behind the woman who resembled her name, for she embodied all the qualities of a curmudgeon—ill tempered and full of resentment. She did not speak again until they came to the end of a long corridor on the third floor. She paused long enough to open the door to one of the one hundred and fifty rooms in Swifford Castle.

"The duke has had this room prepared for you. It is normally reserved for highly distinguished guests."

Sophie said nothing as she stepped over the threshold into the room that was to be her prison, in spite of its exquisite tapestries, painted walls and ceilings.

"The apartments are full of priceless antiques, and rival anything you have in France. Should you require something, pull the silk cord near your bed and someone will attend to you presently."

With a curt nod Mrs. Crabb departed, but not

before Sophie caught a glimpse of the two guards who were now standing on each side of her door.

When the door closed Sophie crossed the room and opened the doors onto a small Juliet balcony. She stepped outside and looked down to the courtyard far below.

The duke had been very careful to assign her a room she could not easily escape from. She thought of the swans and ducks she had seen earlier. How she envied them their freedom to go about, while her life was more like that of a linnet confined in a gilded cage.

Over the roof of the opposite wing of the castle, she could see the treetops of the tranquil, parklike setting beyond. Now comes the waiting, she thought, as she fought against the panic clutching her throat.

Outwardly, Swifford had all the attributes of a fairyland, but inside the confining walls and towering turrets, dwelled something dark and sinister—even monstrous. Beauty and evil...appearance and reality—something was out of balance in this place, jarring her senses like the lyrical harmony of violent poetry.

She could not help wondering how many damned souls had entered this place and never came out.

Weary, Sophie went back inside. She lay across the bed with her clothes on.

She was astounded to discover when she awoke that it was the next afternoon. Who knows how long she might have slept if she had not been awakened by the sound of draperies drawn back, and the burst of brilliant sunlight coming into her room.

She opened her eyes and saw the author of this ignoble awakening was none other than the well-fed Mrs. Crabb.

"His Grace, the duke, wishes to see you, but you cannot expect to see him with the stench of Scotland still on you. There is a tray with a light lunch on your table. Your bath will be brought up shortly. I suggest you do not dawdle. The duke does not like to be kept waiting."

Sophie clenched her jaw and set her chin. "I would think that by now, he would be growing accustomed to it."

"Enjoy your waspish words while you still can, ducky. You will soon be convinced to hold a more civil tongue."

Night had fallen by the time Mrs. Crabb opened the door to her room and told Sophie, "His Grace will see you now."

Accompanied by her guards, Sophie was escorted down the stairs to Rockingham's library—a room as elegant as the rest of the house.

Surrounded by leather-bound volumes that must have numbered into the thousands, Sophie was left to stand on a French Savonnerie carpet, beneath a gilded stucco ceiling. Beyond her, the door closed and she began to wonder how long the illustrious duke would choose to keep her waiting.

Once she tried to sit down in the damask chair behind her, but she was given a sharp poke in the ribs by the guard to her right. "You will remain standing," he said, "for as long as it takes until the duke arrives."

Her hands went up in mock surrender. "I am a statue of patience."

She had to admit she was about to run out of patience by the time the door behind her opened and a maid came into the library to light more candles. It was only a few minutes after the maid departed that a side door she had not noticed before opened, and William Arthur Wentworth, the twelfth Duke of Rockingham, graced her presence.

He was dressed in the role that suited him, with a satin coat and lace-trimmed shirt, and a fashionable wig, powdered and perfectly curled. Affected and foppish, he at first appeared to be the perfect macaroni, well traveled and aping the fashions of the countries he visited.

He gave her a visual going-over that was blatant, carnal and insulting. "So, the flyaway bird has been captured and returned to her cage," he said, after a long and insulting perusal.

"I came of my own accord."

"Do you think me a fool? I know the terms of your surrender, and the Scot you freed in exchange for yourself. An interesting sacrifice and worthy of investigation, which we will discuss later, but first, I want to know why you thought to escape to Norway."

"I did not wish to marry you. I believe I expressed that plainly to you in France."

"I don't recall your opinion being asked for. This was a business agreement between myself and your cousin."

He poured himself a glass of something that looked to be wine or claret and carried it to his desk. He sat down, neither offering her a glass nor a place to sit down.

"You have caused me a great deal of time and difficulty, not to mention money."

"I do not know why you bothered. I am not all that great a prize."

He went on, as if she had not spoken at all. "I

have had men looking for you that I could ill afford to be without. Now I find myself the laughingstock of London, since everyone knows my betrothed gave herself up to save the worthless hide of a bloody Scot."

"I prefer to think of it as saving a great deal of bloodshed, for had you sent troops to bring me back forcibly, there would have been many lives lost on both sides."

"You misjudge me. I am never encumbered with the loss of lives no matter which side they are on."

"I have heard worse about you," she said, forgetting her control and letting her anger show through.

Surprise flashed in his eyes. She wanted to slap herself for baiting him.

"And may I inquire as to what else you have heard?"

"I have heard many things, mostly dealing with the men you have killed, your skill as a swordsman and your insatiable interest in women. Would you care to refute or validate what I have heard?"

"Your smart words and cockiness do little to improve the severity of your situation," he said, his eyes narrowing to a cold stare. "You seem to forget that you are the prisoner here. I will ask the questions."

"I was not aware I was a prisoner," she replied boldly, "for I have committed no crime. I understand that you are displeased with me, and therefore I request to be allowed to return to France. You cannot keep me here indefinitely."

"Oh, but that is where you are wrong. You belong to me, as this castle does, or my horse, or any of a million things I have bought and paid for. I am free to do with you as I like, and that includes marrying you, if I so choose, or simply using you for as long as it pleases me, and you have no say in the matter. You lost all your rights when you ran away to live with barbaric Highlanders."

"I did not set out for Scotland, nor did I cause that storm!" she said hotly. "It was not my fault the ship ran aground."

"Perhaps not, but it was your choice to remain with the Grahams when you knew we were looking for you. You have put me to a great deal of trouble, and marriage will do nothing more than clip your wings. You need to be taught a thing or two, but first I need to answer one question. How many of them had their way with you?"

She was shaking with anger. "You have no right to speak to me like that."

He leaned forward and folded his hands together on the desk. "You are my runaway bride-to-be, and that gives me the right to ask questions. You are also my prisoner, and that gives me the right to ask them in any manner I choose. Just what would you have me do? You show up at my doorstep, looking no worse for the wear, but of course outward appearances have no way of bearing witness to the state of virginity one might find you in. I always inspect my livestock."

"Your daring is only exceeded by your vulgarity."

If ever a smile looked to be painted on silk, it was his as he said, "Is it, now? Well then, why don't you tell me, are you still untouched or have you been thoroughly explored and spoiled?"

She would not respond to such filth. How well she remembered his visits to France, resplendent in his frilly court dress and acting the English dandy. In spite of all his prancing foppishness, she knew him for what he was, a man whose effeminate exterior hid a cunning mind, an insatiable sexual appetite and one of the deadliest sword arms in England.

To him rape was a sport, and murder a way to while away the hours of boredom. She cautioned herself not to rouse his anger any further than she had already, so she clamped her mouth shut.

"If you are no longer a virgin, then I am the one

insulted. Sadly to say, the loss of virtue is irretrievable. And now, as to the state of yours…"

He motioned the guards to take her, and said, "On the desk, if you please, and hold her steady."

She was about to ask what he thought he was doing when, as if he was about to select a peach, he put his hand beneath her skirts and followed the line of her leg, until he reached the top of her thighs. It only took him a moment to find the place he sought.

He examined her roughly then withdrew his hand.

"Just as I thought. A not so surprising absence of a maidenhead." He glanced at the guards. "You may release her."

The two guards helped her off the desk and back to her chair.

Revolted by the thought of him touching her, she sat with her head bowed with shame. She was stunned and shocked, far beyond any mere humiliation. It went far deeper than that.

He had degraded her, in the worst way possible for a woman to be degraded. To do such was unthinkable. To do it on a desk, in a library, in the presence of common guards…was the worst sort of defilement.

Suddenly she felt his hand beneath her chin and

he lifted her face. He studied her coldly. "Have you anything to say?"

She clamped her teeth over his hand and bit down with all her might. He jerked his hand back, and when he saw it was bleeding, he backhanded her.

The blow caught her off guard and knocked her from the chair. A brilliant flash of white light blinded her, and she thought she was going to pass out. Her head spun and a roaring sound whirred in her ears. She tried to get up but only managed to get on all fours. She tried to stand, but could not.

Rockingham nodded at the guards. "Put her in the chair."

Once Sophie was seated, he said, "Now that we have reached an understanding, we can proceed with our marriage arrangements. To prevent your trying to run back to the arms of that bastard in Scotland, we will marry immediately. What say you now, my lovely?"

"Immediately would suit me perfectly," she said, wiping the blood from her mouth, "so the Scot's bastard I carry will be born after our marriage, and therefore be your legal heir."

For a moment she thought he would strike her again. "You are lying."

She lifted her head and stared at him coldly. "You have no way of proving that for some weeks, and a lot can happen in that length of time."

Twenty-Three

It is nought good a slepyng hound to wake.
—Geoffrey Chaucer (c.1342-1400), English poet. *Troilus and Criseyde* (c.1385)

The fire in the Great Hall at Monleigh Castle burned brightly, warming the members of the family gathered there, but their usual teasing banter was absent.

"God love that wee French lassie," Niall said. "If it weren't for her daring, Jamie wouldn't be alive."

"He is barely alive now." Arabella was stabbing the needle into her embroidery, as if by doing so she could ease the anxiety that hovered over the room, and touched every family member present.

"I canna believe anyone who professes to be civilized, as the English do, could inflict such torture on another human being. The worst part of it is, he was guilty of nothing...not even a cattle raid."

"His guilt was being a Highlander," Calum said. "They dinna need a reason to hate us Gaels."

"It proves how badly they wanted Sophie," Bran said.

"They could have asked if she was here before carrying Jamie off," Arabella said. "That only proves they have been waiting for an excuse to arrest him. I want to be thankful that Sophie sacrificed herself to free him, but I dinna want to think of what she suffers now that she is in Rockingham's hands."

"Aye," her brothers agreed.

Arabella went on. "And poor Jamie, it will be some time before he is as good as new. I am thankful that there were no bones broken, save those in his left hand. But to burn him with hot pokers is inhumane."

"Aye, it is heartless and cruel," Bran said, "but 'tis said it is not as painful as being tied for hours by yer thumbs, or having yer flesh laid open with a cattle whip. God's teeth! I could put the length of one finger in the gash on his arm alone. He's got more stitches than Arabella's mending."

The mention of Arabella's lack of perfection when it came to mending was a touch of levity everyone needed.

Arabella stopped her sewing. "I will remember that the next time I'm called to stitch up your stubborn hide." She glanced around the room at each of her brothers. "I wish Tavish were here."

"There's no point in his leaving Edinburgh and his studies to come here," Niall said. "There is naught he could do."

Fraser, who had gone upstairs to see how Jamie fared, walked into the room. He was greeted by anxious glances. "He looks much better. The leeches have reduced the swelling. He can open both eyes now."

Calum, who had remained silent during the discussion, asked, "Is he still restless?"

Fraser shook his head. "No, the laudanum is working. He is sleeping like a bairn."

"I hate to keep him drugged," Arabella said.

Bran nodded. "'Tis the only way to keep him in bed. Once he regains his faculties, there will be no stopping him. He will go after her. We all know that."

"Aye, we know that we canna let him go alone," Niall said.

Bran stood and went to stir the coals in the fire

and then warmed his hands. "Just the same, I don't look forward to the day the laudanum stops and we have to answer to Jamie for allowing his lass to take his place. Not to mention our keeping him drugged while his body healed."

"Or me," Calum said, "for handing Sophie over to the English."

"'Tis true," Arabella agreed. "You will endure the brunt of Jamie's anger. Have you thought about taking a tour of Italy about now?"

"I would have to move to Italy to escape Jamie's wrath for, no matter how long I was gone, he would be waiting for me when I came back."

The bruises were beginning to lighten by the end of the week, and Jamie's mood was as black as his hair.

"It's a sign he is feeling better," Arabella said.

"Is that true, brother? Are ye on the mend?" Fraser asked.

Jamie scowled deeply. "How would you feel if some bastard smashed your hand with a mallet?"

"You should be thankful that it only broke two fingers," Niall said, "and on your left hand."

"Oh, aye, I am thankful all right, and I will be showing ye how bloody thankful I am when I can get out of this bed."

"He's fast becoming his old cheerful self, isn't he?" Bran said.

Jamie's expression of anger and displeasure drew his eyebrows together and a crease formed between his eyes. "There are times when I wish I had been born an only child, and this is one of them," he said. "I dinna need any of you in here. Go on! Get out!"

"Whether you like it or not, you need someone to look after you until you are healed," Fraser said.

It took about all the strength he could muster for Jamie to sit up on the side of the bed, but he did find the energy to give Fraser a withering look. "Someone get my clothes."

"You can't go anywhere until you are fully recovered," Arabella said.

"Like hell. I'm going after her."

"Aye, and we're all going with ye, but first you've got to regain your strength," Niall said. "You couldn't make it to the Borders in your condition."

"I'd be stronger if you'd give me something to eat besides oatmeal."

"There's a joint of beef roasting on the spit right now. Will that suit yer lordship's fancy?" Fraser asked.

"Where is Calum, that bloody traitor?"

"Here, brother."

"Don't call me brother, you turncoat."

"Here now," Niall said. "He had no choice but to take yer lassie. She had already threatened to go alone, and you know her well enough to know she would have."

Jamie started to toss back a reply, but Calum spoke first. "I know you are angry at what I did, but it was my thinking that by going along with Sophie's plan we could save your hide *and* have your lass back."

"How did you come up with that far-fetched idea?"

"By asking myself what would Jamie do?"

When the laughter died down, Calum went on. "I knew that once you were dead, they would come after her. So it seemed the best choice to save your neck from the noose and let Sophie go to England. I did not doubt that once you were free you'd find a way to bring her back."

"And what about Sophie?" Jamie said. "Did you think what might happen to her in the hands of that English bastard?"

"Sophie is resourceful," Fraser said. "You do your lass an injustice to speak of her like she is a witless bit o' fluff. Besides, dinna be forgetting who she is. Rockingham might make her life miserable for a while, but he willna go so far as to harm her. She is still the cousin of the King of France. Rockingham obviously needs that connection."

Jamie scowled at the lot of them. "Aye, she is resourceful, and that is the only thing what's keeping me from throwing the lot of you into the dungeon. And I warn you now, if that bastard marries her before we can get there, I will throw the lot of ye in his dungeon."

Arabella had obviously had enough of Jamie's foul temper. "Hold the big bairn while I give him a little something to soften his growl," she said.

It took all of them to hold Jamie down, and keep him flat on his back.

"Fraser, pinch his nose," she said.

Then to Jamie, she said, "Open your mouth, you big bairn," and when he would not, she said patiently, "We can wait. He has to take a breath sometime."

When Jamie finally did take a gasp of breath, she poured a good dose of laudanum down his throat.

"Keep his nose pinched until he swallows it," she said. "If he throws it back at us, it will have to come out his eyeballs."

* * *

Jamie slept almost two days, rousing only when Arabella cradled his head and spooned a little broth or warmed wine into his mouth.

Gradually she reduced the amount of laudanum she was giving him until stopping it altogether on the fourth day, when he appeared close to being his old self.

"How long have I been sleeping?"

"Long enough that you look much better."

"Tell me truthfully. How long have I been like this?"

Arabella pushed the hair back from his face. "Four days, and before you complain, it was absolutely necessary for your recovery. Your color is much better now, and the swelling almost gone. Even your broken fingers seem to be on the mend. How do you feel?"

"Hungry. I want to chew something…beef."

She smiled. "I will get you some beef and barley soup."

"I don't want soup. I want meat."

"You won't keep it down," she said. "You have to return to your regular way of eating gradually."

"And when did ye become a doctor?"

"About the same time you became so difficult."

He rolled out of the bed and stood, albeit on

shaky legs. "Get me some meat and get it now or, by God, I'll get it myself."

Arabella held her ground. "Take one step and I'll call your brothers to hold you down again, and I'll fill you with enough laudanum that you'll sleep for a week."

She whirled and stomped to the door. "I'll be back with the soup, the laudanum and your brothers, and you can decide which you want."

She marched into the hall and slammed the door.

Fraser came up the stairs about the same time that Jamie let roll with a string of oaths, followed by the sound of something crashing. "I was about to ask how he's feeling, but I can tell he's on the mend."

Arabella smiled at him. "Aye, he's back to his old self."

Twenty-Four

You can deduce it without further evidence
than this,
that no one delights more in vengeance than
a woman.

—Juvenal (c.60-c.128), Roman satirist.
Satires (c.110-127)

During the week that followed Sophie had time to become well acquainted with her quarters.

Confined to her room, she was allowed to take only a short walk each day, accompanied by an escort of six guards. Intermittently, the duke would send word to her that she was invited to dine with him.

On each occasion she sent back her regrets, but

by the end of that first week of confinement, she began to wonder if there was not a better way to gain control of a situation that was completely out of her hands.

After giving it some thought, she decided that if a woman has it in her mind to bring about a change, she might have to play a role that is contrary to her own instincts. This was a roundabout way of saying if her natural inclination was defiance, then she would have to try acquiescence.

Acquiescence…she shuddered at the very sound of the word.

Faith, it would be easier to drink vinegar.

When the next summons to dine with the duke came Sophie stiffened her spine and listened in a way she hoped one would consider demure, as Mrs. Crabb delivered the duke's invitation.

"His Grace will send a guard to escort you to dinner. He expects you to wear the dress he had delivered to you earlier. You are to be there no later than eight."

"Tell His Grace I look forward to dining with him."

Obviously displeased with Sophie's acceptance of the duke's invitation, Mrs. Crabb departed.

Sophie went to the bed and studied the silver-and-blue brocade gown with the décolletage cut dangerously low. She held the dress up in front of her and looked at her reflection in the mirror.

So, that is what he wanted her to wear tonight. In France, she would have called it the dress of a *femme fatale,* an attractive woman who had a destructive effect upon those men foolish enough to succumb to her charms.

Perhaps it was the perfect dress for what she had in mind.

Not wanting to displease the duke on the eve of her first skirmish, Sophie was dressed long before the guard came to escort her to dinner.

Rockingham was standing near the fireplace, with one foot on the fender, when she entered the room. He held a glass of brandy, and something told her it was not his first glass.

Her first impression was that he was preoccupied with something, but when he heard the rustle of her gown he turned toward her, and his sly expression was replaced by one of complete incredulousness.

Feeling a surge of confidence, along with a small amount of power, Sophie withdrew her hand from the guard's arm and smiled at Rockingham. "Your Grace seems surprised to see me."

"I find it is sometimes better to be too believing than too skeptical. I dared not hope you would accept my invitation. I not only wanted you to share dinner, but I also wanted to speak to you about what happened the other day."

"I prefer to forget that," she said, and wished she were a man so she could take that poker standing nearby and run him through.

He nodded. "As you wish, for I had hoped to ask if we might, henceforth, put the past behind us and begin anew."

"I find I am in perfect agreement, for I have harbored a similar hope."

"Shall I pour you a glass of claret?"

"I would prefer to share a glass of brandy with you, Your Grace."

"I knew you would be breathtaking in that gown. I have thought of little else all evening. I have never been able to get that first sight of you out of my mind. You were dancing in the arms of someone else at Versailles."

He placed his glass on the mantel before he poured a glass of brandy and carried it to her. "I shall require all of your dances from now on," he said.

Sophie watched as he came toward her with the glass. She smiled and thought, here comes the trout that can be caught by tickling.

Rockingham had not believed that Sophie would appear for dinner.

He expected another display of her defiance and, because he knew she would not dine with him, he was taken by surprise for a second time when she walked into the room, two minutes early.

The second surprise was seeing her in the dress he sent for her to wear, when he fully expected her to rip it to shreds and toss it over the balcony.

The moment she entered he told himself he had been right to persuade King Louis to accept his offer of marriage. He wanted Sophie. Everything about her was regal, from the mysterious power of her beauty, and the sureness of her carriage, to the sharp consciousness she seemed to have of what went on about her.

Her smile dazzled him, just as her beauty had from the moment he first saw her. That she was here now, in his home, and under his supervision, and coming willingly to dine with him, left him feeling like a schoolboy.

All he could think of was getting her to come willingly to his bed, for he had already decided to marry her the moment she gave birth. That did not mean, however, that he could not make her his mistress in the meantime. Discreetly, of course.

Dinner lasted a long time, and she seemed perfectly relaxed and eager to join into conversation with him. She pleased him immensely, and already he had visions of the envy she would arouse when he took her to London in the fall. That she was such a beauty, with Bourbon blood and royal lineage—it would make her the talk of the ton for the entire season.

He imagined the flabby-armed matrons all vying to have the cousin of the King of France attend their balls.

He was especially courteous throughout dinner, for he did not want to do anything to damage the fragile truce they had established. "As I told you earlier, I did not expect you for dinner. After so many refusals, what made you change your mind and decide to come tonight?"

He had already decided that if she said it was the dress he would not believe her, for he knew she was of too strong a character to succumb to such superficiality. If she said the dress, she was here to play him false.

"I decided there are occasions when it is undoubtedly better to lose graciously than to win defiantly."

"I am delighted to learn that your beauty is matched only by your intelligence."

She ran her fingers down the stem of her champagne glass. "I am sure my cousin will be pleased to hear that. I would hate to think I was a disappointment to my country."

"Never a disappointment. I shall see to it that King Louis is informed that his cousin has skill and tact that outshines his best ambassadors."

After dinner, she agreed to play the piano for him and he watched, entranced, as her fingers floated lightly over the keys. He was filled with imaginings of another talent for those long, lovely fingers of hers.

He was truly disappointed when she finished the last song and closed the lid to the piano. "Oh, my dear, must you stop?"

She smiled and he saw the fire in her eyes that were as blue as crystals. "My father told me it was a sign of greatness to know when to begin and when to stop."

"Then, who am I to argue against anything your father said. He was a great man."

"Yes, he was, and I adored him."

"So I have been told."

She stood across the room from him like temptation, and he had no desire to withstand it. He had been alone too long.

Everything about her shimmered as if her gown had been woven by elves out of moonbeams. He wanted her in every way a man wanted a woman.

He wanted to own her and possess her until she no longer knew where she ended and he began.

But, right now, he wanted to take her in his arms and carry her up to his bed and give her what he had yearned to give her that first time he saw her, five years ago, but he cautioned himself to go slowly with her.

That bloody Scot had abused her, for he was certain now that it was rape, and he would not put himself in the same class as that bloody bastard. She was not a woman to be taken by force, but one to be won with the refinement of courtship. He had realized that the first day she was here when she had infuriated him until his anger was white hot, and he had struck her.

He walked her up to her room, and kissed her hand at the door. "I look forward to dinner again tomorrow night. I hope you will not disappoint me."

She drew her fan down the side of his cheek. "I could never do that, Your Grace. Good night."

The door closed behind her, but he remained in place for a moment longer, until the scent of her perfume had vanished.

Sophie dined with the duke each night for the next four days, and each time she did it became increasingly difficult to hold him at bay.

Thankfully, he set her mind at ease at least for the coming night.

"I am having some gentlemen friends up from London tomorrow night. They will join me for dinner. I do hope you will agree to be present and fulfill the role of hostess."

"If Your Grace desires it," she said, instantly aware that she spoke the magic words, for he took her in his arms and kissed her, calling her "My darling Duchess."

She was surprised the next afternoon, while having tea, to see the duke walk in the room to join her. Through the course of conversation he mentioned that his friends were all members of what he called "the Leicester House Set."

Sophie frowned and stroked the petal of a rose in the arrangement on the table. "I am not familiar with the Leicester House Set," she said. "Is it some sort of gentlemen's club?"

He smiled and placed his hand over hers. "Before I explain that I feel I should give you a little background information, which will help tremendously in the understanding of the Leicester House Set."

"Please do, for I am so terribly uneducated in English ways, and will feel much more comfortable when I am better informed, so I might carry on a more enlightened conversation."

"My dear, you could read King George's decree that put the border of Maine in the middle of the Piscataqua River and have them eating out of your hand."

"Maine? Oh…in America?"

"All this and brilliance, too. You enchanting creature."

She did not relish being called a creature, but she did not let on. Instead, she said, "I believe you were going to give me some background on the Leicester House Set."

"We should start with the king's eldest son, Frederick Louis, who is the Prince of Wales. He was brought to England from Hanover in 1728. He has been despised by his parents, King George II and Queen Caroline, almost from the beginning…so despised, in fact, that the queen often publicly wishes for his death. The royal couple is afraid he will gain popularity at the king's expense. The king even went so far as to consider a scheme to send Frederick to rule Hanover, so his second son, William, could inherit the throne."

"He could do that?"

"He tried. The plan was voted on and defeated. Naturally, Frederick found friends in the circles in opposition to his father. Barred from the palace, Frederick established himself at Leicester House, which has become the meeting place for parliamentary opposition, where we focus on the next king. Those of us who favor putting Frederick on the throne are known as the 'Leicester House Set.'"

"But isn't that dangerous for you?"

He squeezed her hand. "My dove, my heartbeat grows more rapid to think you are concerned for my safety."

Being called his dove sickened her. I must get away from here soon, she was thinking, but she smiled and said, "It is only because I know the danger that lies in wait for those in opposition to the throne. I have known many of those in France who were sent to stand before a firing squad because of it."

"Don't worry for me, *ma petite,* I know what I am doing."

"Do be careful."

The butler interrupted them before Rockingham could say anything more. "Your Grace, the Duke of Worthington and the Earl of Hampshire have arrived."

"I will see them in the library." The duke stood and took Sophie's hand. "Until dinner," he said, and kissed her hand.

Twenty-Five

Out of this nettle, danger, we pluck this flower, safety.

—William Shakespeare (1564-1616), English poet and playwright. *Henry IV, Part 1* (1597), Act 2, Scene 3

The sound of spurs ringing against the stone floors of Monleigh Castle caused those sitting around the fire in the hall to pause in their conversation, as every one of them looked toward the door, each face bearing a look of apprehension.

The doors were thrown back and James Graham strode into the room looking every inch the strong leader he was.

"What are you doing dressed like that?" Arabella asked. "It's too soon for you to be thinking about going out."

"I was thinking about it, but I am no' thinking about it any longer," Jamie said. "I have decided to go out. I am through with languishing in bed. I've something that belongs to me and I intend to get it back."

Niall had been about to take a drink from his tankard but he put it down so hard some of the ale sloshed over the top. "Are you sure you are up to it? It's a long ride to Rockingham's castle."

"We go by boat to Whitby, in Yorkshire. We will take our horses with us, and ride from Whitby to Swifford Castle."

"We will make better time on our own horses," Fraser said.

"How many men do we take with us?" Bran asked.

"Two score, no more," Jamie answered.

He did not tell his brothers that he had no idea if Rockingham had even taken Sophie to his home, but his gut instinct told him he would have taken her to Swifford Castle in Yorkshire, rather than risk taking her to London. The bastard would want to break her spirit first, so she would be the perfect submissive wife when he introduced her to the ton.

"Aye, two score of the Grahams is more than enough to hold off a whole British regiment," Niall said. "When do we sail?"

"At daybreak," Jamie said, "so get a good night's sleep."

"Before we go," Calum said, "I'd like to know something of your plan. Rockingham is bound to know we might try to rescue her. He will have double, even triple guards posted at every nook and cranny."

"If you are frightened of the odds, you are welcome to stay here," Jamie said.

"Hold on, now," Fraser said. "We don't need to have any tempers flaring amongst us. This must be well thought out, and perfectly executed. We don't aim to let you go off to rescue yer lass by yerself, but we do want to have some idea of what we are getting into."

Jamie nodded. "Since none of us have ever been to Yorkshire the best approach is to find a place to make camp, while two or three of us ride over to Swifford Castle. Once we are there, we can explore and gather information about the strength and positioning of the duke's troops. When we have the information we need, we will plan our move and catch them by surprise."

"It's that last part I worry about. Someone is

bound to notice a band of Highlanders riding about Yorkshire."

"We willna be wearing our plaids, if that is what you are thinking," Jamie said. "We will be dressed to look like ordinary Englishmen. Since they will not expect us to have the daring to go that far into England to rescue her, we should raise no suspicion."

"I don't mind saying the odds do not put my mind at ease," Niall said. "It is still a very risky thing we will be doing."

Jamie grinned at Niall and then shared the grin with his other brothers. "The most exhilarating battles are when the odds are no' with us. It is a good way to keep us alert and focused on what we are about. Otherwise, we will be like the man who went out for wool and came home shorn."

It was a welcome laugh they shared and it did much to ease some of the tension, but when the jollity began to fade, the solemnness of the occasion settled over them once more.

"We can't exactly ride in the postern gate and expect to be welcomed," Bran said. "How do you plan to get us inside?"

Jamie lightly cuffed his brother's head. "I ken we will know the answer to that after we visit Swifford."

* * *

Sophie was glad for her time at the French court, for it would have been difficult otherwise for her to carry herself with grace and aplomb while playing hostess to a group of fifteen of England's most influential men. Even when she was most nervous, her experiences enabled her to observe the proprieties easily and without thinking. She almost regretted the many complaints she made against the years of training in what she called paltry decorum.

Seated in the hostess chair at the end of the dining table opposite Rockingham, Sophie was at home in such luxurious surroundings and, because she was comfortable, she fulfilled her role perfectly.

Both of her dinner partners, the Duke of Wyeford seated to her left, and the Earl of Northrop on her left, were well traveled, articulate, and thoroughly enjoyed her presence, although she was not so foolish as to think they might have enjoyed it half as much if she had not been the granddaughter of the Sun King.

After dinner the men turned to their brandy and insisted that Sophie remain in their presence.

At one point Rockingham whispered to her, the pride in his voice reaching pompous levels, "My dear, you have them eating out of your delicate palm. I knew you would make the perfect duchess to grace my table."

She wanted to tell him she was not his duchess, nor would she ever be, but that would have to remain her secret for the time being. Instead, she smiled and said, "I am honored to be of help, Your Grace."

Even the Duke of Bellingham made a similar comment. "I propose a toast to the loveliest, most gracious hostess England has ever had the pleasure of welcoming to her shores."

"Thank you, Your Grace. I feel the honor belongs to all of you, for in order to be a great hostess, one must have great guests, and so I thank each of you."

Soon, the men settled into conversation as if they had quite forgotten Sophie, who was sitting upon a slippered chair a few feet away, quietly listening to everything the Leicester House Set had to say.

They were discussing Frederick Louis, the Prince of Wales, and the strategy for getting him on the throne before George II died.

This discussion caused Sophie to recall Rockingham's diplomatic service in France, and how her cousin Louis said, "Rockingham was sent to

France because King George wanted to get him out of the way."

Instead of serving the English King, Rockingham began to negotiate on his own behalf with Louis. If the French helped him overthrow King George, he and his friends would put the Prince of Wales—who would side with the French—on the throne.

To seal the bargain, Rockingham wanted Sophie as his wife.

Louis was at first reluctant to involve France in such a plot, but King George had declared war on Spain, which was swept up into the Spanish War of Austrian Succession, putting England and France on opposite sides.

In the end Louis said, "We have nothing to lose by going along with Rockingham's plan."

Which was something Sophie balked at, and she told her cousin so. "You cannot mean to go along with Rockingham's idea. How can you, when it means I will be sacrificed in marriage to a man I abhor?"

Instead of being sympathetic, Cousin Louie was very blasé.

As he told Sophie, "Think of it as a way to serve France, dear cousin. You will be married to a very powerful man who will have not only the ear, but also the gratitude of the future King of England."

Sophie saw through that immediately and replied, "The opposite is also possible, for there is an equal chance the Prince Regent might not become king, and Rockingham could lose everything and be imprisoned, or killed. I could even be accused of being part of the plot. What happens then?"

Louis patted her hand and said, "Then all we have lost is our lovely Sophie."

"You would use me, even forfeit my life, to further your schemes against England?"

"That is the way the game is played, cousin. Some of us win, some of us lose, and some of us must be sacrificed."

Even now, the words of Louis brought a sharp pain to her heart. She looked around the room, trying not to let the disgust she felt show.

She had to get out of here.

She wished Jamie were here, with his level head and strength to guide her, but Jamie had never seemed further from her than at this moment.

What difference did it make, she wondered, for she had neither the comfort of his presence, nor a place in his heart.

All she had was her own resources, and it galled

her to think she had to resort to such cheap, womanly tricks as pleading a headache in order to excuse herself from the Leicester House Set.

Two days before the planned rescue attempt, Jamie and his men made a bivouac a mile from Swifford Castle.

During the day, masquerading as various merchants and travelers, he and his men patrolled the area around the castle and nearby hamlets to gain knowledge about the comings and goings, as well as the general layout of the castle itself.

Jamie was fortunate enough to find a man who not only had firsthand knowledge of the castle, but went so far as to cut a limb from a nearby tree and scratch a detailed map of the castle's layout in the dirt, all too happy to fill him in on the most and least-used entrances, and even took the liberty to point the location of a small hidden door few knew about—or so he claimed—in the curtain wall.

The night of the planned penetration of the stronghold arrived. The moonlight made it necessary for everyone to wear black and to leave behind all but the most necessary pieces of armor.

"We dinna want anything that will make noise," Jamie said.

The bridles had been carefully wrapped, as well

as the horse's hooves, and as they rode to Swifford they were careful to stay well within the screen of trees avoiding, whenever possible, the roads and open moors.

When they were close enough to see the lights in the windows of Swifford Jamie held up his hand and the men dismounted.

"I will take two men with me to wait with my horse while I go in alone. I hope to have my lass and be back soon, but if I am not back in an hour you are to leave without me. I will have any man who disobeys that order whipped. Regardless of the circumstances, do not think to play the hero and attempt to storm the castle and rescue me. Rockingham has a well-trained army. Once they know I have breached their walls we will have lost our advantage, and we will not stand a chance."

Bran and Niall rode ahead with Jamie, but once they reached the castle wall the two of them waited in the trees, while Jamie went on alone. He found the door in the curtain wall, which was so difficult to open he decided it must have been several hundred years since anyone even tried. Still, it was good to know it was not a place they would likely guard.

He opened the door at last and entered the castle grounds. Once inside, the moonlight was on his side, for it cast long shadows of the roofs and turrets across the castle keep, and Jamie's own shadow melted into the evening silhouettes.

He made his way into the castle proper, after choosing the area near the privies as the least likely place for guards to congregate. The smell of piss and ordure was almost overpowering, and he took as few breaths as he could until he was well away from there.

His choice was a good one in that the area was poorly lit, and there were no guards to be seen.

From there he went in through the chapel, doubting that Rockingham would be about, devoutly reading or piously engaged in prayer. When he left the chapel he went down a deserted hallway and up a narrow circular stairway that seemed to be seldom used, judging from the cobwebs.

He came above stairs on the main floor of the castle and, to his astonishment, caught nothing more than a glimpse of Sophie's back as she started below stairs. He was about to go after her when two guards came down the hall, and he ducked back into the stairwell until they had passed.

Once the guards were well out of hearing range, he went down the stairs she had taken only moments before.

* * *

After she left the meeting of the Leicester House Set, Sophie was on her way to her room when she passed the salon and saw one of the doors to the small private terrace and garden was slightly ajar.

After all the smoke from the cigars a little fresh air would be welcome, and she slipped quietly through the door.

It was a good choice, for the air was fresh and crisp, and although the roses were not in bloom, the clear sky overhead captured her attention. The stars were out in dazzling array, and the full moon was the texture of cream. She began to feel the chill of the night air, and she was about to return to the house when she noticed a light appear in Rockingham's study.

From where Sophie was standing she could clearly see into the room, as Jeremy Ashford, Rockingham's indomitable factor, entered holding a candle aloft.

He paused long enough to light a girandole on a nearby wall.

From her vantage point on the terrace Sophie watched, in a fascinated way, as he removed the lid from a Chinese urn and withdrew a key, which he used to unlock an ancient stone box.

Once he turned the key, he manipulated the four sides of the box by sliding each of them forward to release the lid.

Sophie was beyond curious now, for the box she recognized was an ossuary, an ancient container to hold the bones of the dead, and she had no inkling why he would be opening it until he withdrew a roll of parchment from his coat and placed it in the box.

After he locked the box and returned the key, he doused the candle and the room was dark once more.

Sophie waited at least five minutes or more before she stepped inside.

Instead of going to her room, she slipped quietly into the duke's study where she immediately withdrew the key from the urn and unlocked the ossuary. Her attention was drawn to an ornate Celtic dragon carved on top, and the markings carved beneath it. It was written in ogham, an ancient Celtic alphabet that consisted of twenty characters.

Hundreds of years ago, it had been a secret religious language used by the Druids. She studied the markings for a moment.

"*Brach Gra*," she said, pronouncing the words that meant eternal love.

Melancholy descended upon her like a weeping cloud. Something she did understand was that at one time, this small stone box had contained the bones of someone beloved.

She had little doubt that Rockingham had disposed of the bones in order to use the box for his own purposes.

She opened the stone box and withdrew the parchment.

To her astonishment it was written in French, and even more surprising was the signature and great seal of her dear cousin, Louis XV, at the bottom.

She quickly scanned the letter and her hands began to tremble, for she was well aware that what she held in her small hands was the means to topple the almighty Rockingham from his powerful perch.

She slipped the letter down the front of her bodice, closed the box, returned the key to the urn and, after dousing the candle, slipped quietly from the room.

Once she was back in her own room, she dressed warmly in her riding clothes and with her cape thrown over her arm she went below stairs to the laundry, where she made her way through a maze of five-legged troughs used for washing, and ducked under a line of clothes drying.

She slipped outside and continued across the lawn while keeping close to the shrubbery, as she headed toward the maze, which was near the stables.

She had almost reached the maze when a hand came around her mouth, and she felt herself yanked backward against a hard, muscular body.

"How do you expect me to rescue you if you won't stay put, lass? I've been following ye around this bloody castle for half the night."

The next thing she knew she was kissing him, or he was kissing her, or maybe it did not matter. All she knew was they were frantically kissing each other.

He is here, she thought, which meant that he did care for her—at least enough that he would risk all to come after her.

It was like being home and, in a way, that is how she felt about being wrapped securely in the protective embrace of the man she loved.

There were a million questions all cramming into her poor brain at the same time, and she could not seem to think straight. All she knew was that this wonderful man was not here by accident, that he must have forgiven her and cared enough about her to risk his life coming here. "What are you doing here?" she finally managed to ask. "I never thought I would see you again."

"I came after you," he said, apparently noticing how she was trembling. "Are you all right, lass?"

"Yes, only I seem to have difficulty breathing. I cannot believe it is truly you." She was holding on to him for dear life, afraid to ease her grip even a little for fear he might disappear.

When he spoke again, he was mumbling the words against her lips. "As much as I'd like to make love to you right here and now, I've got to get you out of here. Where is Rockingham?"

"He is meeting with the members of the Leicester House Set."

"That bunch of dolts who think to put the Prince Regent on the throne?"

"How do you know about that?"

"I make it my business to know as much as possible about the enemy. What are they doing here?"

She began to talk so fast, trying to tell him everything she had wanted to tell him for so long…how she had first met Rockingham at the French Court, and the agreement between her cousin, Louis, and Rockingham, which included her hand in marriage. She kept babbling on and on, unable to stop until Jamie finally had to kiss her to shut her up.

"There will be time for that later, lass. Right now, I must get you out of here."

"Wait! I cannot believe I almost forgot." She began to unlace the top of her bodice.

"As much as I'd like to dally, lass, this isna the time or the place. That will have to wait."

She withdrew the parchment. "It isn't what you think. I found this tonight. It is a letter from my cousin, King Louis. He states that he will send the necessary troops Rockingham has requested, as well as the gold, but only after he receives proof my marriage to Rockingham has taken place. He goes on to say that it is necessary to protect his interests when Rockingham's plan to put himself on the throne succeeds, and I become Queen of England."

Sophie paused, for Jamie seemed not to be listening at all. "Did you hear what I said? He intends to put himself on the throne...to betray the other members of the Leicester House Set."

"Aye, lass, I heard you, dinna worrit about that. Where did you find it?"

She told him how she had watched Jeremy, and then opened the box herself. "It had an ornate dragon carved on top—a Celtic dragon, I assume, since the words written in ogham below it were Celtic. I was sorry I took the time to translate it, for it made me sad...*Brach Gra*," she said. "It means eternal love."

He seemed dumbfounded. "You can read ogham? But...how?"

"My father was a brilliant man. He knew more than a dozen languages, many of them ancient ones—Egyptian, Aramaic, Coptic, Etruscan.... I learned to read the markings from him, but the dragon's significance was puzzling to me."

"It was probably the Celtic dragon, which represents sovereignty, power or a chief. *Pendragon* is the Celtic word for chief...but enough of that for now. I have an idea. Come on." He took her by the hand and started back toward the main part of the castle.

She jerked to a stop and stared at him with a horrified expression. "You are taking me *back?*"

"Never." He smiled beautifully and she almost melted. "I am going back with you, lass."

"But why? We are almost free. Why go back?"

"I ken there is a better way to leave here than slipping over the castle walls."

"Which way is that?"

"I prefer to walk out the front door."

"Jamie Graham, are you daft?"

He kissed her quickly. "Trust me and ask questions later."

By the time they entered the wing of the castle where Rockingham and the others were meeting, Sophie was seriously beginning to doubt Jamie's intelligence. To go in where they were meeting was lunacy. It did not make any sense.

When they approached the door the guards stopped them. Naturally, she thought. What else were guards for?

When Rockingham heard the commotion, he opened the door. "What is going…"

Jamie, with Sophie holding tightly to his arm, walked into the room. "Good eventide, gentlemen."

The Duke of Haversley turned to Rockingham. "What is the meaning of this? Who is this man?"

"The Earl of Monleigh, at your service," Jamie said.

"You have a bloody lot of nerve coming in here, Monleigh," Rockingham said. "I always knew Scots to be thick-headed, but I had no idea they were so stupid."

"Let us decide later, which of us is stupid," Jamie replied, before giving his attention to the other men in the room.

"I have come to deliver a message to you from

the King of France," Jamie said. "He has the gold, and troops, and they are ready to come to Rockingham's aid. The moment he receives proof that Rockingham and the king's cousin, Sophie de Bourbon, have wed, French ships carrying French troops, along with the gold, will be immediately dispatched to England. They come, gentlemen, to assist you with your claim to put your dear friend the Duke of Rockingham on the throne of England."

Rockingham's face was deathly white. He turned to the guards. "He lies. Arrest him."

Jamie turned back to the group of astonished men. "Gentlemen, it would be in your best interest to hear me out. I think it is for you to decide whether I lie or not."

The Duke of Chaffington was the first to say, "Let him speak." The others quickly agreed.

Jamie withdrew the roll of parchment. "Naturally, I did not come here expecting you to believe the word of a lowly Scot, but perhaps some of you might recognize the signature and seal of the King of France."

He handed the document to Chaffington who quickly scanned it, and passed it to Haversley.

"It would seem," Chaffington said, "that our friend Rockingham has ambitions even we did not know about."

Haversley skimmed the document. "Good God! It is true! The bastard intends to become King of England and do away with the Prince Regent."

"It isn't like that," Rockingham said. "You misunderstand."

"Why don't you explain to them how it is," Jamie said, "while I take Sophie away from here. With your permission gentlemen, I will give you the letter from King Louis in exchange for his cousin, Sophie de Bourbon. A worthwhile trade for both of us, do you not agree?"

"Yes, yes," Haversley said, still staring at the letter. "By all means, take your lady. You have done us a great service. Take anything you like…except Rockingham, of course."

"My lass is all I want," Jamie said, and he gave Sophie a look that made her heart flip *tòpsee túrvee.*

He took her hand. "Come, lass, let us be away from this place."

"Wait!" Rockingham called out. "For the love of God, hear me out!"

The duke's pleas fell upon deaf ears. Sophie and Jamie walked to the door, but the guards blocked their exit.

"The Duke of Rockingham is a traitor to the Crown of England. Let them pass," Chaffington said. "We have no quarrel with them. Please accompany them to the door."

The guards stepped back and fell in behind them.

Sophie stole a quick glance behind her, and saw the look of panic that passed over Rockingham's face.

"It is over, lass," Jamie said, with a voice so nonchalant and unruffled she would have thought he was in the habit of calmly walking out of an enemy stronghold on a daily basis.

Sophie felt the warmth of his hand covering hers, and she was comforted by the strength and courage that she could feel emanating from him.

When they saw Sophie and Jamie approach, the guards at the front entrance threw the doors open and stood aside, allowing them to pass.

As they stepped over the threshold and into the night air, Sophie heard the Duke of Chaffington's chilling voice.

"Close the doors, please."

Twenty-Six

> The world was all before them, where to choose
> Their place of rest, and Providence their guide:
> They hand in hand with wandering steps and slow,
> Through Eden took their solitary way.
>
> —John Milton (1608-1674), English poet.
> *Paradise Lost* (1667)

They crossed the grass, Jamie still holding fast to her hand as they walked toward the fringe of trees.

"Do you think we should run? What if they change their minds?"

"Your hour has come, lass. Savor the moment."

"I will, but what if they decide to come after *you?*"

His chuckle was reassuring. "They willna do that, lass, and I wouldn't want to miss this feeling for the world, for there are not many times in a man's life when he can get the best of the peers of England's realm and then, with their blessing, walk away from it."

They did not walk far before Niall and Bran rode out of the dark shadows with such stealth that they were almost upon them before Sophie even realized they were there.

She noticed they led Corrie, but did not have a horse for her.

"Where are ye wounded?" Niall asked.

"I suffered nary a scratch," Jamie replied, "and neither did my lass."

"Then why are ye walking as if you are attending your own coronation? We need to be away from this place before they discover yer lass is gone."

"All is well, for they gave us their leave…and most politely, too."

Niall and Bran exchanged puzzled looks, so Jamie took it upon himself to give them a briefing on what had transpired.

After a few questions from them he said, "Let

us be away from this place. I long for the fresh air o' Scotland."

He lifted Sophie to the saddle and mounted behind her. With his spurs to Corrie's flanks they started off, with Bran riding guard just ahead of them, and Niall acting as the rear guard a few paces back.

There were many questions that needed answers, but there would be time enough for that once they reached Monleigh. There was one question, however, that Sophie wanted to ask him now. "What will happen to Gillian? Do you think she will marry Vilain?"

"Vilain was too smart for that," he said.

"Was? It is over between them?"

"Aye, once Vilain learned of her betrayal it was over between them. I believe his exact words were, 'Once I heard what she did, I knew I could never again lay my head upon that faithless breast.'"

Jamie brushed a kiss across her cheek. "You have nothing to worry about, love. Gillian will never come between us."

Sounds of the night spread over them soft as a cloak. Sophie laid her head against Jamie's chest, and soon became accustomed to the rhythm of hoofbeats and the steady tempo of Jamie's heartbeat.

His brothers remained quiet, alert, keeping to the same pattern as before with an advance guard ahead and a rear guard following behind. The moon was still high in the sky, shining brightly on everything below, as if in competition with the glittering light emitting from a million scattered stars.

They rode without talking, until she saw the first rosy hint of sun balancing itself on the misty top of mountains.

Dawn was fast approaching.

She took a deep breath and burrowed closer to Jamie, his warmth becoming hers, as they rode through the last traces of disappearing night.

Once, she felt him press a kiss upon her head and a tightening of his arms about her as he gathered her closer against him. Corrie's gait was smooth and easy, and Sophie's drowsy head began to nod, until she rested limply against him.

The sounds around her began to dull, and she drifted slowly off to sleep.

She did not wake until the rendezvous with the rest of Jamie's men, when they all turned their faces into the wind and Scotland.

Epilogue

I wish to believe in immortality—I wish to live with you for ever.

—John Keats (1795-1821), English poet. Letter to Fanny Brawne (July 1820). *Letters of John Keats* (H. E. Rollins Ed.; 1958)

Once they were safely ensconced back at Monleigh, Sophie told Jamie everything: how her father had died and how the king had commanded her presence at court, how she arranged her escape, and why she was so foolish as to keep her secret from him for so long.

She was not surprised when he asked her the question she knew he would save for last. "Why did you persuade Calum to hand you over to the English?"

Tears gathered in her eyes. She was not sure she could explain her feelings, or explain how she loved him, more than herself, more than her own life. Perhaps a simple answer was best. "There was no life for me without you."

He reached out and wiped the tears away from her face with his thumbs. He cupped her face in his hands and lifted it, so she had no choice but to look at him.

"Lovely Sophie, your eyes always mirrored your heart," he said.

She sniffed and gave him a watery smile. "Why did you refuse to hand me over to the Black Watch, when you knew it meant you would be imprisoned?"

"Because you were mine, and I could easier pluck out my own eye than give you up." He closed his eyes and she could see the anguish on his face. "The thought of losing you…it was almost more than I could bear. You are part of me… you have been a part of me for so long…since that night Tavish brought you to me, I think. It was a gradual thing, for I never knew when I fell in love with you. I only knew that I had…long before I knew who you were. That is why it hurt so much to learn you did not trust me enough to tell me the truth."

She was crying now. "I am sorry. I know you find it hard to forgive me...."

His arms came around her. "Foolish lass, don't you know forgiving is the cure for suffering? Ease your torment. What is past changing is past grief. I love you. That is all that matters now."

She saw the lopsided grin. "Well, not all that matters," he said, and picked her up. He carried her to his bed and lay down beside her. His mouth came down on hers as his hands caressed her shoulders and he pulled her to him.

She knew he was done with talking and explanations. There would be no more tears now—only the joy of forgiveness and reunion. With the ease and skill that seemed second nature to him, he spoke love words against her throat, and told her how much he wanted her and loved her, and what he wanted to do with her.

Her hands combed through the silky length of his black hair, and when she inhaled the scent of him she recalled those long, dark days when she grieved over the loss of him, and how she thought she would never again lie with him, or feel again the breathtaking thrill of impassioned words whispered against her throat. She had known during that horrible separation that she would grow old, never hearing the sound of his laugh, or seeing the gleam of love and desire in his eyes. But most painful of all was to think she would never again love or know she was loved in return.

His hands tortured her now, and she was mindless with wanting. Everywhere he touched, each place he kissed, she felt on fire. She needed this—the feel of his hands touching her with intense desire, the words of commitment, and knowledge they would share their lives together.

He had taught her about desire and showed her what it meant to love, and now she understood the depth of feeling that moved them even further, to something unfathomable and binding. She felt the first flutterings of it beating soft as a bird's wings in her heart. It was a softer thing than passion, and more enduring.

She was consumed with the flush of loving and being in love, and the quickening drive of his impatience tore her mind away from any further thought. She would always remember this moment, and the silky hardness of him, the purls of sensation rippling through her at his slightest touch.

She gasped when his hand slipped lower to caress her stomach, and then lower still. Her legs opened for him and she moaned when she felt the beloved weight of him pressing her down, and felt the hard press of his prick against her, and the rush of feeling when he slipped inside.

Shafts of fire consumed her in waves, each one coming stronger than the one before. Her hands were on the hard muscles of his buttocks, and she felt the awesome power of him when he shuddered and spilled himself inside her. Her blood flowed in hot torrents as passion worked its miracle, and she called out his name as wave after wave gripped her.

When it was over, she was left with a deep kind of quiet that was as powerful as it was intense. Later, when they lay together, their bodies entwined, in the quiet, comfortable moments that come after the passion is spent, he asked her to marry him.

She said yes, of course, and then asked, "When?"

"I was thinking I had robbed ye of a true courtship, so a summer wedding would give me time to woo my lass properly, and then there is Tavish. He canna come home until summer."

"Ah, Tavish. Sweet, teasing Tavish," she said. "We owe him so much, but we can't wait that long, Jamie."

He kissed her. "Why do you say that? I thought you would have wanted him to be here."

"I do! You know I do, but an old Scottish proverb says, 'Tis better to have a lass unwooed than a bairn born out of wedlock."

"A bairn?"

"Aye, in late summer," she said, and Jamie laughed.

He kissed her softly and said, "I will make a Scot out of you yet. As for Tavish, I will send a message to him so he can arrange to come home for our wedding. He will not want to miss that."

"Nor would I want him to. He must be here for such an event. Besides, I long to see him again. I have written my thanks to him for saving my life, but I want to tell him in person."

His heart was full of love and pride, and he laughed at her with that lazy sort of amusement he always reserved for her. "'Kiss me, Kate, we will be married o' Sunday,'" he said.

Obedient lass that she was, she threw her arms around his neck and kissed him soundly, thinking she was a fortunate lass to have the heart of the Earl of Monleigh, the assurance of a wedding, the joy of a bairn and a few lines of Shakespeare tossed in between.

What woman could ask for more?

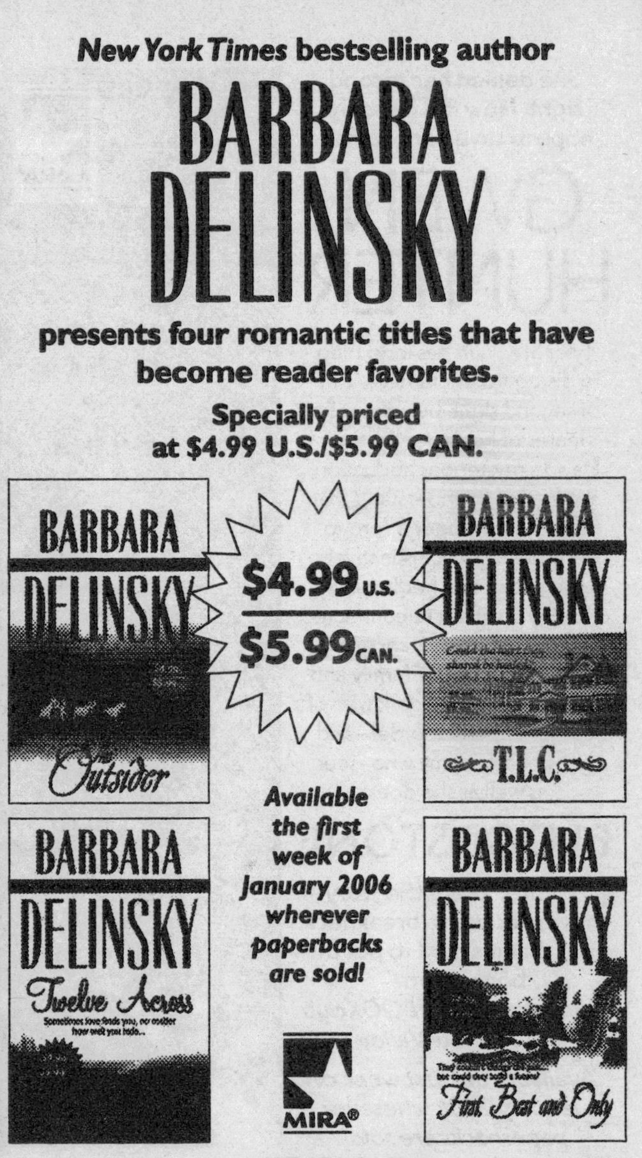
New York Times bestselling author
BARBARA DELINSKY
presents four romantic titles that have become reader favorites.
Specially priced at $4.99 U.S./$5.99 CAN.
BARBARA DELINSKY
Outsider
$4.99 U.S.
$5.99 CAN.
BARBARA DELINSKY
T.L.C.
BARBARA DELINSKY
Twelve Across
Available the first week of January 2006 wherever paperbacks are sold!
MIRA®
BARBARA DELINSKY
First, Best and Only
www.MIRABooks.com
MBDVP0106